SHERLOCK HOLMES
The Spider's Web

ALSO AVAILABLE FROM TITAN BOOKS

SHERLOCK HOLMES

The Spider's Web

PHILIP PURSER-HALLARD

TITAN BOOKS

Sherlock Holmes: The Spider's Web
Print edition ISBN: 9781785658440
Electronic edition ISBN: 9781785658457

Published by Titan Books
A division of Titan Publishing Group Ltd
144 Southwark St, London SE1 0UP
www.titanbooks.com

First edition: September 2020
10 9 8 7 6 5 4 3 2 1

A CIP catalogue record for this title is available from the British Library.

Printed and bound by CPI Group (UK) Ltd, Croydon CR0 4YY.

In memory of my dad, Terry Hallard, who never passed up an opportunity to say 'A *handbag*?'

PREFACE

Many of the cases with which I was privileged to assist my friend Mr Sherlock Holmes require a degree of delicacy in the recounting. In some instances this has been because of the shocking nature of the secrets which our investigations revealed, but in others it is simply that the social status of those involved precludes their publication.

The former kind may, I fear, remain forever unpublishable, but as far as the latter goes it has been my habit to change the names and recognisable details so as to obscure the identities of the principals. This has allowed me to write with discretion about incidents that involved a number of the more eminent personages of our age.

The adventure which I have termed *The Spider's Web* is not amenable to such treatment. One fact of biography was so well publicised at the time, and so unique to the person concerned, that mentioning it would make his identity inescapable. Yet, as it turned out to be of vital importance to the case, I cannot permit myself to obscure it. To do so would entail falsifying some of the links in the chain of reasoning that led Holmes to his conclusions, and he would rightly take grave exception to any such liberty.

Furthermore, the persons in this drama were eminent indeed, including a former Cabinet minister and members of the aristocracy, as well as others prominent in the London society of the nineties. Some were young at the time and are of respectable middle age twenty-three years later, and there is no reason to suppose that their children will not live long and healthy lives.

I have therefore instructed my solicitors that this account must be sealed unread, only to be opened a hundred years from now. At that time it can be supposed that anyone living who still remembers the principals will have other matters to concern them than the protection of their memory.

In any case, by then I can only imagine that the populace at large will have long ago forgotten the name, and the remarkable personal history, of Mr Ernest Worthing.

John H. Watson, MD, 1920

CHAPTER ONE
THE USES OF PALMISTRY

Lord Arthur Savile stared at Sherlock Holmes in dismay. 'What crime?' he asked.

'The most serious of crimes, Lord Arthur.' The detective returned his gaze sternly. 'Ten years ago you murdered Mr Septimus Podgers of West Moon Street, by drowning him in the River Thames close to Cleopatra's Needle.'

The nobleman gasped and turned very pale. His footman, a forbidding, thickset man whose tight-fitting livery bulged as he moved, stepped forward, presumably to throw Holmes and me out into Belgrave Square. Savile waved the man away with a resigned air, however, and said, 'I think perhaps you had better leave us, Francis.' My friend's shot had reached its mark.

'So she's been talking, then,' His Lordship said, with a sigh. 'I had supposed she might.'

Judged by appearances alone, Lord Arthur was an admirable specimen of his class. In his middle thirties, handsome, tall and elegantly presented, he had been charming and scrupulously polite to us since Holmes had requested a private audience with him at his home in Belgrave Square.

The room, too, was furnished elegantly and austerely, even

ascetically, although the carpets looked rather venerable to my eye. Bright forenoon light shone in from the green spaces of the square outside, where early spring flowers were beginning to speckle the earth with colour.

Holmes said sternly, 'I can assure you, Lady Arthur has been the soul of discretion.' I knew, having followed his painstaking investigation of the Winckelkopf case through all its stages, that there had been no information received from any such quarter. Indeed, I had some opportunity to watch the Saviles together at Lady Cissbury's soirée the week before, and their devotion to one another had seemed to me quite exemplary.

Holmes added, gesturing at Savile's hands, 'The chief witnesses against you are these, my lord. You are quite literally betrayed by your own hands.' He clicked his fingers for me to pass him his leather portfolio, which I did without demur. Sherlock Holmes always enjoyed his stagecraft.

'My hands? Good gracious,' said the aristocrat, becoming if anything rather paler. He raised both hands and stared at them as if they bore an ancient inscription he must decipher. He stammered slightly as he enquired, 'May I ask how?'

'These photographs,' Holmes replied, opening the portfolio and brandishing the prints in question. 'I obtained them last week at Lady Cissbury's, under the pretext of photographing your spirit energy. A deplorable and unscientific practice, the feigning of which pained me but proved indispensably useful in this instance.'

Savile looked surprised. 'I say. There was a funny whiskered fellow with glasses and a stoop. Lady Cissbury had him installed in the summer room, so her guests could have their auras photographed. Was that really you?'

Holmes bowed slightly. 'I admit to some small skill in the art of disguise.'

I had been there too, concealed in a closet in case Holmes found himself in need of assistance, but Lord Arthur could hardly be expected to be aware of that.

The aristocrat leaned across to peer at the photographic prints Holmes had placed on the wooden chair beside us, the room being bereft of any writing desk or even a coffee table. Each was a life-sized image of one of Lord Arthur's palms, spread out against the background of a black baize cloth, each line marked clearly in the photographic limelight. In each case Holmes had placed a luggage label next to the little finger, the number written on which distinguished these hands from those of forty-seven other guests. He was still pondering the usefulness of keeping the remainder on file for future use.

'I can't see any spirit energy here,' His Lordship observed peevishly.

Holmes sighed. 'That is what you may expect to see when I take your spirit photograph. More to the point, however, the hands photographed here are indisputably those of the killer of Septimus Podgers.'

'I'm afraid I understand very little of this, Mr Holmes,' Savile said a little plaintively, and I could understand his puzzlement. The Winckelkopf case had been an unusual one even by Holmes's standards, beginning with no more than a name and a time, and leading to a trail of suspicious activity that ended in the death of Podgers the palmist, a decade in the past.

Our involvement in the affair had begun shortly after Inspector Lestrade of Scotland Yard came into possession of a ledger-book, stolen by a cleaning woman from her late employer, an elderly German resident of Soho who had recently died from a severe chill. It seemed that the woman had entertained suspicions that her employer's business was of an illicit nature, and had retained the book in the hope of blackmailing his customers with it, but being unable to locate any of them she had instead turned to the police in hope of a reward. From its contents, Lestrade had realised that the deceased had been a dangerous criminal whom the Yard had been seeking for some decades, a prolific manufacturer of bespoke bombs known by the name 'Herr Winckelkopf'.

The ledger book was a list of sales of explosive devices, and accordingly in many of the entries, alongside the buyer's name or alias and the fee charged (for Winckelkopf had been happy to sell his skills to all comers, whether anarchists, nihilists, Fenians or common assassins, at a price), was a record of the precise time at which the bomb was set to explode.

'Do you mean to say that Winckelkopf wrote down my name?' Lord Arthur asked, when Holmes told him all of this. 'That seems very slipshod practice for a man in his line of business.'

Holmes said, 'On the contrary, you were listed as Mr Robert Smith. It was to identify the owner of that alias that Lestrade asked for my assistance.'

By comparing these times and dates with those of known revolutionary outrages, Lestrade and his men had been able to establish the identities of many of those who had used Winckelkopf's services, but a few eluded him. 'Smith' in particular, who on Tuesday 24th May 1887, ten years previously, had paid the German four pounds, two shillings and sixpence for a mechanism timed to explode at noon on Friday 27th of that month, could not be identified. The police had no record of any explosion occurring at that time, the name was surely a pseudonym, and even if it were not, they could hardly track down and interview every Robert Smith in London. Rather than waste his men's time, Lestrade had invited Holmes to look into the matter.

Holmes had adopted the theory that on this occasion Winckelkopf's normally reliable mechanisms had failed him, and that the bomb had not exploded, or perhaps had exploded sometime later, when its intended target had been absent. He sifted through reports in every newspaper he could find for May and June of 1887, looking for any anomalous occurrences that might indicate something of the kind, until eventually he found, of all things, an account in the *Chichester Express* on Monday 30th May of a sermon preached in the cathedral by the dean at matins on the previous day.

In it the cleric had alluded to an amusing joke played on his family, an ormolu clock sent as a present which had, at that same preset time, emitted a small report and shaken loose an allegorical figure of Liberty, which had broken on the floor. He drew from this some sententious lessons about the limitations of freedom as an ideal, but for Holmes's purposes the important point was that Winckelkopf had been known to use clocks, and ormolu clocks specifically, as a basis for his bombs.

'I can only suppose that the batch of dynamite was defective, or more probably that the explosive was exposed to damp during its journey through the postal service,' Holmes commented.

'I suppose that would explain the outcome,' said Lord Arthur. 'But how did this lead you to Mr Podgers? I confess, Mr Holmes, I am agog.' His enthusiasm seemed sincere, as if he had entirely forgotten the capital predicament in which he found himself.

'Well, the question was naturally who might have wished to assassinate the Dean of Chichester. He is a man of quiet habits, not given to controversy or, as far as I can ascertain, to any firm beliefs at all. But we knew that Herr Winckelkopf was pleased to sell his services to all, and not only those of a political bent. I wondered, then, about the dean's relatives.'

Lord Arthur smiled. 'Ah.'

Like many senior clergymen, the Dean of Chichester was well connected, and with the help of Debrett's *Peerage*, Holmes had been able to compile a comprehensive family tree. This had provided the interesting information that the dean's first cousin once removed, Lady Clementina Beauchamp, had died, apparently of a heart attack, a mere ten days before this putative attempt on the dean's life. Lady Clementina had left much of her property, including a house on Curzon Street, to her cousin's son, Lord Arthur Savile.

Less than six weeks later, Lord Arthur had married the society heiress Sybil Merton, now Lady Arthur Savile, in a ceremony that, according to the gossip columns, had already been twice postponed. His uncle, the Dean of Chichester, had presided.

'The connection between these various events was not altogether clear,' Holmes observed drily. 'As I said, all the indications were that Lady Clementina's death was a natural one. And the dean had issue of his own, meaning that a nephew would have no hope of inheritance and little reason to attempt an assassination. But the connection was sufficient to prompt me to examine all the deaths reported in the papers during May and June that year, in case there were some other pattern linking them.'

'And so Mr Podgers enters the story,' Savile guessed, apparently quite enthralled.

'Indeed. Podgers' body was washed ashore in Greenwich on 2nd June. It was clear that he had drowned. His death was ruled a suicide, ascribed to mental derangement brought on by overwork. As it happened, I recognised the name. Podgers had been a cheiromantist, and was the author of a posthumously published treatise on palmistry that I had read myself, at a stage in my career when I was gauging the merits of physiognomic theories of criminology. It had stuck in my mind because of a vivid account he gave of reading a young man's palm at a party and deducing that its owner would become a murderer.

'Now you may say,' Holmes suggested, 'as Dr Watson did

at this point, that cheiromancy is as nebulous a farrago of poppycock and claptrap as spirit photography.'

I had indeed said as much, quite vocally, when Holmes's investigations reached this stage. As a medical man, I must acknowledge that biometrical descriptions have some validity in predicting criminality – the shape of the skull, for instance, is said to be an indicator of character, and I myself have noticed in my work with Holmes that pickpockets tend to have slim, delicate hands compared to the powerful fists of habitual brawlers – but even at their best, such inferences are general and imprecise. I considered it profoundly improbable that any feature in a man's palm could reliably predict that he would commit a specific misdeed.

Holmes continued, 'Nevertheless, from reading his account of his own theories and practice, I have no doubt that Septimus Podgers believed in it entirely.'

'My wife tells me that Lady Windermere became quite convinced that Podgers was a fraud,' Savile put in. 'The late Lady Windermere, that is, the aunt of the present viscount.'

'Perhaps she did,' said Holmes. 'It was at one of her soirées that you met him, I believe? The society pages place you both at Bentinck House on 29th April.'

Savile nodded, his face paling once more.

Once he had learned of Podgers' connection with Savile, Holmes's interest in the palmist's death was piqued. He had worked out, using tide tables and navigational charts from 1887, along with his compendious knowledge of the Thames's flows, currents and obstacles, approximately where and when the deceased must have entered the water. Accordingly, amid much grumbling from Lestrade about having to chase up the fading paperwork, Holmes had spoken to all the policemen who had been on duty near the Embankment during the 30th and 31st May 1887. At ten years' remove their memories were naturally hazy, but Holmes had the news stories of the day at his fingertips following his perusal of the press archives, and by mentioning contemporary events had been able to jog one man's memory.

This sergeant, though at the time a constable, recalled having seen a gentleman peering over the Embankment by the Needle in the early hours of the morning of the Tuesday, looking as if he had lost something in the river. His memories of the man matched the description of Lord Arthur Savile.

'That is all very well,' Savile pointed out amiably, 'but there must be a good many men in London who match my description. And what reason would you suggest that I had to murder Podgers? I scarcely knew the man.'

'We will come to the question of identification in a moment. In answer to your second question, I do not believe Podgers was your first choice of victim. That was a frail elderly woman who had the misfortune to be connected to you by ties of blood. You were away in Venice at the time of Lady Clementina Beauchamp's death, and while you might have found an agent to murder her on your behalf, I did not think that you would entrust such a vital commission to an intermediary. The easiest way to kill a person in one's absence, without the intervention of a third party, would be by poisoning an item that they would consume at a particular time. It would also be one of the least detectable, if the correct poison were selected.

'It seems you made very little effort to cover your tracks. Mr Pestle, of the apothecaries Pestle and Humbey's, clearly recalls selling you a capsule containing a lethal dose of aconitine in April of that year. He was rather alarmed until you assured him that you needed it to dispose of a sick, though very large, dog. Lady Clementina was known to be a martyr to heartburn, and my conjecture would be that you presented the capsule to her as indigestion medicine.'

'But dear Lady Clem died of natural causes,' Lord Arthur pointed out.

'And so she did. The signs that would distinguish aconitine poisoning from a heart attack are subtle, but I have spoken to Lady Clementina's personal physician, who insists that her body exhibited none of them. She thwarted your plan by dying before it could come into effect, as you must have discovered when you found the capsule untouched while disposing of her effects. Thus you were forced to look for another victim, because while Lady Clementina's death was to your benefit, your motive had never been to profit from her inheritance.'

'I should think not,' agreed Savile with a shudder. Evidently he was of the variety of aristocracy who consider conversation on matters of money to be beneath their dignity.

'And so,' Holmes continued inexorably, 'you turned to your uncle, the dean, and the elaborate assassination scheme you concocted with Herr Winckelkopf, to no ultimate avail after the dynamite in the clock was spoiled. Where, then, to turn? You were running out of relatives, and eager, I am sure, to be married quickly. And so, when a late-night stroll along the Embankment brought a chance encounter with Septimus Podgers, your reaction was immediate. Especially since in many ways Mr Podgers might have been considered the author of all your woes.'

Savile was smiling broadly now. 'And why was that?'

'I have to admit that I am hazy on that point myself, Holmes,' I reminded my friend. Throughout this particular investigation I had been privy to his researches, and thus to more of his thinking than was his habitual practice, but the question of Lord Arthur Savile's incentive for the murder, and his preceding attempts, remained opaque to me.

'It is, I confess, a motive that is unique in my experience,' Holmes admitted. 'Lord Arthur murdered Mr Podgers because

Mr Podgers predicted that Lord Arthur would commit murder.'

'But you said yourself that palmistry's a fraud,' I protested.

'It is. But Mr Podgers was not. In cases of widespread belief, some practitioners of a fraud may also be counted among its victims. I believe Podgers was honest, and sincere in his error. He described in some detail the dilemma he faced in seeing this young man's fate in his palm. Should he tell him, and blight his future, or should he leave him in ignorance, thus failing to warn him of a misfortune he might seek to mitigate, if never to avoid? He tells us that he opted in the end for candour, but not what convinced him to do so.'

'A hundred guineas convinced him, if you must know,' Savile responded haughtily. 'Apparently, I am lucky that he was a less meticulous accounts-keeper than Herr Winckelkopf.'

'Of course, palmistry has no value in predicting the future,' Holmes explained, 'but like any other information, true or false, it can influence it. When a person has their fortune told through any method, however dubious, the knowledge of their supposed fate thenceforth becomes a factor in their decisions. In this case, we must consider the effect produced in the mind of a young man, well-educated but not of exceptional intelligence, in a state of heightened emotion due to his forthcoming marriage and perhaps somewhat impressionable as a result. If such a man came to believe that it was his inescapable destiny to become a murderer, then he might conceivably respond by trying to get this distasteful inevitability over and done with before the wedding.'

'Conceivably he might,' Lord Arthur agreed with a smile. 'But do you suppose that a jury will follow you down such a path, Mr Holmes? Particularly when the accused is a notably handsome man of a wealthy and influential family?'

Despite his lazy defiance, I could hear underlying his words a real concern, if not the fear that I would have felt in his place.

For all his bravado, Savile was seeking Holmes's professional opinion on this point.

'They will believe some of it, I am certain,' Holmes said. 'Ironically, perhaps, they might find the case against you in the matter of Lady Clementina the most damning. You stood to inherit, you bought enough poison to kill a person, and you lied about the reason for it. I fear it would not matter greatly to them that she died before being murdered – you determined that she would die, and her death duly occurred. Attempting to murder someone by poison carries a sentence of lifelong penal servitude. But we have not yet come to the most damning piece of evidence.'

From the portfolio he produced a bound edition of Septimus Podgers' *Treatise on the Human Hand* – Holmes's own copy, singed at the top of the spine from a volatile chemistry experiment conducted somewhat too close to his bookshelves, but perfectly serviceable still.

'The book is illustrated,' he observed, 'with many diagrams of individual palms, showing the points Podgers considered of most interest. For some subjects he illustrates merely the right palm, for some both. These are the lines he found on those of the young man fated to commit murder,' he said, laying open the book on the chair next to the photographs of Lord Arthur's palms. 'You will observe a commendable degree of accuracy in the reproduction,' he said, 'but I imagine these lines were seared into Podgers' memory. We know that Podgers told the owner of these hands that he would kill, and we know that a month later he was dead. It will not be a difficult matter to convince a jury that these were the hands that killed him.'

Lord Arthur sighed. 'It is a shame that the late Lady Windermere never met you, Mr Holmes. She would have so enjoyed lionising you at her parties. Yes, it is all true, exactly as you tell it. I was careless, I suppose, but I never imagined that it could all be connected as you have done. I congratulate you on being that rare yet not always enviable thing: a man whose reputation is perfectly accurate.'

Holmes nodded gravely, accepting the compliment. 'I do not believe that you are an evil man, Lord Arthur. Foolish certainly, impressionable to a grave fault, and lacking the sympathetic connection with others that for most men would have made such crimes unthinkable, but not, I think, with any tendency to spite or malice. But you must see that I cannot fail to pass on what I know to the police.'

Lord Arthur said, 'I am a family man, Mr Holmes. I love my wife extremely, and my son and daughter mean everything to me.' He hesitated, and now I could see real anguish in his eyes. 'I am also, I may say reluctantly but without any undue modesty, extravagantly rich. If there is anything you need, I am in a position to make your life very comfortable indeed.'

'I am not Septimus Podgers, my lord.' Holmes's voice was cold. 'You will not find my professional judgement amenable to the promise of a hundred guineas. Nor do I care to be cast in the role of blackmailer, which is what I should become if I accepted money in return for my silence. Besides, I rather think that you are less solvent than you pretend. Watson, please show Lord Arthur your revolver.'

As instructed, I produced my army service weapon from the pocket of my jacket.

Holmes said, 'I had intended, out of consideration for the feelings of your family, to offer you an opportunity to surrender yourself to the police, but after what you have said I believe that you would take undue advantage of such a courtesy. Instead, I must insist that you accompany us to Scotland Yard, where we shall introduce you to Inspector Lestrade.'

CHAPTER TWO
THE HEIR IN THE HANDBAG

We led His Lordship to our waiting cab, the threat of my firearm overcoming the objections of the grim footman Francis. As we left the house, under the gaze of passing pedestrians and nursemaids with perambulators, another cab drew up carrying Lord Arthur's wife and their two children. I feared recriminations, but Lady Arthur was far too well-bred to cause a scene in sight of all their neighbours on the square. She listened tight-lipped as her husband told her of our suspicions, in precise, cheerful tones that spoke eloquently of his guilt. She did not, I thought, look especially surprised. Then, glaring at us with eyes that held tears but dropped none, she led her children inside and we took her husband away to his appointment with Lestrade.

'It is hard on them, of course,' Holmes observed that evening, over an excellent plate of roast beef and Yorkshire pudding at Simpsons-in-the-Strand. 'But a man with such a deed in his past cannot be allowed to walk free.'

'I suppose not,' I said. 'And yet he seems to have led a harmless enough life since his crime. Was he really a danger to the public?'

Holmes said, 'A man who has murdered once may do so again, if a reason presents itself. The cause of Savile's downfall was his gullibility, and I saw no sign that he has become wiser during the past ten years. He could be easily led into criminal acts on behalf of others, if those others were persuasive enough. Besides, he is in financial difficulty, and the effect of that on a man of Lord Arthur's background must not be underestimated. If I had accepted his generous offer of a bribe, he would have been obliged to pay me with money somehow ill-gotten, or, more likely, to arrange to meet me for payment on the Embankment, late at night and at high tide.'

I said, 'I had been under the impression that his wealth was beyond question. You said he came into the late Lord Rugby's fortune when he turned twenty-one.' Holmes had ruled out from his considerations the death of that nobleman, another of Lord Arthur's uncles, in a hunting accident witnessed by many when Savile was a mere boy.

'Come, Watson, you know there are many ways in which a gentleman may lose a fortune, or even several of them. A gullible gentleman especially so. Besides, you have the evidence of your eyes. Did Lord Arthur's house look like that of a wealthy man to you?'

'It's in Belgrave Square,' I protested mildly.

Holmes tutted. 'That he was moneyed in the past is not in dispute. Certainly the property has considerable capital value, but it is also one of the last possessions that a man, especially a man with a family to house, would divest himself of. I suspect that if we made enquiries, we might yet find it heavily mortgaged. Did you not note the absences on the walls where pictures would have hung?'

'The room did seem rather sparse,' I admitted. 'And there was very little furniture.'

'And even fewer ornaments,' Holmes pointed out.

'Perhaps he simply dislikes antiques,' I said. 'He's obviously a man who knows his own taste.'

'He dresses well,' Holmes allowed, 'though in last season's clothes, which I imagine must pain him. He cannot afford new clothes for his servants either, even when the servants themselves are new. Francis seemed faithful enough, but he was not of the more refined species of footman, which is to say the more expensive. And dressed, if I am not mistaken, in a recent predecessor's livery.'

Holmes's points seemed indisputable, as they were wont to be. It would not do to let him become complacent, however, and I was casting around for some counterargument when a voice hailed us from close by. 'Have I the honour of addressing Mr Sherlock Holmes and Dr Watson?'

I looked up into the studiedly nonchalant face of another gentleman of about Savile's age. Not as tall as Lord Arthur and somewhat less good-looking, he was nonetheless a more striking figure, impeccably turned out in white tie, white gloves and a dove-grey tailcoat, with a pale peach carnation in his buttonhole. My knowledge of the most expensive fashions is sadly limited by my means, but it was clear to any observer that this man's appearance was of the utmost concern to him.

He said, 'Forgive me, gentlemen, but your landlady told me that I might find you here. I've been searching for you rather urgently.' His expression radiated well-bred impassivity, but the strain in his voice betrayed his agitation.

Holmes had risen, and so did I. 'Pray join us,' my friend said. 'Do please partake of the Beaune. How may we be of service, Mr...?'

'Goring,' replied the newcomer, sitting with us. 'Viscount Goring, if we must be precise about it. And I suppose we must.'

'Ah yes, Lord Goring,' said Holmes, shaking his hand. 'Your father is the Earl of Caversham, I believe. I had the honour of being of some small service to him during his time in the Cabinet.'

Lord Goring nodded. 'Yes, he has mentioned you approvingly. Apparently you are a fine example of what a man may achieve if he applies himself, something I persistently refuse to do. The general theme is a perennial one with him, although you are one of its less commonly heard variations. His high opinion explains why I thought of coming to you tonight under what are, I'm afraid, somewhat trying circumstances.'

'It appears to be our day for interfering in the affairs of the aristocracy,' Holmes observed. 'Pray tell us about these trying circumstances, Lord Goring.'

Waving away a renewed offer of wine, Lord Goring said, 'I come to you by a rather circuitous route. Before speaking to your landlady at Baker Street, I was briefly at my brother-in-law's house at Grosvenor Square. But for most of the evening, I was in Belgrave Square.'

From this I assumed that he must be a friend of Lord or Lady Arthur Savile, come to berate or plead with us on their behalf. Holmes must have been thinking something similar, as before the viscount could say more, he asked, 'What number Belgrave Square, please?'

Lord Goring blinked in surprise. 'Number 149, the home of the Moncrieff family.' This was, I remembered, the opposite side from the Savile house.

'Thank you,' said Holmes. 'It is as well to have all the facts at hand. Pray continue.'

'There was a ball there this evening. The Honourable Gwendolen Moncrieff is an old schoolfriend of my wife's sister-in-law, and we were all invited. Up to a point it was a pleasant enough occasion, with many of the best type of people there, and many of the worst as well, which I always find the best combination for enjoyable company. The latter are amusing, the former instructive, and those who are neither may occupy themselves in attempting to distinguish the best and the worst apart.'

Rather irritably, Holmes said, 'I assume you to be of the second type, Lord Goring, for your conversation has not been greatly instructive so far. If you have brought me nothing more than epigrams, I will ask your leave to enjoy our meal in peace.'

His Lordship accepted the rebuke calmly. 'Forgive me,' he said again. 'I often speak frivolously in times of difficulty. I've said that the evening was pleasant up to a point, and that point was the discovery of a body.'

'A body!' I exclaimed. 'Discovered where?'

'In the back garden of the house, beneath a balcony. It appears the fellow fell. A tragedy, no doubt, for those who knew him, but appearances conspire to make the matter more immediately troublesome to one much closer to me.'

'And who is that?' Holmes asked, an eyebrow arched.

Lord Goring looked grave. 'I am speaking of my wife. I left her at her brother's house on my way to Baker Street, but I fear that will avert the unpleasantness only temporarily. The police were being summoned to Belgrave Square as we left.'

I said, 'You fear they will suspect that she was involved in the death?'

'I can hardly suppose that they will not. She assures me the deceased was unknown to her. Certainly he is a stranger to me, which many might say is to his credit. But it doesn't explain how he came to be clutching my wife's brooch as he fell. And neither, I am afraid, can I.'

'Ah,' said Holmes. 'That, certainly, is a complication which our friends at Scotland Yard are unlikely to ignore. Watson and I will accompany you at once to Belgrave Square.'

'I am exceedingly grateful.' He clicked his fingers for a waiter. 'Allow me to answer for your interrupted meal.'

'I regret I must refuse, Lord Goring,' Holmes said. 'My business is to uncover the truth, and that you may rely on me to do without fear or favour. Whether or not my findings absolve Lady Goring of blame, it will compromise them if I am seen to have begun the case in your debt, even to the tune of dinner and a bottle of a middling wine.'

Lord Goring accepted the truth of this, and we collected our coats, our hats and his elegant antique walking-cane, and stepped out into the chilly spring evening, where His Lordship's landau awaited us. It took us along the Strand, where hotel guests and theatregoers strolled in the warm amber glow of the gas-lamps, past Nelson's Column and the Admiralty and between the majestic rows of plane trees on the Mall, in the direction of Belgravia.

On the way, Holmes asked Lord Goring about his hosts for the evening. 'I believe I have heard of the family,' he said. 'Who is the Honourable Mrs Moncrieff's husband?'

'Oh,' Goring replied easily, 'his name's Ernest Moncrieff. I'm not surprised that you've heard of him, he was rather famous for a little while. He used to be known, in London at least, as Ernest Worthing.'

'Good heavens!' I exclaimed. I remembered the case well – it had been widely reported in the newspapers at the time.

John Worthing had been a country squire and Justice of the Peace, usually known at his home in Hertfordshire as Jack, but to his friends in town by the name Ernest. He had been adopted as an infant and brought up by a philanthropic gentleman named Thomas Cardew, who on his death had left his country seat and much of his wealth to Worthing. With them came the guardianship of Cardew's granddaughter, Cecily Cardew, who received the rest of his fortune.

Two years before our encounter with Lord Goring, Worthing had discovered that he was by birth the elder son and heir of the late General Ernest Moncrieff, and thereby that his Christian name was, indeed, Ernest. Unknown to any of them, the Honourable Gwendolen Fairfax, to whom Worthing had recently become engaged, was in fact his cousin, while his close friend Algernon Moncrieff, through whom he had met Miss Fairfax, was none other than his younger brother.

In itself, this assortment of coincidences would have been enough to make headlines, especially when it transpired that Algernon Moncrieff had also become engaged to his brother's ward, Cecily Cardew. However, it had been the details of John Worthing's (or rather, Ernest Moncrieff's) early history that had especially captured the imaginations of both journalists and the reading public. He had learned of his true identity from the information of a former employee in the household of the then-Colonel Moncrieff, the nursemaid who had thoughtlessly misplaced him as a baby. Thomas Cardew had found the child in a cloakroom at Victoria Station, where this inept woman had accidentally deposited him in a handbag. The name 'John Worthing' had been bestowed by Cardew after the seaside resort to which he had been bound that day, although his discovery of the infant had naturally caused his plans to change.

Some of these details sprang immediately to my mind when Goring mentioned the name, while my memory of others I refreshed later with the help of Holmes's comprehensive Index. The case of the so-called 'Handbag Heir' and his relatives had become something of an obsession with the popular press during the summer of 1895, though they soon moved on to celebrating some other sensation.

'Quite so,' said Goring drily in response to my involuntary utterance. 'I need hardly say that great delicacy must be exercised in discussing Ernest Moncrieff's family history.'

'Of course,' I agreed.

'It is point of discretion among his friends to avoid mentioning it at all, in fact, as it is naturally a subject that causes him the greatest excitement.'

He said this with an air of amusement that it took me a moment to puzzle out. 'You mean that if it's mentioned he talks about it incessantly?'

Coolly, Goring replied, 'I would not like to say so, Dr Watson. Certainly not in so many words.'

Passing the Palace, we shortly entered that district where so many of our nation's most august and honoured families have their London homes, and in a brief while we found ourselves once more at Belgrave Square.

This close consists of a leafy, landscaped central area of greenery surrounded by beautiful cream-coloured terraces in the Georgian style. Four separate mansions stand at its corners, marking the cardinal points of the compass, but Number 149 was one of the terraced houses, standing six storeys high including attic and basement, with a pillared front entrance and balconies at several levels, front and rear.

These details were familiar to me, of course, both from my long residence in London and more particularly from our visit to Lord Arthur Savile's house that morning. I glanced across the square towards the Saviles' house in the far terrace as our cab drew up, but my view was blocked by the trees thronging the central park.

Seeing me looking, Lord Goring observed, 'A few years ago, fashion favoured the far side of the square, but she is an inconstant mistress. Lady Bloxham, to whom Cardew and then Moncrieff let this house for many years, wouldn't have cared to be on the fashionable side, but Moncrieff's mother-in-law has a different view.'

I was briefly surprised by the idea that one of London's

most exclusive addresses could be subject to such gradations of prestige, but by then our cab was coming to a halt. As we climbed out, one of a brace of police constables came across to us, leaving his colleague stationed at the doorstep of Number 149. He touched the brim of his helmet and said, 'Party's over, I'm afraid, gents. There's been an accident.'

Goring said easily, 'Nonsense, my man. I told you when Lady Goring and I left that I would be back.'

Recognising him then, the constable said, 'That's as may be, my lord, but my inspector's orders is that there's not to be all these comings and goings. It's all we can do to stop any more guests leaving than has already. We had to let Lady Bracknell go just now,' he added, shuddering slightly at the memory.

'Then I suppose your inspector should be delighted to see one of us returning. Let us in, there's a good fellow.' Lord Goring strode towards the front door with that unquestioning assumption of entitlement that aristocratic breeding uniquely confers – although I have observed that Holmes effects a very passable imitation. He did so now, leaving me following both of them rather more diffidently.

The policeman on the door stepped readily aside. We followed, and as this second man touched his helmet to us I realised I recognised him from some past case of Holmes's. He said, 'Mr Holmes, Dr Watson. We wondered if we'd be seeing you here. The inspector's out the back with the body.'

Holmes paused for just a moment. 'Which inspector, Constable Northbrook?'

'Inspector Gregson, sir.'

Holmes nodded thoughtfully, then declared, 'He will do.'

A butler met us in the entrance lobby and began to show us through to the rear of the house. As we passed along the main hallway, however, a side-door burst open emitting a surge of chatter and cigar smoke, and a handsome moustached man emerged. He was rather younger than Lord Goring and wore a white gardenia in his buttonhole. 'Are these *more* policemen, Merriman?' he asked the butler irritably. 'Oh, it's you, Goring. I thought you were the police again. There's an absolute legion of them infesting my lawn. I don't believe I've ever seen so many together in one place. I keep expecting them to break into a comic chorus. Who are these fellows?' It was clear that this man was our unwitting host, Mr Ernest Moncrieff, formerly known as Ernest or Jack Worthing.

Lord Goring smiled. 'Auxiliaries for the legion, I am afraid, Moncrieff. This is Mr Sherlock Holmes, and this is Dr John Watson.'

'Very probably they are, but what on earth do you mean by bringing them here?' Moncrieff demanded, shaking our hands peevishly. Behind him, in what must have been the house's diminutive ballroom, a band struck up a waltz. 'It's outrageous that I should be besieged by official detectives in my own home, without amateurs, even gentleman amateurs, coming to reinforce them.'

'My dear fellow, I've brought them here to do the police's work for them,' Goring explained patiently. 'If they can uncover the truth of this matter then you will no longer be besieged.'

Another man, slighter, darker and a few years younger than Moncrieff, had emerged from the ballroom behind him, holding a plateful of small chocolate éclairs. This man said airily, 'In my experience the truth, like brick walls and bathers, is generally better covered up. In all cases a tasteful drapery is more acceptable than the brute reality.' He popped one of the pastries into his mouth.

'The dead man might feel otherwise,' Holmes observed, 'were he in a position to feel anything at all, Mr…?'

Ernest sighed. 'Oh, this is my preposterous brother,

Algernon.' Though I would not have taken them for blood relations, Ernest's voice was full of the impatience and affection that men feel for their brothers, or for their closest friends.

Algernon Moncrieff fastidiously finished his éclair before saying, 'Not one of us knows what the chap was even doing here. I consider it unconscionably presumptuous to fall to one's death from the balcony of a perfect stranger. Even if a man has no balcony of his own from which to arrange a mortal fall, many of our public buildings are designed to afford every facility for such occasions. Oh, are you leaving us, Mrs Teville?'

This was addressed to a woman dressed very glamorously in a deep purple ballgown with lace at the cuffs, embellished with pearls and a slightly faded mink stole. Though the colour of the gown indicated mourning, the impression made by the ensemble was anything but sombre. To my practised eye she looked to be around my own age, which is to say no longer by any means in the bloom of youth; but her attire and hair, and the powder and rouge she wore on her face, were artfully contrived to make her seem ten or more years younger.

She said, in a low-pitched, rather dramatic voice, 'I am afraid I must. It has been a most pleasant evening, apart from those parts of it that have been frightful. But really, such a misfortune as has occurred tonight might happen to anybody. You have my condolences, Mr Moncrieff.'

'Our misfortune is as nothing compared with the loss of your company,' Ernest gallantly assured her. She snapped open a prettily decorated fan to mask her smile.

'Now, Mr Moncrieff, you must not flirt with me,' Mrs Teville said, severely gratified. 'My late husband would not have cared for it, and I am quite certain that your dear wife would not.'

Ernest replied gravely, 'Since a man may not flirt with his wife, Mrs Teville, he is left with no choice but to flirt without her.'

'My dear fellow,' Algernon remonstrated, 'Cecily and I flirt constantly. The alternative would be to talk seriously to one another, and if that were to happen I could hardly answer for the survival of our marriage.'

The partygoers were still impeding our path, and Holmes was becoming visibly irritated with their badinage. Lord Goring said, 'If you will excuse us, Mrs Teville, I have brought these gentlemen to assist the police in the garden.'

'Oh,' Mrs Teville declared, showing no inclination to move. 'And who are these very helpful gentlemen?'

Holmes bowed stiffly. 'Sherlock Holmes, madam, at your service. And this is Dr Watson.'

Mrs Teville gasped in excitement, unless it was alarm, and fanned herself quickly. 'Sherlock Holmes, the adventurer and sleuth? Sir, if I have need of your services I shall most certainly call upon them.'

'I trust that you never will,' Holmes replied.

'Oh, but I hope I shall,' she laughed. 'I should far rather you were investigating someone else on my behalf than investigating me on theirs.'

'Allow me to accompany you to your carriage, Mrs Teville,' a man of around her age suggested smoothly as he, too, emerged from the ballroom, and claimed the widow's arm as if Holmes were not there. 'The police, puritans that they are, try to keep us here on the grounds that we may be guilty. Guilty!' he laughed. 'Speaking for myself, I hardly know the meaning of the word.' He was grey-haired but very attractive, tall and obviously strong, and like Goring clearly prided himself on his appearance.

'I thank you, Lord Illingworth,' Mrs Teville replied, rather coldly. 'I hardly think the services of an experienced diplomat such as yourself are necessary for such a simple venture. Perhaps Mr Holmes or Dr Watson would instead oblige?'

By now Holmes was looking extremely impatient. 'I regret, madam, that we are both required most urgently on other business.'

'Then it shall have to be Lord Illingworth. I am delighted to have met you, Mr Holmes, nevertheless.' She allowed herself to be led to the front door.

'Will the police let her through?' I wondered.

'After their encounter with our aunt, I doubt they will have the heart to refuse,' observed Ernest, with a sympathetic shudder.

'Indeed,' Algernon agreed. 'If the demoralising effect she has on policemen were somehow to be applied to their opponents, I should expect the capital's crime statistics to halve overnight.'

As we followed Lord Goring to the back door, I heard Ernest retort, 'Algy, I can't see how you can possibly eat éclairs at a time like this.'

'I can't see how you can possibly expect me to eat these particular éclairs at any other time,' Algernon protested as they retreated into the ballroom.

Goring led us out into the rear garden, which was indeed full of policemen. It was not, however, a large garden, and this initial impression soon gave way to a realisation that there were only a handful of uniformed men there, a sergeant and four constables, together with the tall, pale figure of Inspector Tobias Gregson.

The terraced houses in Belgrave Square are narrow, and extend a long way to the rear as well as vertically. Since all are equipped with a mews giving onto a lane at the back, for stables and additional servants' accommodation, the space available for a garden is limited, and indeed many of the houses lack one altogether. Number 149's garden was in a tight L shape surrounding one end of the house, little more than a thin green strip of lawn running around this end of the long ballroom. Its longer section was interrupted in the middle by a square of flagstones surrounding a granite plinth. As Algernon Moncrieff had suggested, one of the floors above boasted a balcony, and it was from this that the man who lay dead upon the flagstones had evidently fallen.

'Well, well, Mr Holmes, Dr Watson,' Inspector Gregson said. 'I am surprised to see you here.'

'Lord Goring was kind enough to involve me in this case,' Holmes explained smoothly, 'but I have explained to him that my interest is exclusively in finding out the truth.'

'Ah, Lord Goring,' Gregson replied, unhappily. 'I'm glad you have returned. We will need to speak to you later, you know, and to Lady Goring also. I have people talking to the servants downstairs, but the guests are going to need to make their statements when they're ready.'

'For my own part, I am at your service,' His Lordship replied. 'For Lady Goring, the morning will have to suffice.'

'May I examine the body?' I asked the inspector.

'Surely, Dr Watson. In fact, gentlemen, to be frank I would appreciate both of your opinions,' Gregson said, drawing us a little away from Lord Goring. 'This is something of a ticklish situation. There are more earls and viscounts and honourables at this event than you can shake a stick at, and if I put a foot wrong and arrest the incorrect person, my superiors will not be best pleased. Your presence here may be unexpected, but I cannot pretend that it is unwelcome.'

I crossed over to the dead man. 'Do you have any idea who he is?' Holmes asked.

'A stranger to the household, as it seems,' said Gregson. 'The butler says he turned up for the first time this evening, asking to speak to Mr Moncrieff. He gave his name as… what was it, sergeant? I didn't make a note.'

The sergeant murmured in his ear.

'Ah yes,' said Gregson. 'Apparently the deceased's name is Bunbury.'

CHAPTER THREE
THE UNEXPECTED GUEST

The unfortunate Mr Bunbury was a slight man of about thirty, clean shaven with his black hair closely cropped, dressed in a cheap suit that nevertheless fitted him tolerably well. He lay on his back on the flagstones, his limbs splayed, his eyes regarding the starry sky with appalled horror. The state of his cranium, and a bloodstain on the plinth, suggested that a collision between them had been the immediate cause of his demise.

The dead man's attire marked him out as neither a servant, all of whom were garbed in appropriate livery for the ball, nor a musician or guest, as they naturally wore evening dress. In his left hand he clutched a scrap of white lace on which a cluster of jewels gleamed duskily.

'What is that plinth for?' I heard Holmes ask as I knelt on the chilly grass.

'I'm told it used to hold a sundial,' Gregson replied. 'The previous resident liked to keep one, though this garden must get very little sun. Apparently Mr Moncrieff had an idea of installing some sculpture there, so has never had it removed.'

I quickly established that the cause of death was as it appeared. I said, 'The poor fellow would have died immediately.'

The ground was hard and frosty tonight, but had he fallen onto the lawn instead I thought that he would probably have survived.

'Who found him?' Holmes asked Gregson.

'The Earl of Illingworth,' the inspector replied heavily, and I remembered the man who had offered to escort Mrs Teville from the premises. 'A bachelor, so he's here on his own. He is something distinguished in the diplomatic service, though I think he's between assignments just now. He had just stepped out to take the air in the garden with Mrs Moncrieff, and, well, they couldn't have missed him lying there.'

This end of the house was separated from the garden by French windows. As it was a cold night these were closed and curtained off inside, but I was aware of those curtains twitching and eyes periodically observing us from the ballroom.

Holmes said, 'Please be specific, Inspector. Which Mrs Moncrieff?'

'Oh – Mrs Algernon Moncrieff, I gather. Cecily. The host's sister-in-law.'

'Also his former ward and his wife's cousin by marriage,' Holmes noted. 'The family history is a convoluted one.'

'That's often the way of it in these aristocratic families, isn't it?' said Gregson. 'Saving your presence, Lord Goring.'

'Oh, please don't mind me,' His Lordship said, a little impatiently. 'I had the very good fortune to marry a woman to whom I am no relation whatsoever.'

'Nor to the Moncrieffs?' Holmes asked.

'No, neither of us. My wife's family are the Chilterns. Her brother is Sir Robert Chiltern, the parliamentarian.'

I had been examining the late Bunbury for other injuries, but had found little out of the ordinary. I closed the man's eyes now, and stood up. 'The only recent wound is the one that killed him,' I said, 'although there's a scratch on the back of his right hand that's a few days old. If he was pushed, it looks like an unexpected shove rather than a protracted fight. But equally he might have fallen unassisted.'

'It's hard to see how,' Gregson observed practically, peering up at the second-floor balcony. The metal railing looked as if it would come up to a little below waist height. 'Unless he was blind drunk, of course.'

'If so, it is hardly likely that the servants would have admitted him,' said Holmes. 'Did you find anything else, Watson?'

'Well, if his hands are any guide, he's no gentleman,' I said. 'The fingers are calloused and the fingernails roughly trimmed, and there's a strong smell of carbolic soap about them. Though he's scrawny, his muscles are well developed. I'd say he was some kind of manual labourer – the scratch might well be from a nail or a thorn.'

Holmes knelt beside me and leaned close to sniff the dead man's face. The suddenness of the action made me recoil a little. 'I detect no odour of alcohol,' my friend observed coolly. 'Bring your lantern nearer, will you, sergeant?' Lifting the man's right hand, he pulled the sleeve up slightly, then quickly loosened the tie and unbuttoned the collar of the shirt. 'His hands and wrists are rather darker than his arms, as is his face. It is early in the year for a suntan to appear, yet this suggests the beginnings of one. It continues somewhat below the neckline, as if he habitually wears an open shirt or smock. A soldier might catch the sun on the parade ground, but that would stop strictly at the collar. An outdoor worker, then, though he lacks the muscular development of one whose main work is hefting and carrying.'

He sat back on his heels. 'Though cheap, the suit is new. The shave and haircut are also recent. He had a little money, saved from his wages perhaps, and wished to present himself well.' He ran his quick, deft fingers across the man's body, probing his pockets, but his search turned up nothing out of the ordinary: a handkerchief, matches, a few loose coppers.

'A labouring man, washed, trimmed and turned out neatly in a suit, calling at a gentleman's house in the evening and asking to speak to him,' Holmes repeated. 'Whoever he was, he must have felt he had some compelling reason to seek out Ernest Moncrieff, and something to say that would command his attention. Or was it Algernon Moncrieff he expected to see?'

Gregson checked his own notebook and conferred with his sergeant, but neither of them could be clear on this point. 'It sounds as if we'll need to talk to the fellow who let him in,' the inspector said.

'Then let us turn our attention from his hands to their contents,' suggested Holmes. He gently prised from the dead man's left hand the cloth with its jewellery. The material was a delicate white lace, torn raggedly free from some larger garment, and the brooch, which had been mostly hidden by the fabric and by the corpse's fingers, now shone in the moonlight with a bright, clear, faceted light.

Despite his previous comment, Holmes scrutinised the corpse's hand carefully before allowing it to fall. He then stood and showed us all the brooch.

It was six-sided, with radial spokes of silver set with diamonds, and parallel strings of similar stones forming a hexagonal spiral around and across them, from the centre to the outer edge. In that centre sat an eight-legged spider, intricately constructed from darker metal and sapphires. It was a beautiful piece, despite the perverse choice of subject matter, and I thought that any young woman not prey to a fear of the species would be delighted to wear it.

'It is an heirloom piece,' Lord Goring noted, 'belonging to my mother's family. It's valuable, of course, but not scandalously so. I would wager that it was not the most expensive item being worn here tonight.'

'Worth stealing, even so,' Gregson pointed out.

'Oh, undoubtedly, Inspector.'

'And the lace?' Holmes asked. 'It is from a lady's shawl, if I am not mistaken. Had Lady Goring such an article of clothing with her tonight?'

'Oh, yes,' said Goring again. 'She was wearing the shawl, and the brooch was pinned to it.'

'And is that the rest of it?' Holmes asked, pointing.

So focused had my attention been on the ground where the corpse lay, and the balcony from which we assumed he had fallen, that I had barely glanced in the other direction, towards the grounds of the neighbouring house. Had I done so, I could hardly have failed to notice the white shape hanging, like a ghost's discarded shroud, from the tall beech tree which in daylight must have shaded most of Number 148's garden.

'It could well be,' Lord Goring agreed. 'I should have to see it more closely.'

'Perhaps an adventurous constable might be prevailed upon to retrieve it, Gregson?' Holmes suggested, oblivious to the nervous glances this provoked from the uniformed policemen. 'In the meantime, I should like to inspect that balcony.'

As we returned to the house, he confided to me, 'I do not think that the late Mr Bunbury tore the brooch from the shawl himself. The corners of the spider's web are sharp, but he had no scratches on either of his palms, only the partially healed one you found on the back of his right hand. Nor were there any strands of lace beneath his fingernails.'

The Moncrieffs' butler had been waiting to assist, and he now showed Holmes and myself up to the second floor of the house. On this level the space above the garden end of the ballroom

was occupied by a rather fine library, three of its walls lined with
shelves of books and periodicals in leather-bound editions. A fire
burned low in an ornate fireplace, and the faint sound of music
drifted up from beneath us. There were two armchairs and a sofa,
upholstered in the softest red leather, a writing desk and a table
bearing an antique globe. The fourth wall bore pictures and two
sets of floor-length curtains in red velvet, the nearer of which
Holmes drew aside to reveal another pair of French windows.

He tried the handles, and tutted. 'Locked.' Crossing to the
other pair of curtains, he threw them open to find the second set
of windows slightly ajar. He pulled the handles and they opened
easily. 'Merriman, has this room been used during the ball?'

'No, sir,' the butler replied. 'That is to say, it has not been
locked, but the guests have not been directed here. The music
room has been in use,' he added, gesturing to the room beneath
us, the door of which had stood wide open as we passed to show
empty chairs, 'but the string quartet has now left. Mr Moncrieff
is fond of music.'

I said, 'But someone who knew the house could have found
their way in there?'

'Yes, sir.'

Holmes said, 'Are these windows normally kept locked?'

'As a rule, but Mr Moncrieff smokes on the balcony when
the mood takes him. He keeps his own key. I generally check
them last thing at night, sir, and lock them if necessary.'

'I saw another balcony, up on the third floor,' Holmes said.
I had too, but it had been much smaller and projected from the
foremost wall of the garden, facing directly to the rear. Bunbury
would have had to have leaped, not merely fallen, to have reached
the flagstoned area from there.

'The master bedroom, sir. That room *is* locked, and the floor
is out of bounds to guests.'

'Yes, I see. Thank you, Merriman. Wait here a moment, will you?' Holmes stepped through the curtains onto the balcony and I joined him, not without a certain reluctance to plunge back into the cold night air. Beneath us in the narrow garden the body had been covered with a blanket, and two of the policemen were assembling a stretcher.

I said, 'It sounds as if anyone could have been up here with Bunbury. The servants as well as the houseguests. Even the musicians.'

Holmes nodded. 'Some will be accounted for, of course. The musicians will have been in view for most of the time, and the absence of any of them would have been audible as well as visible. An event like this is an onerous affair for servants, and they too will have been kept occupied for much of the time. It would also have been noticed if the host or hostess, or any of the more conspicuous guests, had been out of the view of the others for very long. But nothing we have seen here narrows the possibilities significantly.'

We peered down at the lawn again, perhaps eight yards below us. One of the constables had found a ladder and a rake, and now was balanced above the garden wall, gingerly trying to hook the shawl down from the neighbour's tree. Gregson stood nearby, calling up with helpful advice. The music from the ballroom was louder out here, a ghoulishly cheery accompaniment to the scene below.

'It's a survivable fall if one landed on the grass,' I said.

'Quite,' Holmes agreed. 'A lucky man might even escape injury. But… face me, Watson. I want to recreate the scene.'

At his instruction, I turned my back upon Bunbury's body and faced the French windows. He positioned me leaning back upon the metal railing balustrade, which, as I had supposed, ended a little below my waist. 'Let me see,' he said. 'If a man were standing there... and were pushed – *thus*...' Suddenly, to my alarm, his palms were against my chest, and pressing hard. The force was not great, but it was inexorable, and I immediately felt myself overbalancing.

'Steady on, Holmes!' I cried, clutching at his lapels to steady myself. The pressure relented immediately, and Holmes stepped back from me. I moved away from the edge at once.

'Yes, quite,' Holmes said, calmly. 'Forgive me, Watson. If I had warned you of my intentions, your response would not have been the spontaneous one I needed to see. I think a man pushed thus would try, as you did, to save himself from falling by seizing his attacker's clothing. If that failed, he would have no further opportunity to arrest his fall. He would topple backwards over the balustrade, and would, I submit, end up exactly where we found Bunbury, and with equivalent injuries.'

'And if his attacker's clothing were flimsy, with some of it in his hand,' I agreed, shivering slightly. Though I was used by now to Holmes's occasional need to re-enact crimes for his own satisfaction, I wished he had felt less need for psychological realism.

Holmes nodded, oblivious to my continuing discomfiture. 'Whether he would have had time to grasp it if he were pushed more sharply is not a question we can safely test,' he noted. 'And there is the matter of Bunbury's unscratched palms.'

We stepped back into the library, where Merriman had been joined by a very nervous youth whom he introduced as Peter, the pageboy who had let the deceased into the house. He had, the butler explained to us, just completed his statement to the police, and had come to tell us what he had told them.

'The poor bloke come to the tradesmen's entrance, sirs,' the boy stammered. 'Down in the area, what you get to through the gate in the railings next to the front door. He said as his name was Mr Bunbury, and how I should be sure to tell Mr Moncrieff that.'

'How did he speak?' Holmes asked.

'Not sure what you mean, sir,' said Peter.

'Did he sound like an educated man? Had he any noticeable accent?'

'No, sir, nothing like that. He just sounded like an ordinary bloke.'

'A working Londoner, then. Did he appear drunk to you?' Holmes asked.

Peter shook his head. 'Not to notice, sir. For all I'd know he could have had a couple before he came, but he wasn't talking funny or wobbly on his pins or nothing.'

'Which Moncrieff brother did he ask for?' Holmes continued.

Peter hung his head. 'I didn't even think to find out, sir – I just thought it must be the master he wanted. I clean forgot Mr Algernon was here for the do.'

'Peter has only been with us a few weeks, sir,' Merriman explained, a little defensively.

'Did you suggest that Mr Bunbury should wait here in the library?' Holmes asked.

Peter smiled gratefully. 'That's right, sir. He said as he didn't want to get mixed up with the guests, though that would never have been allowed in any case, sir. I remembered when a tailor's man came here last week with some bills to pay, Mr Merriman asked him to wait in the library. Then he told the master the bloke was here, and the master went straight out to his club.'

The butler had been clearing his throat loudly during this last, but Peter ploughed on, oblivious. 'So I put Mr Bunbury in here, sir, see, then I went to see if I could find the master, only then Lady Caroline Pontefract wanted her coat, sir, and when Lady Caroline wants something you don't keep her waiting, so I went to deal with that and—'

'Yes, well, never mind all of that, Peter. Did you tell Mr Moncrieff that he had a caller waiting for him?'

'Well, sir, what with one thing and other, sir, I didn't get to it, no. I did tell Mr Merriman, and he said I should find the master and let him know, but then cook needed some fetching and carrying done, and then – well, like you say, sir, never mind all of that – as I says, what with one thing and another I… well, I forgot about it all. I did remember later on, see, but that was only after someone had shouted about finding a body and I'd gone out to the garden to see, and it was him. And by then it was too late, of course.'

'Yes, I see,' said Holmes. 'Merriman, did *you* tell either Mr Moncrieff that this man was in the library?'

'I did mention it to our employer, sir, but he was with several of his guests at the time. He told me he had no intention of interrupting pleasure for business. Mr Moncrieff has views on such things.'

Holmes turned his attention back to the pageboy. 'Peter, this may become important. Do you remember noticing what time it was when Mr Bunbury arrived?'

'Why yes, sir. The kitchen clock had just chimed the quarter past ten, sir.'

'And when was the body found, Merriman?'

'Quite close to quarter to eleven, sir.'

I fished out my pocket-watch and glanced at it. It was half past midnight now. From what I understood of such things, the Moncrieffs' ball would normally have had at least an hour left to run.

Holmes thanked both servants and we went down past the music room to the ground floor, hoping to confer with Gregson in the garden. Once again, however, before we could reach the back door the ballroom door opened to disgorge one of the revellers.

This time it was a woman who emerged, in her late twenties, with a strikingly attractive face to which I imagined laughter and hauteur would come equally readily. She fixed us with a stern glance and said to us, 'Mr Holmes, Dr Watson, I am Gwendolen Moncrieff. You are so busy that I cannot bear not to interrupt you. Won't you join me for a while and meet our guests? I have already promised them that you will, and I am sure you would not wish me to disappoint them again this evening.' She softened the admonishment with a charming smile.

Holmes looked annoyed, but he knew as I did that it would be as well to obtain what information we could from talking to the guests, or at least those who remained. Indifferently, he replied, 'It would be an honour, madam,' and allowed himself to be led into the ballroom while I tagged along awkwardly behind.

Though inevitably small as such venues go, the room was much longer than it was wide, with a polished floor and intricate gold curlicues on the ceiling and walls, draped here and there in the red velvet that curtained off the French windows to the garden. It could comfortably have accommodated several dozen guests, but only a few were left, and on the dais at the far end the band were packing away their instruments. Among those present I saw Lord Goring, speaking to a couple of markedly differing ages, and Lord Illingworth with a pretty blonde woman.

'Mr Holmes,' said Ernest as he and Algernon sidled up to us. 'Have you any idea who my mysterious houseguest is? Or I suppose I should say "was", now that he has been good enough to vacate my garden. Although I see there are still multiple policemen occupying my flower beds.'

'Please forgive my husband's impatience, Mr Holmes,' Gwendolen suggested smoothly. 'He is very protective of his borders.'

'So far we know very little,' said Holmes. 'He came here to

speak to either you or your brother, we believe, giving the name Bunbury. Does that name mean anything to either of you?'

I could tell that Holmes was watching closely for a reaction, but even without his powers of observation it did not escape me that the brothers exchanged a startled look. Ernest glanced also at his wife, and then said carefully, stroking his moustache, 'I have certainly never known anyone of that name. What about you, Algy?'

Algernon said lightly, 'Frankly, I doubt that any such person exists. Bunbury? It is quite the unlikeliest name I have ever heard.'

'Well, it may yet prove an alias,' Holmes acknowledged.

'If so, it is a very feeble one,' opined Algernon. 'I consider it an insult to the intelligence.'

'I'm sure that makes you very clever, Algy,' Ernest replied, rather shortly.

Gwendolen was still discharging her hostess's responsibilities. 'Mr Holmes, Dr Watson, I do not think you know Algernon's wife, Cecily.'

The blonde girl stepped up, slipped her arm into Algernon's and smiled charmingly at us. Cecily was by far the youngest of the Moncrieffs, a sweet-faced lass surely no more than twenty. She wore a dark blue-green ballgown that seemed to me alarmingly décolleté, although doubtless my views on such matters were terribly out of date. It was plain that she was also expecting a child, though in my professional judgement the happy event remained several months away.

'Mr Holmes,' said Cecily Moncrieff née Cardew, 'and Dr Watson. I am very excited to meet you. I always read your adventures in *The Strand* with great interest. I do not believe I have met any literary characters before.'

'As a status, it has its drawbacks,' Holmes replied, with a stern glance at me.

'My governess, Miss Prism, used to tell me that in fiction, the good end happily and the bad unhappily,' said Cecily Moncrieff. 'I am glad that I live in real life, not in a book, for many of my friends are very bad people and I should hate them to come to equally horrid ends. Dear Lord Illingworth, for instance, is excessively wicked.'

The peer, whom Cecily had been talking to previously, had been hovering nearby and now obtruded himself into our circle. 'That may be so,' he said. 'Yet I am responsible for great good. For in society to be wicked is to be talked about, and there is no greater good in society than to provoke conversation.'

Cecily laughed prettily. 'But if the talk one provokes is also wicked?'

'There is no wicked talk, my dear, only wicked deeds. And the wickeder the deeds, the more improving the conversation.'

'I confess that that has not been universally my experience,' said Holmes coldly. 'Watson and I have witnessed some acts the mention of which would put a stop to all polite discussion. Lord Illingworth, Mrs Moncrieff, I believe the two of you discovered the body earlier this evening.'

'Why, yes,' said Cecily brightly. 'It has been quite the night for new experiences.'

'I blame myself for persuading Mrs Moncrieff to take the night air with me,' Lord Illingworth confided playfully. 'Young ladies should be exposed to agreeable sights exclusively.'

'On the contrary, I feel that every young woman should be shown what a dead body looks like,' Cecily declared with spirit. 'How else is she to recognise one should she stumble upon one alone? Without looking closely, I should have thought the man asleep or drunk. To be sure, it would be most unusual for anyone to be asleep or drunk in Ernest's garden, but it is hardly to be expected that somebody should be dead there either.'

'Nevertheless, it must have been a most distressing experience,' I suggested gently. So keen were those around her to armour themselves with wit and flippancy against any expression of genuine feeling, that it seemed to me that Cecily was feeling obliged to suppress the horror she must surely have felt at such a disagreeable sight. This, I thought, could hardly be healthy for her nerves, especially in her delicate condition, although she showed no outward sign of being troubled.

'Oh, it was horrid,' she agreed sincerely. 'Distressing, and frightening, and thrilling too. I have led a sheltered life, Dr Watson, and that prepares one for a great many things. When excitement has been so rare, one savours what one finds. And, of course, it means that I have read a great deal of sensational fiction, though only when my governess was otherwise occupied.'

'So you knew what to do on finding a body, at least,' I said.

'Of course. I knew not to move it or interfere with the scene of the crime, and all those important things. And I asked Merriman to call the police at once.'

'What about you, Lord Illingworth? Was this your first dead body?' Holmes asked.

The diplomat blanched a little. 'I have seen my share of misfortune, Mr Holmes. I try not to dwell on it. It is one of the principles of good taste.'

'You have been in Vienna, I perceive,' Holmes noted. 'Your cufflinks were made there, and you still wear your whiskers in the style the Austrians favour.'

'Indeed I have,' the peer boasted. 'I have spent the best part of the last four years as the ambassador to Austria-Hungary.'

'Dr Watson, you must meet Major and Mrs Nepcote,' suggested Gwendolen, drawing me gently away. 'Major Roderick Nepcote has spent considerable time in Afghanistan, I believe. I am sure you will have very little in common.'

'Oh, excellent,' I said, with little enthusiasm. The hour was late, and I was in no mood to swap stories of the subcontinent with some old warhorse.

'To tell you the truth, you need not meet them if you don't wish it,' said Gwendolen more quietly. 'Mrs Nepcote is a lady of the highest breeding, and always perfectly shameless in her treatment of the gentlemen to whom she is introduced. It is very amusing to watch, especially for those of us who were at school with her, but I will spare you if you would prefer it. I wanted to speak to you about this business in the garden. I am exceedingly concerned about it.'

'It's a very concerning matter,' I agreed. 'But your questions would be better directed towards Inspector Gregson. There is very little Holmes or I can tell you.'

However, the Honourable Gwendolen Moncrieff was not a woman to be diverted from her chosen conversational path. 'Does Mr Holmes have any idea who this Mr Bunbury was? Such an unusual name,' she added quickly. 'I am certain Algy must be right that it is an invented one. I expect you will find out nothing at all if you enquire after him. But does anybody know why he called at such an inconvenient hour, asking to speak to my husband?'

'We are not even sure it was your husband he wanted to speak to,' I said. 'Inspector Gregson will be doing his best to find out who the poor man was, of course, whatever his name may have been. As I'm only a medical man, all I can tell you is that he fell, struck his head, and died.'

'You found nothing to identify him?' Gwendolen asked. 'No papers or personal items?'

'We must trust the police to know their business, Mrs Moncrieff,' I said, concerned by her persistence, 'and Holmes to know his. They are the experts in their profession. We mustn't carry coal to Newcastle.'

Gwendolen looked at me with sudden chilly disdain. 'I assure you, Dr Watson, I am not in the habit of carrying coal anywhere.'

I heard a voice call, 'Watson!' I looked hopefully for Holmes, but it was Lord Goring beckoning me over. I crossed the floor to him in the hope of respite, which evaporated when the viscount said, 'Dr Watson, I'd like you to meet Major and Mrs Nepcote.'

'Dr Watson, I'm so pleased to meet you,' Mrs Nepcote purred. She was an auburn-haired woman of around Gwendolen's age, rather plump and with a manner that was, as her friend had implied, embarrassingly forward. 'I can't understand why you've never been invited to any party I've attended before. You would be quite the ornament at any of them.'

'My blushes, madam,' I protested as Goring slipped away with evident relief, but Mrs Nepcote seemed unstoppable. In the space of five minutes she praised my 'military' physique, my presumed bravery on the battlefield, my selfless devotion to medicine, my writings (which it was perfectly apparent she had never read), my wonderfully practical attire and, in the end, my moustache, which she even went so far as to stroke, all while her husband the major, who might have been anywhere between two and three times her age, smiled indulgently at her every antic.

'Mr Holmes, too, is a fascinating man,' she went on, finally exhausting her first subject and turning without pause to the next. 'A man of his accomplishments and adventures will always be enthralling, but I did not expect him to be so handsome in the flesh!' She glanced across to where my friend was still in conversation with Lord Illingworth and Algernon Moncrieff. 'I am always fascinated by the private lives of prominent men. I am sure he must have had many lady friends not mentioned in your discreet stories, Dr Watson.'

I spluttered afresh at this absurd characterisation of my friend, and she showed me a calculating frown. 'Or perhaps,' she said, 'his interests do not lie in such directions. In your stories—'

'His interests,' I said, very stiffly, 'lie entirely in the arena of detection, and my accounts reflect this with the most faithful factual accuracy.'

Mercifully, at this juncture Inspector Gregson entered, carrying the torn and somewhat soiled shawl that the constable had finally retrieved from the tree, and I excused myself hastily. Holmes also gravitated towards the inspector, as did Lord Goring, and we reconvened in the passageway.

'That is certainly my wife's shawl,' Goring confirmed when asked, and Gregson showed us how the torn section fitted into the hole. The spider's-web brooch, the inspector told us, had already been taken to Scotland Yard for safekeeping.

'Well, my lord, you will see how this looks,' Gregson said, apologetically.

'Naturally,' Goring confirmed. 'It looks just as it would if my wife had met with this Bunbury fellow on the balcony outside the library and pushed him to his death. That was what you were about to suggest, was it not, Inspector?'

'I can hardly ignore the facts, my lord,' Gregson replied, more defiantly this time.

'You accuse Lady Goring of murder,' the viscount insisted.

'I would not say *accuse*, my lord. Not at this stage. But, as I say, you must understand how this looks.'

'If I may, Inspector,' said Holmes, and Gregson gave way to him at once. 'The scenario you outline raises significant questions.'

Lord Goring said, 'Go on,' but Holmes had not been waiting for his permission.

He said, 'Firstly, why would Lady Goring make such an ineffectual attempt to conceal the shawl? She might instead have hidden it, perhaps up the chimney in the library or behind some books, to be retrieved at her later convenience. She might indeed have stirred up the library fire and burnt it, all unobserved. Instead, you ask us to believe that she threw it across the garden onto a tree where it would hang for the world to see.

'Nor is it an easy feat to throw such a light object such a long distance, unless it be from a greater height. The shawl would naturally unfurl as it flew, increasing its resistance to the air. Unless thrown with considerable force, it would have simply fluttered and alighted on the lawn. To me the position looks far more as if it were thrown *down* from an upper window, perhaps even an attic room – those being the servants' quarters, I assume?'

'I believe so,' said Gregson slowly. 'I'll grant you those are objections, Mr Holmes, but—'

'There is another,' Holmes said, 'and it is the largest of all. Why would Lady Goring make concealing the shawl her priority, when the far more distinctive brooch that she had been wearing all evening was clearly visible in the deceased's hand? There are any number of ways in which a lace shawl might become torn, but a corpse clutching a unique item of jewellery is a good deal more difficult to explain away. And yet your supposed murderess seems to have made no attempt to remove this far more incriminating piece of evidence.'

Holmes was, I knew, overstating his case. I had been by his side during enough murder investigations to know how rare it is for a criminal to act rationally in the aftermath of a homicide. Not even the most hard-headed of killers can always manage it. The point about the ballistics of a thrown shawl might be valid, though Holmes would normally have preferred to confirm this by experiment rather than asserting it so boldly, but the arguments relying on Lady Goring's state of mind after putatively committing murder were tenuous at best.

Of course, Gregson had been a policeman long enough to

know this as well. However, while never a detective of Holmes's calibre (as if there were ever any other such), the man was no fool. Holmes was not seeking to convince him, merely to establish grounds for doubt… and if it meant that Gregson did not have to arrest the wife of a viscount without first obtaining his superiors' approval, the inspector would be very willing to go along with the pretence.

He said, 'Well, I dare say those points would benefit from further consideration, Mr Holmes. Very well then, if you insist then I'll do nothing precipitate tonight. Lord Goring, may I assume that Lady Goring will remain at your brother-in-law's house until we have spoken to her?'

'I believe I can give you that assurance, Inspector,' Goring said, and I understood that he, too, comprehended Holmes's subterfuge and was allowing it for now. Though it could surely not be hoped that it would last, Holmes had for the moment brokered a truce between the inspector and the viscount.

Goring gave us Sir Robert Chiltern's address in Grosvenor Square, and Gregson said, 'Well, then. My men still have a number of statements to collect, but I can let you gentlemen know what we find out in the morning. I suggest that we all might get whatever sleep we can, and approach this afresh on the morrow.'

As we left Ernest Moncrieff's house and looked for a cab, I espied a man loitering next to one of the trees in the small park that occupied the centre of the square. He wore an ordinary suit rather than evening dress, and seemed otherwise out of place, with a noticeably scarred face and a misshapen nose. He stood in the shadows, where he could watch the house without Constable Northbrook or his colleague, standing in the well-lit doorway, seeing him.

Seeing me staring, the man scowled, spat and sloped off into the bushes. I turned to point him out to Holmes, who sighed.

'I saw him also, Watson,' he said, 'but I made my scrutiny less obvious. An incident such as this will naturally draw idle observers, however, and his presence is not necessarily suspicious. I suggest that we remember his face, all the same.'

CHAPTER FOUR
INSPECTOR GREGSON MAKES AN ARREST

'What is your opinion of the celebrated "Ernest Worthing" and his circle, Watson?' Sherlock Holmes asked me at breakfast the next day.

'Well, it's hard to say,' I mused, grateful for the excuse to put down my newspaper. I had been scanning an article about the government's forthcoming financial regulation bill, but the details were beyond me. 'On the surface they seemed utterly frivolous, but I can't believe that they could really be so unfeeling about a man's death. The trouble is that they all seem so unwilling to reveal anything of their feelings that it's as if they are nothing but that surface. Even Lord Goring seemed to be putting up a front most of the time, for all his concern for his wife.'

'Quite so, Watson, quite so. Their social milieu prizes a calm and imperturbable demeanour, and they are so repulsed by vulgar sentiment that even conventional expressions of shock or horror seem tawdry to them. I sometimes think that Mr Wells is right, and that the rich really are becoming a separate species.'

We shook our heads at the obliviousness of the rich as Mrs Hudson bustled around us, clearing away our breakfasts. A moment later, she returned and announced that Inspector

Gregson was waiting outside. I finished my coffee hurriedly while pulling on my coat.

'It's not looking rosy for Lady Goring this morning, I am afraid, gentlemen,' Gregson revealed grimly in the cab on the way to Grosvenor Square. He looked rumpled, and no less pale in the morning sunshine than he had at midnight. 'I've talked to the commissioner already, and it seems Sir Robert Chiltern's influence goes less far than it used to. So does Lord Caversham's, her father-in-law.'

The interviews Gregson's sergeant and constables had held with the servants and, eventually, with those guests who could be persuaded to comply, had continued into the small hours and had turned up some points of significance. Gregson told us that the overfriendly Mrs Nepcote claimed to have seen Lady Goring climbing the stairs to the library at around half past ten, midway between when Bunbury had been left to wait there and when his body was found. A housemaid by the name of Dora Steyne, who had returned briefly with a headache to her room at the top of the house, had looked out soon after that time, and seen a woman dressed similarly on the library balcony, with a man in a suit who she was now sure had been Bunbury.

'A woman dressed similarly to what?' Holmes asked. 'What exactly was Lady Goring wearing?'

Ponderously, Gregson read from his notes. 'A ballgown in midnight-blue satin, with flared chiffon sleeves and a pompadour neck with pearl-bead trimming at the side-fronts, a satin sash and bow. That description's put together from a number of conversations with the ladies and their maids, so we can probably trust it. As far as I can make out, it means a dark blue dress with frills stuck onto it. And the lace shawl, of course.'

'The maid saw the shawl?'

'She was not altogether clear on that point. In fact, she

became a bit flustered when we asked her. You know how these girls are. She's worried about getting into trouble if she says the wrong thing.'

Holmes considered. 'It would be difficult to distinguish between dark hues by moonlight,' he pointed out.

'That's true,' Gregson agreed. 'This Dora says she recognised the dress by its cut. The trouble is, that sort of thing's the height of fashion at the moment, and half the women present were wearing something similar.'

'Most of those we saw were in different colours, though,' I said. 'Although wasn't Mrs Teville's dress a quite dark purple?' I recalled the glamorous widow in her perfunctory mourning.

'Very observant, Watson,' Holmes replied. 'Indeed it was, a royal purple, I should say. Gwendolen Moncrieff was in a much lighter powder-blue, and Cecily Moncrieff in teal. The former could never have been mistaken in moonlight for such a dress as you describe, Gregson. The latter might, were it not for the fact that its wearer was in the family way. Mrs Nepcote's dress was of a rather dark red.'

Gregson sighed heavily. 'I've a list here of what the other female guests were wearing, too. I dare say, when we manage to speak to the guests who skipped out on us, they'll give us even more detail.'

'Did Mrs Nepcote recognise Lady Goring by her dress?'

'No, she swears she saw her face before she mounted the stairs. There's nothing else up on that floor except the guest bedrooms, and they were all locked. So, either Mrs Nepcote's lying, or Her Ladyship was in the library after Bunbury was settled there.'

'Not that that makes her a murderess, of course,' Holmes observed, 'but it is suggestive, nonetheless. Well, let us see what Lady Goring has to say in her defence.'

There are few addresses in London grander than Belgrave Square, but Grosvenor Square is among them. Rather than

Belgravia it is in Mayfair, a neighbouring district built at the commission of the same aristocratic family, but earlier, in the eighteenth century rather than the early nineteenth. Its houses are older, therefore, and a little less elaborately decorated, but their luxury, wealth and exclusiveness are wholly comparable. When we arrived, we found Sir Robert Chiltern's house to be more imposing than either of those we had been in the day before. Not only was it more spacious in every dimension, but its interior was quite as befitted its owner's station, with chandeliers and marble floors, and a grand staircase leading to the upper levels.

Robert Chiltern was not one of the idle rich, like Savile and the Moncrieffs, but an able politician who had served as a Cabinet minister under the Earl of Rosebery and was at present one of the leading lights of Her Majesty's Opposition. As a baronet he was, of course, ineligible to sit in the House of Lords, but was a leading figure in the Commons, speaking often on matters of finance and foreign affairs, and his colleagues and opponents alike considered him a man of great integrity and principle. As well as a testament to his personal wealth, his house had served as a venue for affairs of state, hosting receptions involving ambassadors, royalty and other dignitaries.

The great man himself was waiting for us on the landing in the great hallway of the house, along with his wife and Lord Goring. Sir Robert had finely sculpted features, a firm chin and dark eyes, and an air of great dignity tempered somewhat by world-weariness. Gertrude, Lady Chiltern, matched him well, a beauty significantly younger than her husband but no less solemn, like a classical statue in modern dress.

They greeted us with punctilious politeness but some reserve. Sir Robert thanked Inspector Gregson for his service in the police force, the details of which he recalled with the ease of a man briefed recently by an excellent secretary.

He then said, 'Mr Holmes, I know that you have often been of service to the state as well as to the police, often with Dr Watson's help, and I thank you both for it. However, I am at a loss to account for your involvement in this tragic case of the death at the Moncrieffs'. I quite understand why Inspector Gregson must speak to my sister on the matter in his official capacity, but speaking for myself, I would prefer to have her troubled by as few people as possible.'

With a sigh, Lord Goring said, 'We've been through this already, Robert. I myself invited Mr Holmes's interest in the case, as I feel it is in Mabel's best interests.' He wore a morning-suit as exquisite as his evening dress of the night before, with a fresh carnation at the lapel.

'You speak as her husband, Arthur,' Sir Robert said with a frown, 'but I must think of the whole family's reputation.' I had not realised that the viscount shared a Christian name with Lord Arthur Savile, but it was not, after all, a particularly rare one.

'By which you mean your career,' Lord Goring replied calmly.

Lady Chiltern interjected. 'The fortunes of the family are tied up inextricably with Robert's career. If his sister is wrongly accused of a crime, naturally it will damage that career. Were she to be wrongly convicted, it would destroy it.'

'That is not what I mean, Gertrude,' protested Sir Robert. 'If Mabel became the victim of such a miscarriage of justice, I should make it my business to spend my every waking hour righting that wrong, and so, I am sure, would you. No doubt it would affect my career, but it would affect our home life far more severely. We still have hopes of—' He seemed suddenly to recall that Holmes, Gregson and I were there. 'Well, never mind that for now.'

Holmes bowed and said, 'Sir Robert, your reputation holds you to be a man of honesty and rectitude. Mine, such as it is, is that of one whose skills lie in discovering the truth. In that respect we are both on the same side.'

Lord Goring said, 'Mabel is innocent, Robert. You don't doubt that, I am sure. We have nothing to fear from the truth, only from error. I admire Inspector Gregson's record as much as you do, but Mr Holmes's speaks for itself. The chance of such a miscarriage as you mention is greatly reduced by his involvement, and that is all that should be important to us.'

'Unless…' said Lady Chiltern abruptly, and stopped.

'Unless what, Gertrude?' Goring asked gently. 'Unless my wife is guilty? It is true that those we love turn out sometimes to be less blameless than we believed. But you cannot suppose it of Mabel, surely?'

'No,' she said at once, then shook her head. Resolutely, she repeated, 'No, I cannot.'

'It is settled, then,' said Sir Robert shortly. 'My sister is upstairs in the Octagon Room, Inspector, Mr Holmes. You will question her in the presence of my brother-in-law, please.'

Lord Goring led the way to a large and sumptuous room, eight-cornered and two-storeyed, with its own internal staircase leading up to further reception rooms. Its chandelier was surrounded by four light-wells which filled it with morning sunlight. A tapestry above the stairs reproduced a painting I vaguely remembered seeing other copies of, nymphs and cupids disporting themselves *déshabillé* in the sea-foam next to some hazardous-looking rocks.

Mabel, Lady Goring, sat on a sofa that I guessed must date to one of the Louis's reigns, cradling an infant. Despite this pose of a Madonna, she looked something like a nymph herself, with the same pink cheeks and sunshine hair that the artist had evidently admired in his models. She was a slight figure and very much younger than her brother, barely half his age, as I thought, and

I could see why he and Lady Chiltern felt so protective of her. The child, an infant only a few months old, she handed over to a nursemaid as we arrived.

'Mr Holmes,' she said to my friend, with a perfectly charming smile, as the nurse and baby left us. 'How delightful to meet you. You look so like Dr Watson's descriptions of you! And these worried-looking gentlemen must be Dr Watson, who so rarely describes himself, and Inspector… Gregson, was it? Won't you please sit down, all of you?'

The three of us sat in the chairs arranged nearby, while Lord Goring crossed to stand behind the sofa and put a protective hand on his wife's shoulder. She covered it with her own.

Holmes said, 'We are pleased to meet you, too, Lady Goring, but I am afraid that pleasure is not the reason for our visit today.'

'We need,' said Gregson, exerting his authority as the official police presence without much grace, 'to ask you some questions, Lady Goring. About the death last night.'

'Yes, I'm quite prepared to answer them. What a horrid business that was!' she exclaimed. 'It made me feel quite wretched for the poor man's family. Have they been told?'

'Not yet, my lady,' Gregson replied. 'We're still trying to identify him at present. Did you talk to him at all last night?'

Mabel Goring shook her head emphatically. 'No, I didn't see him at all. I spoke only to Mr and Mrs Moncrieff's other guests, and to a few of the servants. Then I heard that a tradesman of some sort had fallen from a balcony and died.'

'You are quite sure about that?' Gregson asked, frowning.

'Of course I am,' she replied firmly. 'If I had spoken to a strange tradesman during a society ball, I should certainly have remembered such a novelty. It would have been such a refreshing change.'

I thought that our hostess of the previous evening would probably agree about the novelty, but might find other words to describe it than 'refreshing'. I asked, 'How well do you know the Moncrieffs, Lady Goring?'

She smiled. 'Oh, fairly well. Gwendolen is an old schoolfriend of Gertrude's, so she and her mother, Lady Bracknell, used to visit our family often. Then, at around the same time I was engaged to Arthur, Gwendolen and Ernest became affianced too, and so did Algy, who I knew a little, and Cecily, who I met only after their engagement was announced but liked immensely. Cecily is very near my own age, and we saw a great deal of each other when we were planning our weddings.'

Mabel Goring reminded me somewhat of Cecily Moncrieff, I thought. But whereas Cecily had all the sophistication of a girl brought up in the countryside, Mabel was a natural, unspoiled city lass.

I sighed inwardly. After spending even such a little time with Lord Goring and the Moncrieffs, I too was beginning to think in paradoxes.

Holmes asked, 'What is your opinion of the Moncrieff brothers?'

'They're both very sweet,' she said. 'Ernest can be quite irritable, but Algy will needle him so. But they are both perfectly obedient to their wives, exactly as a husband ought to be.' She patted her own husband's hand fondly.

Embarrassed by the show of affection, Gregson fumbled in the carpetbag he was carrying and extracted the torn shawl, which he held up in one plump hand. 'Were you wearing this shawl last night, Lady Goring?'

'Oh, but it's filthy!' she exclaimed in dismay. 'And torn, too.'

'But it is yours?' he persisted.

'Oh, yes. Yes, I arrived wearing it.'

'And was this brooch attached?' Gregson asked, producing it in turn.

Mabel gave a delighted gasp. 'Oh, I thought it must be lost! And Arthur would have been so understanding about my losing it, it would have driven me quite distracted. May I have it back?'

'Well, I can see no reason why not,' said the inspector a little doubtfully. 'There's probably nothing more it can tell us down at the Yard.'

'I am obliged to you, Inspector,' said Lord Goring as Gregson passed his wife the brooch.

'Please don't mention it, my lord. And were you wearing – by which I mean you, Lady Goring...' Gregson inspected his notebook warily, '...a midnight-blue satin ballgown with a pompadour neck and—'

'And various other frills and fripperies?' Mabel smiled again. 'Yes, Inspector, I was.' Gregson marked a large tick in his notebook. 'I intended to wear a perfectly ravishing frock in eau de Nil, but my maid was rather careless as I was dressing and spilled scent on it, so I had to change.'

Holmes asked, 'Lady Goring, the shawl and brooch parted company with you, and with one another, during the course of the evening. Do you recall when that might have happened, and why?'

She considered carefully. 'Well, let me see... I believe I became too warm when I was in the music room, and removed the shawl then. I didn't consider at the time that the brooch was still pinned to it. When I came to look for it later, I couldn't see it, and neither could any of the servants.'

'Did you wonder then whether the brooch had been stolen?'

She shook her head. 'No, it didn't cross my mind. I thought it must have been tidied away somewhere, and I could send round for it today.'

'You left in rather a hurry, as I understand it, rather soon after the body was discovered,' Gregson said. 'You had gone by the time my men arrived.'

Mabel leaned forward confidingly. 'To tell you the truth, Inspector, I would have felt perfectly comfortable in staying, but Arthur felt it his duty as a husband to protect me from distress. Men are the more emotional sex, and we women must always consider their feelings.' She leaned back, patting Lord Goring's hand once again.

Holmes asked, 'During the course of the evening, Lady Goring, did you enter the library at all?'

She seemed surprised. 'I did, but not for very long. After I felt too warm, I went upstairs to the library for a moment. I might have stayed there five minutes, but no longer.'

'Were you alone there?' Holmes asked.

'Yes, there was nobody else.' Mabel Goring gave the impression of perfect sincerity.

Inspector Gregson said, 'Do you remember what o'clock this was?'

'Not really, but I recall that Lady Caroline Pontefract was leaving just as I came downstairs again, so I was able to bid her goodbye.'

Gregson thumbed through his notebook, and I remembered that Lady Caroline's imminent departure had distracted Peter the pageboy from telling Ernest that Bunbury was waiting for him in the library. I knew from experience, though, that a certain type of woman could maintain the state of imminently leaving a party for a surprisingly long time.

Mrs Nepcote had put Lady Goring's ascent of the stairs at half past ten. By that time Bunbury had supposedly been settled in the library for a quarter of an hour, and the maid, Dora Steyne, had seen Bunbury and a woman on the balcony around then. Either time might have been imprecise, of course, and conceivably while Mabel was in the library Bunbury had been prowling elsewhere in the house, perhaps collecting the brooch and shawl on his travels, returning to the library and meeting his end only after she left. But the explanation that Mabel Goring was lying about meeting him would, I knew, strike Gregson as at least equally likely.

The inspector said, 'So, to be clear, you didn't see this Mr Bunbury in the library, nor any other person?'

She frowned. 'No, Inspector, I did not. I am beginning to think that your questions have an import which, while I find it quite exciting, my husband and my brother will not appreciate. Could you tell me plainly what you suspect, please?'

'In good time, my lady,' said Gregson awkwardly. I could sympathise with his discomfort. Whatever his superiors' views of the waning influence of her relatives, it went against the grain to accuse any member of the aristocracy of such a serious crime, let alone one so young, pleasant and personable as Lady Goring. But Gregson was a dogged policeman, and not one to let personal sentiment get in the way of his job. I feared that Sir Robert and Lord Goring might indeed disapprove of what he had in mind.

He said, 'Can you account for your shawl being found in a tree, Lady Goring?'

Mabel laughed. 'In a *tree*? How extraordinary! No, I am afraid I can't. I suppose it must have been thrown there, unless someone climbed up to place it there. Why anyone should have done either, I have no idea.'

Gregson said, 'And the brooch? Are you aware that it was found clutched in the hands of the deceased after he fell to his death from the balcony outside the library?'

Lady Goring gasped in dismay, and dropped the brooch on the floor. 'I was not,' she whispered.

Lord Goring said coldly, 'I had understandably kept that detail to myself, Inspector, to spare my wife's feelings.'

'You can hardly expect me to do the same, my lord,' said the policeman stoutly. 'Lady Goring, can you account for the facts that I have outlined?'

Mabel said quietly, 'No, I can't. I know nothing of what happened to the shawl or the brooch after I took them off in the music room.'

Gregson persisted. 'You said that you felt too warm in the music room, but going into the library would not have helped with that. There had been a fire burning all afternoon. The air was close and stuffy.' I saw Holmes's eyebrows twitch, and I wondered whether he had expected that the policeman would not detect this inconsistency.

Mabel seemed surprised. 'Really? I am afraid I didn't notice.'

'Come, Lady Goring. If you felt heated the library would only have been warmer still, as you must have realised from the moment when you entered. Why did you really go in there, and stay for five whole minutes?'

She paused. 'I thought,' she said tentatively, 'that perhaps it was not just the temperature, but that I was perhaps feeling oppressed by being surrounded by so many people. Such a thing would be quite unlike me, I admit, but that only means that I am not really sure what the sensation would feel like. As it was, five minutes were all I could bear before I started to feel lonely again.'

'You sat there alone in a hot room for five minutes, simply to try out the sensation of being alone?' Gregson repeated sceptically.

'It must sound absurd, Inspector. I expect it was absurd of me. But yes, that is what I did.'

'Were you already aware that the library has a balcony?' Gregson asked.

She thought for a moment. 'Yes, I remember stepping out there with Gwendolen one afternoon last summer. I didn't suppose that it would be unlocked on such a chilly evening, though.'

'Did you not think to check? The fresh air would have quickly cooled you down.'

Mabel smiled again. 'I am sorry, Inspector. I obviously lack your admirable common sense.' In Gwendolen Moncrieff's mouth the comment would have been a cutting one, but Mabel delivered it as charmingly as she had everything else.

'Indeed,' said Gregson heavily. 'It would have been common sense to cover your tracks, my lady.'

'Ah,' said Lady Goring a little sadly. 'Now I suppose we will come to it. Do go on, Inspector.'

Gregson said sternly, 'It is clear to me that you met this Bunbury in the library, despite what you have said. Either you stepped out onto the balcony and found him already there, or you and he stepped out together. Whether you were already acquainted I don't know, and nor do I know what you quarrelled about, but whatever it was, you pushed him over the balustrade onto the plinth below. He grasped your brooch before falling to his death, and tore your shawl, which you threw away in disgust, as hard as you could, so that it got stuck in that tree. And then you went back to the party and tried your hardest to pretend to yourself, as murderers sometimes do, that the whole business had never happened.'

Lady Goring had been shaking her head all this while, her rosy cheeks turned pale as paper. She whispered, 'It's not true,' and stared at Holmes, and then at me, in mute appeal.

I had nothing to offer. Holmes's objections of the night before had been paper-thin, and Gregson's accusation had thrust its way brutally through them. The case was far from proven, of course, but with her brooch in the victim's hand and the testimony of the two witnesses, it was perfectly clear that it must be answered.

Lord Goring said icily, 'I assure you that you will regret this very much, Inspector.' The hand that was not holding his wife's was clutching his cane very hard.

'I shouldn't be in the least surprised, my lord,' Gregson acknowledged. 'But regretting it is not the same thing as being wrong, is it? I dare say we will find out in time. For now, Lady Goring, it is my solemn duty to arrest you on suspicion of the murder of one Mr Bunbury, address unknown. I must ask you to accompany me at once to Scotland Yard.'

CHAPTER FIVE
THE ELUSIVE MR BUNBURY

'That was a most upsetting scene,' I said after we left the Grosvenor Square house. The Gorings had left with Inspector Gregson, and in their absence Sir Robert and Lady Chiltern had not made us welcome. Indeed, Sir Robert had been proposing as we left to take a cab directly to the office of the Commissioner of Scotland Yard and to demand his sister's immediate release.

'Distressing but necessary, Watson,' Holmes replied.

'She has a child!' I exclaimed. 'Indeed, she is scarcely more than a child herself.'

'The infant will do well enough with his nursemaid,' Holmes observed disinterestedly. 'That is considered perfectly natural in children of his class. Meanwhile, the evidence Gregson holds appears to implicate Lady Goring. He would be derelict in his duty not to act as he has done, and it is to his credit that he has. Ladies are no more above the law than lords are, and if a policeman will not uphold that law when it becomes a hazard to his career, then he does not deserve a career at all.'

'But surely you do not believe that Lady Goring is guilty, Holmes?'

'Believe? I believe nothing, Watson, except that we are not

yet in possession of all the facts. So far, Inspector Gregson has offered no motive for the crime on Lady Goring's part, nor any proof that the death was not accidental even if she was involved. We have not established whether the shawl could indeed have been tossed into the tree from the balcony. We have no idea who the dead man was, nor why he came to the house.' He had been ticking off points on his bony fingers. 'Such information may, as you and Lord Goring hope, exonerate Lady Goring. On the other hand, it may convict her. Without it, we have no hope of making a case for either outcome.'

I fell into a gloomy silence for a few minutes, as we strolled by unspoken consent in the direction of Hyde Park.

'On the question of Bunbury's identity,' I said, 'the name meant something to the Moncrieffs, I'm sure of it. The brothers, at least, and I think Gwendolen as well.'

'That point was clear to me also,' Holmes agreed. 'I wondered only how long it would take for you to voice it.'

I said, 'We should return to Belgrave Square and speak to Ernest and Gwendolen.'

'There are times, Watson, when our minds are as one.' He smiled, and produced from a pocket Mabel Goring's torn shawl. 'While we are there, we should also experiment with throwing this from the balcony. We can return it to the good inspector later. I suspect he'll not miss it in the meantime.'

It being a fine morning, though cold, we wrapped ourselves in our mufflers and walked through the park, past the ornamental fountain that stands near Grosvenor Gate and down past the statue of Achilles, that peculiar memorial to the Duke of Wellington from the women of Britain, which eschews the traditional equestrian figure in favour of a classical bronze hero scarcely more decorously clad than those cavorting nymphs on Sir Robert Chiltern's Octagon Room tapestry.

From there we passed through the great colonnaded gateway that marks Hyde Park Corner, and crossed to Grosvenor Crescent, named, like the square, the gate and much of the rest of that region of London, for the aristocratic family who have owned it for generations. At length we arrived once more at Belgrave Square, the name of which derives from another of the same family's titles, and knocked at the door of Number 149.

We were shown by Merriman the butler into a first-floor drawing room, where we found both Moncrieff brothers and their wives entertaining a woman dressed all in black, with a veil concealing the upper part of her face. For a moment I thought that it might be Mrs Teville, the widow from the previous night, but this lady's figure suggested that the youth which Mrs Teville was battling against the passage of time to retain was hers by right of birth. She was introduced to us as Mrs Winterbourne, their next-door neighbour, who must, I realised, own the tree in which Mabel Goring's shawl had become lodged.

'How concerning it is to meet you here, Mr Holmes,' she said in a light, trilling voice once we were settled among them with cups of tea. Her deeper mourning betokened a loss recent enough that convention would not expect her to be abroad, but the Moncrieffs were a young family with modern ideas. As a widower myself, I sympathised. Though it may protect society from the distress of seeing their grief, I have never considered enforced solitude to be healthy or constructive for the bereaved. 'It was you, was it not, who took Lord Arthur Savile away to Scotland Yard yesterday morning? I shall be most unhappy if the same fate awaits dear Mr Moncrieff.'

Ernest insisted, 'My conscience is at ease, Mrs Winterbourne. Unless Mr Holmes has been engaged by my tailor to investigate the matter of his unpaid bills, I am in no danger.'

'I read about Lord Arthur in the newspaper,' Cecily said. 'I hope what he did was very wicked, Mr Holmes. I should hate to think that you had wasted your time.'

'A jury will determine that,' Holmes replied shortly. 'I am not here to investigate Mr Moncrieff, Mrs Winterbourne. However, as his house is the scene of last night's crime, if crime it were, I can hardly ignore it.'

'And so you return here,' the widow said. 'How interesting, that what they say of murderers should be true of detectives also.'

Gwendolen said, 'Lord Arthur always seemed to be a perfect gentleman: quiet, respectable and a devoted family man. I am not in the least surprised to learn that he had a skeleton in his closet.'

'Most men have, you know,' said Mrs Winterbourne, 'if one only steels oneself to open the door and look. My first and second husbands both did.'

'And your third?' asked Holmes.

The young widow's veil made it difficult to be sure, but I thought that she looked appraisingly at Holmes. 'In his case I felt it best not to enquire,' she replied. 'Twice bitten, one is entitled to be once shy at the very least. All the late Mr Winterbourne's skeletons went to the grave with him, and I have no interest in disinterring them.'

'It's quite a coincidence, though, my dear fellow,' Algernon observed to Holmes, 'you investigating two cases in Belgrave Square in so many days.'

'We must certainly hope so,' Holmes replied smoothly. 'May I ask if you also learned about Lord Arthur from today's papers, Mrs Winterbourne?'

'Oh, no. There is little that escapes me, Mr Holmes. I am always on the lookout for comings and goings in the square. I watched all the arrivals and departures from the occasion last night, for instance – including your own and that of Dr Watson, in Lord Goring's landau. As a recent widow it would not be fitting for me to attend society events, even when they occur in the house next door to mine, but I miss the company. I intend, when I return to society, to bring the very best information with me.'

'Good heavens!' exclaimed Ernest. 'I do hope your information isn't *too* accurate, Mrs Winterbourne.'

'If it were accurate, Mr Moncrieff,' she replied with a small smile, 'it would hardly be the best.'

'In such matters, sensation, not accuracy, is the vital thing,' Gwendolen agreed.

'If you were watching the front door all night, Mrs Winterbourne,' said Holmes, 'then your testimony may be invaluable.'

Gregson had supplied us with a list of known times of arrival and departure for the various guests, which Holmes now proceeded to confirm with the widow.

We had already known that Ernest and Gwendolen Moncrieff were present throughout the evening. Gregson's itinerary, which Mrs Winterbourne now confirmed, had Algernon and Cecily as the first guests to arrive, with the Gorings following them at around eight o'clock, then a steady flow of others until around ten. The last guest to enter was Mrs Teville, the widow of the night before, who had arrived only shortly before Bunbury. Finally, there was Bunbury himself, whom Mrs Winterbourne had seen arrive on foot. Those others who had turned up after the discovery of the body had been politely turned away by the servants.

There were some guests who had already left by then, such as Lady Caroline Pontefract and her husband Sir John, whose protracted departure had begun roughly with Bunbury's arrival but who had not left until shortly before the unpleasant scene in the garden, and the present Lord and Lady Windermere, who had left still earlier, at around nine-thirty. Sir Robert and Lady Chiltern had arrived with the Gorings, but had departed by ten and could, Gregson assumed, be ruled out of our enquiries. Around twenty guests had been present throughout the half-hour between Bunbury's arrival and the discovery of his body, including Mr and Mrs Algernon Moncrieff, Lord and Lady Goring, Major and Mrs Nepcote, Mrs Teville, Lord Illingworth and Gwendolen's mother, Lady Bracknell.

The musicians, both the band in the ballroom and the string quartet in the music room, had been playing throughout the same half-hour, with only brief intervals between pieces. Gregson had a separate list which charted the few occasions when the servants had been on solitary errands in empty parts of the house, but Mrs Winterbourne could hardly be expected to corroborate those, and besides, by this time the evident boredom of the Moncrieff family was getting the better of them. The young widow excused herself decorously and returned next door, leaving us alone with our hosts.

'How did you know Mrs Winterbourne had been thrice widowed?' I asked Holmes after she left, as a footman poured me some more tea.

'The language she used,' Holmes explained. 'Had she been married but twice, she would have referred to "both my husbands", or something similar. Whether she chose her words deliberately or not, "my first and second husbands" suggests further husbands from whom a distinction must be made. I concluded that Mrs Winterbourne has had the misfortune to lose not two, but three spouses, or even more.'

'To lose one husband is certainly a misfortune,' Gwendolen agreed. 'To lose three smacks of policy. The reason is that Mrs Winterbourne has a charitable fondness for invalids, Mr Holmes, especially wealthy ones.'

'And speaking of invalids,' Ernest said with a glance at Algernon, who smiled lazily, 'or rather, I should say, of jumping to invalid conclusions... have the police thought better yet of their absurd idea that the man who fell was murdered?'

'They have not,' said Holmes coolly. 'Indeed, I believe they have a suspect in mind for the crime. Tell me, Mr Moncrieff, were you aware that Mr Bunbury was waiting for you in the library last night?'

Ernest played nervously with his moustache. 'No, I was not aware that Mr Bunbury was waiting for me in the library last night. That is to say, I believe Merriman did mention something about somebody waiting for someone somewhere, but he certainly didn't allude to the name Bunbury. In any case, I told him that it was the height of bad manners to interrupt pleasure for business.'

'A servant's duties may sometimes force them into what would be bad manners among their betters,' Holmes observed.

'Merriman's position requires him to be a paragon of rectitude,' drawled Algernon. 'If the lower orders won't set us a good example, what is the use of them?'

'Were you with your brother when Merriman made this announcement, Mr Moncrieff?' Holmes asked Algernon.

'Certainly not.'

'Oh, come, Algy,' Ernest remonstrated. 'We were in the music room at the time, with Cecily, Aunt Augusta, Lord Illingworth and Mabel Goring... I believe Mrs Teville was there, too.'

'My dear fellow, if that's true then I might as well have been in Stevenage. The music those fellows were playing was so thunderously German that I couldn't have heard a word if Merriman had bellowed at me through an ear-trumpet.'

'I do remember Merriman talking to Ernest,' said Cecily, 'but I was distracted by some particularly aggressive arpeggios.'

Holmes turned his attention to Gwendolen. 'You were not there at the time, Mrs Moncrieff?'

'No, I remained downstairs in the ballroom. I wasn't even

aware that there was a stranger in the house until after his precipitate departure.'

Holmes looked carefully around at the assembled Moncrieffs and asked, 'So you are all quite certain that he was a stranger?'

'Of course,' said Ernest peevishly. 'Although I can't imagine why such a person would think I would speak to him on any kind of business matter during a ball. My friends are all atrociously ill-bred, but I would expect a stranger to know better.'

'Of the four of you, I believe only your sister-in-law saw him,' Holmes persisted. 'How can you be so certain that you didn't know the man?'

Ernest was taken aback. 'Well, as I've said, someone who actually knew me would have had better taste.'

'Forgive me, Mr Moncrieff, but that is the exact opposite of what you said.'

Flustered, Ernest picked a different conversational tack. 'Well, if you want my view, the man was a common thief. He gained access to the house under false pretences, stole poor Lady Goring's brooch, then tried to make his escape by the balcony. If he hadn't slipped and killed himself we might never have been the wiser.'

'The objections to that idea are so numerous and obvious that I do believe Watson could enumerate them,' said Holmes languidly.

He raised his eyebrow at me in expectation, and I said something like, 'Oh. Ah.' I had been enjoying my tea and watching Holmes work, and felt rather put on the spot by his suddenly conscripting me into the conversation.

I said, 'Well… there's the position the body was found in, and its injuries. Those are far more consistent with a sudden backward fall. If he had slipped while climbing he'd have ended up huddled underneath the balcony with his legs twisted or broken, but probably he would have survived. But why would he have risked leaving that way at all, when he arrived openly through the tradesmen's entrance and could have left the same way without arousing suspicion?'

I was unsure whether to mention the other point that sprung to mind, which was that a thief could have either neatly detached Mabel Goring's brooch from the shawl or else just pocketed the whole garment. Though the Moncrieffs had evidently heard about the brooch, I was unsure whether the evidence of the torn shawl would be known to them. Instead, I asked, 'Have I missed anything, Holmes?'

'Only that this house contains a great many other valuable objects, many of them not attached to people, which it would have been easier for a thief to steal,' my friend said. He gestured around at the drawing room, which did indeed hold a number of expensive ornaments. 'A thief, or an unscrupulous debt-collector,' he added.

'Mr Holmes!' Gwendolen exclaimed, aghast. 'That insinuation is most objectionable.'

Ernest shrugged and said, 'If you're thinking of my tailors, you may certainly ask them if they know the fellow. Use my name if you like.' He gave the address of a Jermyn Street firm into whose windows I had occasionally peered with envy as I walked past. 'You might mention that my latest order of shirt collars is deplorably late.'

'Forgive me,' Holmes asked with very little evidence of contrition, 'but do you owe any other debts?'

'An unpaid restaurant bill here, a tobacconist's account there. Nothing of sufficient substance that my creditors would send thugs to extract it with menaces. Although you remind me that I should pay my church tithes as a matter of urgency.'

Holmes tutted, a sure sign that his reserves of tact were running dry. He said, 'There is one further question I must ask, before I prevail upon you to allow the use of your balcony for an experiment in ballistics. What, please, is the actual significance of the name Bunbury?'

All four of the Moncrieffs looked at one another with exaggerated bafflement. 'There's no significance to it at all,' Algernon said at last. 'As I've said, it's not the sort of name one's likely to come across in real life.'

'On the contrary,' insisted Holmes, who I knew had spent some time before breakfast consulting his Index, 'there is a lineage of baronets of that name, the incumbent being Sir Henry Bunbury, a naval officer. Two entirely unrelated Thomas Bunburys have served with distinction both in the army and as colonial governors. A third is the Dean of Limerick. There is nothing implausible about the name, so why are you so certain that it is an alias?'

Algernon raised his eyebrows in surprise. 'Oh, really?' he said. 'Well then, I suppose I'm mistaken. Maybe it was the chap's real name after all. Rather a leaden one, though. It has a heavy, dull quality to it, don't you think? Rather like the sound made by dropping a really solid teacake. I detest teacakes.'

'It has none of the romance or dash of Moncrieff,' Cecily agreed. 'I wonder what his Christian name was?'

'At this stage his Christian name is hardly germane,' Holmes objected.

'No, I should think not,' Algernon scoffed. 'A Bunbury he may have been, but a Germain Bunbury would be taking things altogether too far. No, he would have a stolid English name, I fancy, like Kenneth. No Kenneth could compose a piano concerto, or tie a really elegant necktie. A Kenneth Bunbury would be practically born to fall off a balcony.'

'Enough, sir!' snapped Holmes, and I could see that he was, an enormous rarity for him, genuinely angry. 'A man died here last night, very probably as the victim of murderous violence, and you are making pleasantries out of his name! He may not have been of much account by your reckoning, but he was a man nonetheless, and his death should be weighing heavily upon you all. Dr Watson and I intend to find out who killed him. Will we have your cooperation, or do you intend to offer us nothing but facetiousness and flippancy?'

There was a silence, and it became clear that the family's show of imperviousness had been somewhat dented by my friend's censure.

Cecily gave me a shamefaced glance. Ernest shifted awkwardly in his seat and avoided looking at Holmes or myself. Even Gwendolen's composure appeared a little ruffled. Algernon was the most embarrassed of them all. He cleared his throat twice, then, in a chastised tone, began, 'Well, you see—' Then his eyes became suddenly wide, and he leapt to his feet as if electrified. His brother and their womenfolk followed suit at once, as, alarmed, did I.

Behind us, a voice like an indignant French horn demanded, 'What, sir, is the meaning of this importunate interrogation?'

As I turned to the door, Merriman coughed awkwardly and belatedly announced the arrival of Lady Bracknell.

CHAPTER SIX
ENTER LADY BRACKNELL

Gwendolen Moncrieff's mother was a statuesque woman in the latest of late middle age, wearing a purple floral dress and a purple feathered hat. Her face bore a resemblance to Gwendolen's which, though at present merely a hint of what the daughter might grow into, made it difficult to look at Gwendolen in quite the same light afterwards.

The same face also bore an expression of grave disapproval and distaste, which I would soon learn was a fixture rather than a reaction.

Holmes had already been standing during his righteous tirade, and had not yet resumed his seat. He bowed, and said calmly, 'Lady Bracknell, I believe your nephew was about to tell me some information of significance.'

'I sincerely hope not,' Lady Bracknell replied. Her tones called to mind the trumpeting of a haughty elephant. 'Information of significance is invariably vulgar. The safest particulars are those pertaining to nothing of importance whatsoever.'

'I beg leave to differ, my lady,' Holmes replied quietly.

Lady Bracknell retrieved a lorgnette which hung from a gold chain pinned to her breast, and examined my friend through it for a lengthy interval. He lowered his eyes and politely submitted to her stare.

Finally, she asked, 'Ernest, who is this controversial gentleman?'

Ernest stammered a little in his hurry to explain. 'This is Sherlock Holmes, Aunt Augusta. He's a consulting detective working with Scotland Yard. He's here about the... *occurrence* last night. Oh, and this is Dr John Watson.'

'We have been helping Mr Holmes with his inquiries, Aunt Augusta,' Algernon supplied smoothly.

'That shows very poor judgement,' Lady Bracknell decreed. 'A perfectly successful inquiry would be one which elicited no information at all. It would do nothing to imperil the established order, yet satisfy all concerned that nothing more could have been done.'

'I assure you, Lady Bracknell,' Holmes sighed, 'that that is precisely the kind of success towards which your young relatives have been endeavouring to assist me.'

'I feel bound to tell you that you are not a person I should have chosen to find in their company, Mr Holmes.' Lady Bracknell's tone was like a frozen waterfall. 'Your influence upon them is unlikely to be admirable, and may prove alarmingly instructive.'

Holmes said, 'This is not a social call. As Mr Moncrieff says, I am here on behalf of the police.'

'That in itself,' Her Ladyship decreed, 'is hardly a sign of respectability. No doubt the excesses of the constabulary classes must be tolerated until such time as they can be eliminated or reformed, but for a gentleman to interest himself in their activities is to risk overturning a status quo decreed by providence and statistics. And that, Mr Holmes, smacks of a revolutionary tendency that I cannot condone.'

Holmes smiled. 'I am pleased to say that the only revolutions which interest me are in the sphere of knowledge.'

'Indeed,' tolled Lady Bracknell sceptically. She crossed to a divan and settled herself upon it. Gratefully, the rest of us sat. 'Mr Holmes, my nephews have been wayward at times.' Algernon and Ernest looked embarrassed. 'Their smoking and drinking, their gambling, their frequenting low forms of the theatre, reputable pursuits though they are for a young gentleman, cannot hide that fact from me. But it is quite impossible that they should be so vulgar as to turn to crime, just as you should have had better taste than to turn to its suppression.'

Holmes reiterated, 'Nobody in this house is under suspicion at present, Lady Bracknell. I am here merely in search of information – though I am afraid it may turn out to be of significance,' he added with a small smile.

'Last night's events are much to be regretted,' Her Ladyship stated sternly. 'Poor Lady Harbury was so overcome by shock that she fainted into the arms of three separate footmen, and it is the purest good fortune that she had absented herself before the policemen arrived. The decent course now is to put the deplorable affair behind us and do our utmost to ensure that it is forgotten. To indulge any further curiosity on the topic seems to me incorrigibly morbid.'

'That surely cannot be the course of action you would recommend to the police?'

'Even the police may hardly be allowed to satisfy their inquisitiveness on every trifling matter. It will only give them an exaggerated sense of their own importance. If there is any particular fact that it would be instructive for them to know, they may be sure that we shall tell them. Their judgement can hardly be allowed to hold sway in the matter.'

Holmes's smile became a little steely. 'Perhaps not. But they have me acting on their behalf.'

'Indeed,' Lady Bracknell intoned, her disapproval palpably

intensifying. 'I am told that your name is in the newspapers this morning, Mr Holmes. I read only the society columns myself, but I allow Lord Bracknell to indulge himself, strictly during the hour of breakfast, in more sensational fare. He tells me that you and this Dr James, or John, Watson, arrested Lord Arthur Savile yesterday on a charge of murder. Tell me, sir, is this lamentable aspersion correct?'

'That I arrested him is true enough,' Holmes replied. 'The murder charge will be decided in court.'

'And what evidence have you for his culpability?'

'His handprint,' said my friend.

'A *handprint*?' Lady Bracknell's voice elevated itself several octaves in disbelief.

Holmes did not flinch, but his voice sounded a little tighter as he said, 'The case is a complicated one and I would not wish to pre-empt its presentation in court. Suffice it to say that I am quite satisfied of Lord Arthur's guilt.'

'If the only safeguard against young gentlemen being carried away from their homes and turned over to the police is to be their innocence,' Lady Bracknell intoned, 'then we live in an era the depredations of which may only be compared to the iniquities of the French Revolution.'

'I can assure you, it is not a general principle. The facts of the case took some effort to uncover, but I am quite convinced of them. Lord Arthur is a murderer. So far I have found no indication that this is true of any of your relatives.' Holmes was pre-empting the truth here, at least as I understood it, but it was clear that Lady Bracknell would need to be placated if we were to make any headway here today.

Undeterred, she replied, 'Then I advise you to desist from your investigations at once, while such a happy state of affairs still pertains, and take up some inoffensive pastime such as stamp-collecting or a career in the church.'

'Lady Bracknell, are you suggesting that if I continue, I will find some evidence against your family?'

'I never suggest, Mr Holmes. When I wish to make something known, be it information or instruction, there is no element of suggestion whatsoever. Unlike yours, my principle is a general one. I do not approve of this modern obsession with discovering the facts when a multitude of pleasing illusions is available. Misconceptions are both simple and reassuring. Facts are neither.'

'Mama believes that ignorance is like a delicate exotic fruit,' Gwendolen put in. 'If you touch it, it loses its bloom.'

'Whereas I regard ignorance as the most stubborn of weeds,' replied Holmes stiffly, 'and any garden the worse for its growing there. But there, again, I am afraid we must agree to differ.'

'I shall agree to no such thing,' said Lady Bracknell decidedly. 'My view is that which I have stated. If you choose to differ from it, that is entirely your own affair.'

Holmes bowed again. 'As you say, Lady Bracknell. In that case, Dr Watson and I will bid you good day.'

Confused, I stumbled to my feet and followed Holmes as he strode towards the door. A footman held it open for us, but at the last moment, my friend turned.

'Incidentally, Lady Bracknell,' he asked, 'the dead man gave his name as Bunbury. Does that have any meaning for you?'

Lady Bracknell's eyes widened, and she deployed the lorgnette once again. 'I am quite positive,' she told us with ringing conviction, 'that none of my family has ever had dealings with any person of that name. Good *day*, Mr Holmes.'

Behind her I saw Algernon steel himself in anticipation as she turned, but at that point the footman closed the door behind us. Merriman appeared, in readiness to show us out, but Holmes held up a hand.

'A moment, Merriman,' he said. 'I think the family will be distracted for a few minutes at least. I shall need admittance to the library balcony once again, if you please.'

The butler paled. 'Mr Holmes, sir, I do not believe that Lady Bracknell would be best pleased if I—'

Holmes fixed him with a stern eye. 'You know I represent the police in this matter, Merriman. Besides, who has authority in this house, your employer or his aunt?'

'On the second question,' said Merriman stiffly, 'to offer an opinion would hardly be within the purview of my position, nor advisable should I wish to keep it. As it happens, however,' he added hesitantly, 'I find that I am unavoidably called away at present, and must ask you to wait upstairs in the library for a short time, while a footman is found to escort you from the premises. I believe that Mr Moncrieff has spent some time smoking on the balcony this morning.'

The butler showed us up to the landing, nodded curtly, and left us outside the library, which Holmes immediately bustled me into.

I said, 'Holmes, this is extraordinarily rude even for you. We are guests in Mr Moncrieff's house, and we've been left in no doubt that we are no longer welcome. Nobody is in danger, nor are we expecting to effect an arrest. Politeness surely dictates that we should withdraw, rather than placing the servants in such an impossible position.'

Holmes gazed quizzically at me. 'Watson, in the name of justice you have committed more burglaries and impersonations at my side than I can immediately recall. Outstaying one's welcome in order to ascertain a fact or two is a mild solecism by comparison.'

Saying this, he opened the French windows and steered me out once more onto the balcony. In the daylight the garden below us looked a much cheerier place, with spring flowers bursting forth in bunches across its well-kept borders, although the grisly stain on the sundial's former plinth remained. The drawing room where Lady Bracknell was presumably even now haranguing her younger relatives overlooked the square at the front of the house, so we stood unobserved for the moment.

'Attend carefully, Watson,' said Holmes, withdrawing Mabel Goring's tattered and dirty shawl from an inner pocket of his jacket. 'It is likely that we will have but one opportunity.'

He spent a long moment sizing up the distance to Mrs Winterbourne's tree and hefting the crumpled ball of the shawl, then hurled the grubby bundle in an arc up and across the garden with all his might. At first it hurtled as swiftly as a cricket ball towards a batsman's willow, but as it did so it unfurled rapidly, slowing itself down as more of it was presented to the resisting air, until after a few seconds it was more fluttering than flying. It sank gently, alighting at last on the bottommost branches of the tree, a good six feet beneath where it had hung the night before.

'A different initial angle and speed would make a difference, of course,' said Holmes, 'but not, I think, a very significant one. A demon bowler might perhaps reach the position where we saw the garment last night, or it might be done with some kind of catapult, but neither of those would have been easily obtainable by Lady Goring last night. No, if she threw it, it was not done from here.'

He hurried out onto the landing, where a footman with a pinched and worried look was waiting to usher us from the house with indecent haste.

'I think you were right when you suggested that I was being unnecessarily cautious, Holmes,' I conceded, though not before we were standing safely outside on the pavement. 'Frankly, though, Lady Bracknell is a rather intimidating person.'

'Oh, nonsense, Watson,' Holmes replied, and his voice was

suspiciously firm. For a moment I thought that Her Ladyship had oppressed him as much as she had me, but looking at him I saw that he was concealing a smile. I realised with surprise that during his conversation with the Moncrieff family's matriarch, my friend, mercurial as ever, had gone from his incandescent anger to a wary amusement. Perverse though her views were, he had actually enjoyed exchanging conversational sallies with that formidable woman.

I suddenly had a sense of what it might be like to be Holmes: always the most dynamic and forceful person in a room, always the centre of everybody's attention. He revelled in it, of course – his inclinations were nothing if not dramatic – but it must be refreshing nevertheless on the rare occasions when he encountered a rival for that status.

'But what we suspected is true,' he said decidedly. 'It is quite clear that Bunbury's name is known to them all, and is of some especial significance to Algernon Moncrieff.'

'But who was he?' I asked. 'Was the dead man the same Bunbury that they knew, or some relative? From their first reaction to the name, I would have supposed they thought him dead already.'

'Perhaps a stranger merely gave a name they knew in order to gain their attention. At present we simply do not have sufficient knowledge to guess. We must ask Gregson whether he has made any headway in identifying the dead man.'

By now we were strolling back along Grosvenor Crescent. I glanced back nervously towards Belgrave Square and said, 'They were all there last night, even Lady Bracknell. If they thought the man knew some shameful family secret, might they not have tried to silence him?'

'It is a rather extreme hypothesis, Watson. But you're right, it is not one we may altogether discount. The family's conspicuous refusal to acknowledge any moral dimension to the situation, and Lady Bracknell's attempts to discourage my investigation, might point in its favour. The Moncrieffs have already had some embarrassing family history revealed in the popular newspapers, but whether that will have inured them to the experience or made them more averse to having it repeated, I cannot tell. Nor is it obvious what further secrets the family might hold.'

'Well, that is the nature of secrets,' I said. 'Would they really be so malicious as to cast the blame onto Lady Goring, though?' I could perhaps imagine the Moncrieffs acting individually or collectively to eliminate a threat, but none of them seemed actively spiteful.

'Not everyone is as chivalrous as you, Watson,' Holmes said chidingly, but he looked thoughtful, nonetheless.

A hundred yards later, I said, 'The problem is that we know so little about these people.'

Holmes sighed. 'True enough,' he said. 'If they belonged to the criminal classes we could draw on my Index or the police records, but at their level of society one must rely on *Burke's* or *Debrett's*, and they carry little information that is useful for purposes such as ours. For that we must either listen to gossip or suborn the servants. We may yet need to fall back on the latter.'

We were entering Green Park now, passing beneath another monument to the Duke of Wellington, the gigantic equestrian statue that surmounts the arch bearing his name. It was not the most direct route back to Baker Street, and I realised what Holmes had in mind.

'You intend to try gossip first?' I guessed.

'Indeed, Watson. Our current path will take us to the Albany, where I suggest we avail ourselves of luncheon. After that, I propose we repair to Bradley's Club on St James's Street, and speak to our friend Langdale Pike. Of all the men in

London, he is best situated to tell us all that is known about the Moncrieffs and their guests.'

I ate well, though Holmes was restless and picked irritably at his food, refusing wine and drinking only water. After lunch, on our way from Piccadilly to St James's Street, I espied a figure crossing the road some distance ahead of us.

'Isn't that Lord Illingworth?' I asked Holmes, noting the man's height, broad build and steel-grey whiskers. He appeared not to see a speeding hansom, and the cabbie yelled imprecations while hurriedly changing course to avoid him, nearly running into a grocer's dray.

'None other, Watson,' Holmes agreed. 'He seems somewhat distracted.' The diplomat was carrying an envelope, and as we watched he disappeared into a post office, emerging shortly afterwards without it. 'I am surprised, also, that he is running his own errands.'

'Should we follow him?' I asked.

Holmes said, 'No. He knows us, and I have no disguise to hand.' He glanced around for any sign of his Irregulars, the motley force of street urchins whose offices and loyalty he was able to rely upon in return for regular cash payments, but none of them was in evidence. By now Illingworth had almost disappeared in the direction of Trafalgar Square and the Embankment.

Holmes shrugged. 'I admit his demeanour is intriguing, but pursuing a peer of the realm whom we have no special reason to suspect is unlikely to be the best use of our time. Let us follow our plan and pay our visit to Langdale Pike.'

We found Holmes's confederate, as always, sitting in the bow window at Bradley's, where he received visitors of all kinds and, as I understood it, rewarded them lavishly for the information they brought him. He greeted us with the listless, slightly acerbic humour that was the nearest he came to warmth, and bade us sit across from him. Holmes stretched himself out at perfect ease but again refused the offer of wine. I called for tea, settled myself uncomfortably, and tried not to pay attention to the passers-by gawking at us from the pavement of St James's Street.

I have not often written of Pike, Holmes's longest-serving and most reliable source of hearsay, chitchat and particularly scandal relating to the upper echelons of London life. A languid, dandified figure, he made a profligate living writing columns of society tittle-tattle for all the worst papers, and had a memory almost as formidable as Holmes's own, despite the trivial use to which he put it.

'So, Bunbury's reared his head again?' was his first comment when Holmes asked him whether he had heard the name in connection with the Moncrieff family. 'How amusing. We all thought we'd heard the last of Bunbury when young Algy became engaged to Cecily. Not least Algy himself, I imagine.'

'Well, he's dead now,' I said, a little harshly.

I regret to say that, when Holmes called Pike 'our friend', he exaggerated. I confess that I did not care greatly for the man. I considered his profession a parasitical one, and felt that their association did Holmes little credit. Still, it could not be denied that he was the prime conduit for all the gossip worth knowing in London; its one-man intelligence headquarters or, if one were feeling less charitable, its primary effluent pipe.

Pike said, 'Oh, Bunbury has long since passed far beyond our mortal ken, Doctor. He was a close friend of Algy's, a fearful invalid who needed constant attention and companionship, and Algy was frequently obliged to run down to the country and stay with him at a moment's notice. These relapses of Bunbury's often coincided fortuitously with dreary social occasions or other burdensome commitments which Algy would have been obliged to honour, had he remained in London rather than being at his sick friend's beck and call. It was, I have no doubt, a tremendous trial to him.'

'So this Bunbury was a fiction?' I asked.

Pike smiled lazily. 'He was far more than that. He was an alibi for whatever whim Algy might choose to follow at any particular time. Alas, I haven't the details of precisely what wild oats the lad was sowing while he was away Bunburying, but I am sure that his aunt would not have approved of them. The day he became engaged to Cecily Cardew, he announced that Bunbury's health had finally given out altogether. I've often wondered whether he would regret that impulsive decision.'

Holmes asked, 'How widely is this known, Langdale?'

'Oh, it was one of the worst-kept secrets in London,' Pike assured us. 'It was so popular it was hardly worth gossiping about. My guess would be that even Lady Bracknell suspected it, but preferred to allow her nephew the leeway afforded by the fabrication. Perhaps Algy chose to kill Bunbury off, not because he was a reformed character, but because he apprehended that Cecily would never believe in him.'

'There was no foundation for the lie?' Holmes asked. 'No real Mr Bunbury languishing unvisited?'

'Not that I ever heard,' Pike replied. 'I must say, this is most intriguing. What has been going on, Sherlock?' Pike was one of the very few people who routinely called Holmes by his first name, something that, in sixteen years of friendship, I had done only to distinguish him from his brother Mycroft. I still felt somewhat affronted by the overfamiliarity.

Briefly, Holmes set out the facts of the case before Pike, admonishing him that the evidence against Mabel Goring and the matter of her arrest must remain confidential for the moment. This seemed to me a fantastically optimistic stipulation given to whom we were talking, but I am bound to report that Holmes's trust did not prove misplaced.

After Pike had listened to the story, he said, 'Well, I can tell you little to the discredit of the rest of the family. Ernest, like Algy, enjoyed something of a wild youth, but I have heard nothing exceptional about him, beyond the quite splendid story that is already public knowledge. Cecily Cardew seems to have led a disappointingly blameless life, both before and since her marriage. And if Lady Bracknell or her daughter have any guilty secrets, those in the know are too terrified to confide them even to me.'

'What of Lord Bracknell?' I asked.

'Exceedingly rich, but in poor health,' said Pike. 'After more than thirty years married to Lady Bracknell, I should say he has shown remarkable stamina in surviving at all. He was ennobled from the commonalty, having made his money in some kind of commerce, although you would never think it from speaking to his wife or daughter. The heir is his son, Gwendolen's brother Gerald, who I understand used to propose marriage rather often, but has had the habit curtailed since one of the young ladies unexpectedly took him up on the offer.'

Holmes gave a selective list of the other guests at the ball, and asked Pike whether he had anything to report of them.

'There is little of interest concerning Major and Mrs Nepcote,' said Pike. 'She wears her nature openly and he tolerates it, and so they put themselves beyond the scope of scandal. The rest are dull at best and foolish at worst, with three exceptions.'

Holmes leaned back in his chair, tapping a long forefinger against his chin. 'Pray tell.'

Pike glanced dubiously at me. I seldom accompanied Holmes on his visits to Bradley's Club, and I had noticed a certain reserve in the gossipmonger's behaviour towards me compared with his easier manner with Holmes.

'Come now, Langdale,' Holmes smiled. 'You know you may rely on Watson's discretion.'

'May I? There are certain things I should prefer not to see published in *The Strand*,' Pike said peevishly, 'or *Beeton's* or *Lippincott's*, come to that. I have my professional standards, Sherlock, just as you do.'

I began to splutter in protest, but Holmes calmed me. 'Now, now, Watson, Langdale is right to be cautious, though I promise him that he has every reason to trust you. He keeps a lot of the information that he holds from the public. Why, if that were not the case, would I have any need to consult him at all, rather than merely reading his columns?'

'I suppose he must be wary of legal repercussions,' I grudgingly acknowledged. 'But so must I, and I resent—'

'Not just that, John,' said Pike insolently. 'I may call you John?' He continued, without the slightest pause for my assent, 'Of course, I am often given material that would be actionable if published, or that is insufficiently interesting for my readers, but I also have an obligation to protect my sources. Much of my information comes from servants, whom the upper classes will often leave out of their considerations when attempting to keep secrets. When a particular morsel of gossip could only come from one source, I must be circumspect lest I leave that source without a roof over their head or a livelihood.

'I also exercise some judgement in the matter of culpability. In certain types of scandal I make a clear distinction between perpetrators and victims, one which is rarely drawn so clearly by society at large. In such cases it would hardly be right to expose the latter to the forces of public opprobrium. Unfortunately, there are instances where naming the perpetrator would make the victim's name obvious, and those are consequently of no use to me at all. In such cases, in fact, I often pass what I know on to Sherlock in case there is anything he can achieve with them.'

I was surprised, I must admit, to discover that London's telltale-in-chief had scruples, but it made more sense of his friendship with Holmes.

I said, 'Whatever you may tell me, I promise you I will not publish it in any way that might allow the individuals to be identified during their lifetimes. I do have some experience of this sort of thing, you know.'

Pike smiled. 'Good enough,' he said. 'Very well, then. I may be able to provide some further details on three of your... principals? Suspects? Persons of interest in the case?'

Holmes said, 'Any of those terms will do. Pray proceed. Watson and I are all ears.'

Pike said, 'To take the simplest and least pleasant to tell first... Lord Illingworth is an awful man, a notorious seducer and rake. He was ruining impressionable young women when he was plain Mr George Harford, long before he succeeded to his noble title. I have knowledge of at least one illegitimate child, a young man who fled to America four years ago with his mother and fiancée rather than reconcile with his natural father.'

'Who was the mother?' I asked.

'Oh, a woman of no importance,' Pike replied blithely, leaving me in no doubt that he knew her name. 'This was shortly before Illingworth was dispatched to his embassy, where I imagine he continued in much the same vein. I have no doubt that there are other children, nor should I be at all surprised to discover worse things in his past.'

Well, Cecily Moncrieff had said that Lord Illingworth was very wicked. I wondered, though, whether she could possibly be aware of how wicked. I supposed that such a character might at least account for the coldness that Mrs Teville had shown towards the earl.

'Who else?' asked Holmes.

'Well, there is the matter of Lord Goring.'

'Ah!' Holmes was intrigued. 'This promises to be of interest.'

'In recent years he has done little to warrant any ill reputation, beyond being idle and a constant cause of annoyance to his father. As far as little Mabel is concerned, he has shown every sign of being an ideal husband to her. The scandal in his case comes in his past. Twelve years ago, in 1885, he was engaged to a schoolfellow of Gertrude Chiltern's, an engagement that lasted only a few days before he broke it off.'

'Surely not Gwendolen Fairfax?' I asked, astonished.

Pike shook his head. 'No, another girl. Her name was Laura Hungerford. She was seventeen, Goring twenty-four. The whole affair displeased his family greatly, although the accounts I've heard suggest that the fault was on his side rather than hers. After their estrangement she vanished altogether from public view.'

'A youthful folly on Goring's part,' suggested Holmes. 'Of no lasting consequence, surely. And the third guest?'

'Patience, Sherlock, there is more. Two years ago, Miss Hungerford resurfaced under a married name. She returned to London as a wealthy woman, calling herself Mrs Cheveley and claiming to have spent time in Vienna. Whether there was ever a Mr Cheveley is a moot point. Her path crossed Lord Goring's at that time, and that of Robert Chiltern. There was some unpleasantness that I never did reach the bottom of, though it culminated in Goring's engagement to Mabel Chiltern. It may have concerned Mrs Cheveley's business interests.'

'Is this Mrs Cheveley in business?' Holmes asked, surprised.

'Before she disappeared once more from my sphere of knowledge, she was an active investor of her fortune, and a shareholder in a number of dubious ventures. Financial scandal isn't really my area, I'm afraid, but I gather that her name had a habit of arising in peripheral connections when fraud, malpractice, embezzlement and the like were discovered, always in ways which left her blameless legally, but morally implicated.'

'Interesting,' Holmes said again. 'Although as yet we have no evidence of any fiscal dimension to this case. Is that everything?'

'As far as the Gorings and Chilterns are concerned, yes. Mrs Teville is a more interesting case. I know of her, of course. She has been a fixture at balls and parties among the Moncrieffs' circle this season. But I have been quite unable to identify her.'

'Identify her?' I repeated, confused. 'Do you suppose she's using a false name?'

'Oh John, these much-married women are a dreadful trial in my line of work. They go through so many names, some of them doubtless as fictitious as Mr Bunbury's. It is far easier for a woman to reinvent herself than for a man, as Laura Cheveley shows us.'

'And is that all you can tell us of her? That you can tell us nothing?'

'Very nearly,' Pike confirmed. 'However, there is a rumour that Mrs Teville has one particular interest in London society. A younger woman whom she has met in private at a number of houses in London, and to whom she is more closely related than is generally known.'

'And who is that?' I could tell Holmes scented an avenue of inquiry.

'Unfortunately I have no idea, and neither have my informants. The only one who could perhaps have told me more, a maid in a respectable household with a laudably open ear for her betters' conversation, was too scrupulous to do so. She has heard them together, but like me, she feels that the identity of an innocent is not for general ears. The scent of scandal attaching to Mrs Teville, whom she dislikes, was quite another matter.'

'Interesting,' Holmes reflected, 'most interesting. How old would you say Mrs Teville was, Watson?'

'Her mid-forties,' I said promptly. 'Although she covers it up well.'

'Such was my impression also. And this mysterious woman – her daughter, surely, Langdale?'

Pike nodded. 'My informant seems to believe so.'

'In that case it seems unlikely that she can be older than her mid-twenties, and she might well be younger. This may have some bearing on our case.'

I said, 'Gwendolen Moncrieff is twenty-nine, I think.' I had looked the family up in *Debrett's* that morning. 'Lady Chiltern must be around the same age. They must be too old, surely.'

Holmes agreed. 'Mabel Goring is more the correct age, but she, like them, has a firmly attested family history. Cecily Moncrieff, however, is a possible candidate.'

'By Jove, yes,' I said. 'She's Thomas Cardew's granddaughter, isn't she? But Ernest was her guardian, so she must have no living parents. Or none known, at any rate.'

'Well, we must not get too excited. There may be no connection at all, except that the family knows Mrs Teville now.'

'You know I make no guarantee as to the relevance of any of this, or even of its veracity,' Pike observed lethargically. 'I merely offer it for what it may be worth. The use you make of it is your affair.'

'You have given us sufficient for our current needs, Langdale, and I am grateful.'

'You will forward the usual fee?' Pike asked, a hard glint in his eye. 'We may be friends, Sherlock, but it is important to me that our business affairs be on a professional footing.'

Holmes responded with a far more friendly smile than this impolite request deserved. 'Never doubt it, old fellow.'

'One other thing,' Pike suggested as we stood up to go. 'That story about the infant in the handbag has always seemed... incomplete to me. How likely it is that a nursemaid might mistakenly place a baby in a piece of luggage I can't say, but no reason was ever given for why she should deposit the bag at Victoria Station. Nor, having realised her mistake, why she would get rid of the perambulator and run rather than attempting to make amends. A child's life could have been at stake, after all, and she would have lost her position in any case.'

Holmes nodded thoughtfully. 'The latter point might be explained if the late Mrs Moncrieff, the nursemaid's employer, were as imposing as her sister, Lady Bracknell. But you're right, the story is a queer one. I have never seen any reason to examine the matter in depth, as its outcome seemed to be so satisfactory to all concerned, but you may be right that there are questions to be answered. Whether they are relevant to the business in hand is another matter, of course.'

CHAPTER SEVEN
EXCURSION TO WOOLTON MANOR

Holmes and I spent the evening at home, I catching up with my correspondence, he alternating between wordlessly playing the violin and smoking in the meditative silence which was typical of his cogitations when in the early stages of a case. In its companionable familiarity our enclosure was a thoroughly pleasant one, but I could not help comparing it with that of Lady Goring, separated from her husband and child and consigned to the privations of a police cell, or worse, a prison, and shivering a little in sympathy with her.

In the morning Holmes outlined his plan for the day. He purposed to prevail upon our comrades at Scotland Yard to provide him with the police accounts of the infant Ernest Moncrieff's disappearance in 1867, while I took a trip to Woolton in Hertfordshire, the site of the Cardew family home, to make discreet enquiries of the locals regarding the history of the family, and particularly of Cecily's parentage.

I had been in Scotland Yard's record room before, and Holmes's share of the work sounded unenviably dull to me. For my part I was perfectly content to accept a respite from the capital, and enjoy the train journey through the leafy

countryside to the north of London. The intrigues and the verbal
fencing of the past days fell away behind me and I basked in the
spring sunshine through my carriage window. The air was clear,
the sky blue, and as we passed from buildings through fields
and into woodland, birdsong could be heard over the bearlike
huffing and grunting of the engine.

The journey from King's Cross took little more than an
hour, and soon I was alighting at Woolton, a charming village
that enjoyed its own station purely because it happened to lie
directly upon the branch line. A row of rustic cottages with
flowers flourishing in baskets faced the main street, a stream
babbled under a humpbacked bridge towards a mill-race, and
hens scratched at the pavement in front of the village post office. I
stepped into an old half-timbered public house, the Spotted Calf,
and left half an hour later, the better for a bottle of the local ale
and with directions to the Manor House and the parish church.
For the convenience of the local nobility, the latter, as is often
the way in such places, lay in the grounds of the former. The
landlord assured me that the rector, one Reverend Canon Doctor
Chasuble, was a most learned gentleman and something of a
local historian, as well as a personal friend of the bishop, so I had
hopes that he might be able to supply the information I needed.

I strolled along the church path past the boys' and girls'
schools to the church, a compact affair nestled in a churchyard
surrounded on three sides by woodland, with its own small
bell-tower and what the verger assured me was a much-
admired octagonal marble font. This gentleman also informed
me that the rector would be making his rounds of the parish,
but suggested a time later that day when I might find him at
home with Mrs Chasuble.

I filled the time with a ramble through the manor grounds,
both verger and publican having assured me that Mr Moncrieff

had no great objections to visitors on his land. The estate was larger than I had expected, including a modest farm and several hundred acres of woods replete with pheasant and deer. It seemed neat, orderly and well kept, which I assumed reflected better on Ernest's, or perhaps more likely Gwendolen's, choice of estate manager than on any labours of his own.

The Manor House was also large, with a grand Regency frontage concealing an older building behind. It was shut up in the family's absence, presumably housing only the minimum of servants required to keep it in order, but I saw several groundsmen, gamekeepers and gardeners, including a chatty fellow who I happened upon digging a new flower bed in a lavish rose garden, and who introduced himself as Moulton. He was perfectly delighted to give me the standard potted history of Ernest Moncrieff's life in exchange for half a crown, but became understandably wary when I ventured onto the subject of his master's former ward.

I considered loosening his tongue with further emoluments, but reflected that I was likely in any case to find a more informed account at the rectory. Moulton willingly directed me there, and felt free enough to vouchsafe that the rector had only recently married, and that the new Mrs Chasuble had previously been Miss Cecily's governess. This vindicated my determination to speak to the canon and his wife, so I bade farewell to Moulton and set off back towards the village.

After a hearty lunch at the Spotted Calf, I found Woolton Rectory easily enough, a forbidding grey building that had clearly been built under the assumption that the incumbent might bring with him a sizeable family, and now stood with most of its rooms unused.

Announcing myself as an amateur student of English rural history, eager to learn more about the annals of Woolton and its prominent families, earned me an effusive welcome from Dr and Mrs Chasuble in their slate-floored, stone-hearthed parlour. The canon was an eagerly sincere man, heavily whiskered, academic in tone and manner but with a generous nature. He was considerably more elderly than I had expected, although his wife was younger, perhaps in her mid-fifties. Her plain but expressive face made her seem severe yet rather anxious.

The canon told me a great deal about Woolton's early history before I could work the conversation around to more recent matters. The village, I learned, had been settled since Saxon times and appeared in the Domesday Book, but was renamed in the fourteenth century after the Woolton family. It was they who had built the original manor house, and whose descendants had fallen on hard times hundreds of years later, eventually selling it to one Thomas Cardew, whose nineteenth-century descendant of the same name had been in residence when Chasuble first took up the benefice in Woolton.

'The late Mr Cardew was a great credit to our little community in every way,' Chasuble reminisced. 'He was a most philanthropic gentleman, greatly inclined to benevolent gestures in every part of his life. Did you see the baptistery in the parish church, Dr Watson? A splendid piece, is it not, and thoroughly canonical in shape and inscription?'

'It certainly is,' I hazarded.

'That was a gift, and a most generous one, from Mr Thomas Cardew,' the canon enthused. 'He also endowed both our village schools. The man was a true cornucopia of charity.'

I said, 'I believe I've heard something of the kind. Didn't he adopt a foundling child?'

Dr Chasuble smiled beatifically. 'Oh, yes. He was a veritable Nicholas.'

'I thought the name given to the boy was John or Jack?' I asked, confused.

The canon frowned. 'I spoke allusively. My allusion was to the patron saint of children.'

'Oh, I see,' I said. 'And I understand he left the adopted child his estate. That was even more generous, although I suppose he had no family of his own.'

'Ah, that is not quite correct. John Worthing, as the boy was named by Mr Cardew, inherited his house and land, and some of his considerable fortune. But the greater part of the latter went to Thomas's granddaughter, Cecily, on the occasion of her marriage. She and her husband plighted their troth on the same day as Laetitia and I,' he added, beaming.

His wife seemed less pleased. 'Frederick, I expect that Dr Watson's interest does not extend to our personal histories, still less those of Cecily and her relatives.'

'Naturally, naturally,' the canon said. 'Forgive me, Doctor, I am afraid that there are times when I exceed the boundaries of my interlocutor's patience. It is an instructive lesson in humility, and one upon which I have preached at length in my sermons. To return to the history of the village, then, this rectory was built in 1815, shortly before the Battle of Waterloo, and quite interestingly the architect was a veteran of Trafalgar. His name was—'

'Actually,' I said as politely as I could, 'I am somewhat interested in the history of the Cardew family. Did Miss Cecily Cardew live at the manor until her marriage?'

'Ah yes. She was under Laetitia's tutelage until the age of nineteen,' Dr Chasuble confirmed, but once again his wife had other ideas.

She said, 'Dr Watson, local history is one matter. Local biography is quite another. If you are familiar with the background of Mr Worthing – that is to say, Mr Ernest Moncrieff – then you will understand that we have been at times much pestered by persons of the journalistic persuasion, seeking unsuitable tales regarding my former employer. You will also understand that considerations of loyalty and propriety quite forbid us from indulging in any such indiscretion.'

'My wife is quite correct, sir,' Dr Chasuble confirmed, a little sadly, 'as I am afraid she often is. If your interest is in stories of the family for publication in the periodicals, then we can be of no help to you, and I can only entreat you to repent of the scurrilous and defamatory ways endemic to your profession before it is too late.'

This was the second time in as many days that I had been suspected of gutter journalism, and I might well have taken offence, had it not been for these people's evident good intentions. Instead I said, 'I must admit, I have deceived you a little, for which I can only apologise. I am here in the furtherance of an official police investigation. The story has been kept out of the papers, so you have probably not heard that there has been an unpleasant incident at Mr Ernest Moncrieff's London house.'

I sketched out as rough and vague an outline of the case as I could, concluding, 'So if I am asking you to be indiscreet, you must understand that it is from the best of motives. Indeed, I do not exaggerate when I say that further lives may conceivably be at stake.'

'Mr Sherlock Holmes?' Dr Chasuble was impressed. 'So you are the Dr Watson who chronicles his emprises? Remarkable, quite remarkable. In that case, I am sure there can be no objection, my dear…?'

Mrs Chasuble, however, looked positively alarmed. 'I hope Mr Holmes has not accompanied you here?'

'No, he remains in London,' I assured her.

'I am pleased to hear it,' she said. 'I should not like to imagine him conducting himself so trivially. I fail to see what good can come of our intelligence. Surely Mr Wor— Mr Moncrieff and his family can tell you all you need to know?'

'Holmes wished me to seek out another perspective,' I said. 'Those not directly involved in the family affairs may have greater objectivity. The fact is, we suspect... that is,' I amended, not wishing to overstate the matter, 'it is perhaps possible, that the family background of Mrs Cecily Moncrieff, the former Cecily Cardew, may be of some significance. Anything you might tell me about her parentage, for instance, could be most helpful.'

'I always strongly discouraged Cecily from asking about such things,' Mrs Chasuble said sternly. 'Excessive curiosity in personal matters is of no credit to any person, Dr Watson, and it is rightly considered unbecoming in a young girl. Cecily was most obedient to my wishes in this matter.'

'In this instance, though, my curiosity is not idle,' I argued. 'As I have said, it's possible that the knowledge might help us to catch a murderer.' As tactfully as I could, I asked, 'Is Cecily really Thomas Cardew's granddaughter, Dr Chasuble, or did he adopt her as he did the boy he named John Worthing?'

'Oh, no such thing, I can assure you.' Dr Chasuble seemed rather agitated at the suggestion. 'Cecily is the daughter of Thomas Cardew's daughter Violet Cardew, who married a distant cousin. She moved away when young Jack was barely a denarian. That is to say,' he added, seeing my befuddled expression, 'he was little more than ten years old.'

'What was the cousin's name?' I asked.

'It was Cardew, naturally. I do not believe I ever knew his first name. Certainly I never met the gentleman. The wedding took place elsewhere.'

'Did you meet him, Mrs Chasuble?'

'No, nor did I ever meet Miss Violet Cardew herself,' she said reluctantly. 'Mr Cardew employed me only sometime later, to teach Cecily.'

'How old was Violet Cardew at the time of her marriage?' I asked.

Dr Chasuble sighed. 'The poor child was twenty-two. She was but twenty-three when she died.'

'So she died?' I echoed. 'I suppose that is how Cecily came to live at the Manor House with her grandfather and adoptive uncle. What became of her father?'

'Ah, the whole affair was a grievous one,' Dr Chasuble told me with regret. 'Both Cecily's parents left this mortal coil when she was but a babe in arms. I believe it was scarlet fever that carried them away; either that or a runaway carthorse.' He paused, a little confused. 'It is possible that there was some ambiguity in the matter.'

'But you are certain they died?' I asked. 'There was no ambiguity on that point?'

'Oh, none at all, none at all. It was a great tragedy for young Cecily, though I am pleased to say that she has not suffered by it. She, too, benefited greatly from her late grandfather's generosity.'

'Forgive me, Dr Chasuble, but had you any proof of her parents' demise? Beyond the word of Mr Thomas Cardew, I mean.'

'Proof?' The canon seemed confused. 'It did not seem to be a matter that called for proof, Dr Watson. In philosophy or mathematics a proof may be both necessary and enjoyable, but in family relations they are not generally considered de rigueur.'

'No, I hardly suppose so,' I said. 'So Cecily was born when Violet was twenty-two or twenty-three? And she was married last year at nineteen?' Forty-three was a perfectly plausible age for our enigmatic Mrs Teville, although her affectations of youth made the question a difficult one to judge.

I searched my mind for further questions to ask, but I felt I had discovered all I could here. It was possible that Ernest Moncrieff knew more of his adopted sister's fate, but given his age at the time he would remember little of it. Indeed, the theory that was germinating in my mind required him not to recognise her now. His behaviour towards Mrs Teville did not seem like that of a brother to his sister, even an adopted one.

I stood to thank the canon and his wife for their hospitality, but was interrupted by a thunderous knocking at the rectory door.

'Whoever can that be, Frederick?' Mrs Chasuble asked, unnerved.

'I suppose there is some crisis in the parish,' Dr Chasuble sighed. 'If there has been an accident, I may be called upon to administer extreme unction.'

I heard the sound of the Chasubles' aged servant opening the door, then arguing with a voice whose presence surprised me enormously.

A moment later Dr Chasuble gave a gasp of surprise, and Mrs Chasuble a very audible shriek, as Sherlock Holmes burst into the parlour.

'Holmes!' I expostulated. 'What on earth are you doing here?'

'Ah, Watson,' he replied, entirely unsurprised. 'I am impressed by your good thinking. These would be the ideal people in the village to ask about Cecily Cardew's parentage.'

'That's what I thought,' I said, aggrieved. 'But I understood that you wished me to handle your enquires in Woolton. Why are you here so suddenly?'

'I have come hotfoot from Scotland Yard,' he said, as Mrs Chasuble clutched her husband's arm with a tiny moan, 'to confront the kidnapper of Ernest Moncrieff. Yes, madam,' he added as she gave vent to a full-throated wail, 'I said the *kidnapper*.'

'Have you altogether lost your mind, Holmes?' I protested. 'This is Mrs Chasuble, Cecily's governess.'

'Yes and no, Watson, yes and no. This is Mrs Chasuble, but before that she was Miss Laetitia Prism. And before she was Cecily's governess, she was Ernest's nursemaid!'

I frowned. From nursemaid to governess was a considerable promotion, bringing with it an improvement in social class normally quite beyond the reach of such servants. Besides, the time when Thomas Cardew would have required a nursemaid for Ernest would have been when he was quite a young child, before Violet Cardew left home, and Mrs Chasuble had just been denying that she had ever met Violet.

Holmes sighed, impatient with my slowness. 'Not in the household of Thomas Cardew, Watson, but that of Ernest's father, General Moncrieff, or Colonel Moncrieff as he was at the time.'

'*That* nursemaid?' I gaped. 'Mrs Chasuble was the handbag woman?' The name of the servant whose unfortunate error had set Ernest Moncrieff on his unusual course in life had not appeared in any of the newspaper reports I had seen, though it was possible that Langdale Pike could have supplied it had we asked. While I knew that the woman in question had been the one to identify John Worthing as Ernest Moncrieff, I had had no inkling that she was still involved in his life in any other capacity.

Holmes said, 'The name of Prism is prominent in the police reports, and I recognised it as the most unusual one which Cecily had employed when speaking of her governess.'

'By Jove!' was all I could think of to say.

But the Revd Canon Dr Chasuble had more to contribute. 'Mr Holmes, sir, for shame and for pity!' he protested. 'My wife has suffered quite enough for her lamentable error. She has borne agonies of remorse and regret for what she has done, and like the Magdalen she has been forgiven!'

'Frederick!' objected Mrs Chasuble primly.

'My apologies, my dear. I spoke analogically. My analogy pertained to the forgiveness of the sin, not the character of the sinner. But sir, the living person most injured by Mrs Chasuble's regrettable mnemonic lapse was Ernest Moncrieff himself, and he has shown great magnanimity in absolving her of all blame. If he can make his peace with her, then surely it is for us to follow his Christian example, and not to throw around expressions like "kidnap" indiscriminately!'

Sombrely Holmes replied, 'Dr Chasuble, I assure you that I am never indiscriminate when it comes to matters of crime. I spoke literally. My terminology was drawn from the criminal lexicon. Was that not correct of me, Mrs Chasuble?'

By now Mrs Chasuble had overcome her immediate panic, and her head was drooping miserably. 'Mr Holmes,' she said, 'I admit with shame that it was. My earlier confession to Lady Bracknell was pusillanimously incomplete. I sought merely to set the record straight upon Mr Worthing's identity, and evaded my responsibility for a more profound crime.'

'Good Lord!' I declared. 'So Pike was right. There was more to the story than we were told at the time.'

'Laetitia, you must confess now,' Dr Chasuble implored her, in great distress. 'The weight of such a transgression upon the soul can only be lifted through honest disclosure.'

'I think I may spare Mrs Chasuble the pain,' said Holmes. 'Much of the story I know already, though she may be able to fill in some of the details. May I tell you what I know?'

She nodded her head, and he began.

'In 1867, you were twenty-five or thereabouts, and employed as nursemaid in the household of Colonel Ernest Moncrieff and his wife Claudia, sister to Lady Bracknell, both of them now deceased. Your duties entailed the care of their infant son, also named Ernest, then less than a year old. His younger brother, Algernon, would not be born for several years, so Ernest was your only charge.

'In time you might have gained the experience to apply for a more senior situation as a nanny, but you had ambitions to better yourself beyond that. You had intellectual pretensions, and even hopes of becoming a published novelist. In short, while conscientious in your duties, you were dissatisfied with your lot, as well you might be. It was at this time that you met Sergeant William Durrington.'

The name was unknown to me, but I could see from Mrs Chasuble's pained expression that it had very particular meaning for her.

Holmes went on. 'Durrington had until recently served in Colonel Moncrieff's regiment. He had been dismissed, unless I am mistaken, by the colonel personally, and consequently bore a grudge against his former commanding officer. What was the cause of his dismissal, do you know?'

Mrs Chasuble spoke quietly. 'He told me that he was punished for selling cigarettes to the troops, but I now believe that he was dealing in opium. The regiment was fortunate not to see active combat duty under the colonel's command, but young men can be extremely foolish. Their boredom had a deleterious effect on morale.'

'Indeed. Well, that would certainly be grounds for a summary discharge, if not a court martial. In any case, this Durrington wished revenge upon Colonel Moncrieff, and to that end he chose to prey upon a blameless young woman, a domestic servant in the colonel's employ. What occurred between the two of you so long ago is for you alone to know, and not a matter any of us is fit to judge.'

'Amen,' murmured Dr Chasuble fervently, embarrassed by

this speculation. He was about to say more, probably a great deal more, but Holmes was determined to continue.

'Whatever occurred, it was enough to put you in his power. With what he knew, he could have had you dismissed without a reference, which would have put an end to all your hopes. This enabled him to manipulate you to his own ends, which were vengeful and villainous. It was at his behest, not through any moment of mental abstraction, that you placed the infant Ernest Moncrieff in a handbag and deposited him in the cloakroom at Victoria Station, so that Durrington could collect the child and demand a substantial ransom from his former commanding officer for his return.'

'But Holmes,' I said, 'that's not what happened.'

'As far as Miss Prism knew at the time, it was what was to happen. But although she could not risk frustrating Sergeant Durrington's scheme, she was a woman of conscience. She felt, as Dr Chasuble has said, agonies of remorse.

'You had left the perambulator which should have contained the baby outside Victoria Station while you deposited the handbag, so that your entry and withdrawal from the cloakroom could be quick and stealthy. I can only assume that you waited until the baby was sleeping peacefully in the luggage, or his wails would hardly have been inconspicuous. He was, in any case, to wait there only minutes before your accomplice collected him.'

'But Holmes!' I said again.

Holmes sighed. 'You show a remarkable lack of patience, Watson. The plan was thwarted when William Durrington became involved in a trivial altercation with one of the passengers on the Brighton line platform. The argument developed into a fight, and resulted in Durrington being pushed onto the tracks just as a train arrived. He was badly injured and did not survive.'

'Good heavens,' said Mrs Chasuble. 'I had no idea of that,

though I am not in the least sorry to hear it. As a man sows, so shall he reap. When I realised that the scheme had gone awry, I supposed that he had merely mistaken the time or the day.'

'You knew nothing at the time of his failure to collect the child, of course.'

'Naturally not. I left the station to reacquire the perambulator. My instructions were that I should walk back through Hyde Park, as if returning to the Moncrieffs' Upper Grosvenor Street home, before ridding myself of the encumbering conveyance in Bayswater. I was then to hide at an agreed address while I awaited my share of the proceeds. With them I intended to start a new life as a governess, with the proceeds of authorship as my nest egg. I fear now, however, that I was sadly deceived in believing that Sergeant Durrington intended to deliver them to me at all.'

'I see that your understanding of human nature has matured with the years. For the moment, however, I am more interested in the events of that day. As you left the station, you were quite understandably in a state of some distress. As I have said, you are not a monster. You were, I imagine, quite visibly upset. And it was at that point that you met a kind gentleman who gave you his card.'

'That is correct, although I cannot imagine how you know it. I admit that I was quite overcome by womanly tears, and Mr Thomas Cardew, though a stranger, was good enough to comfort me. As you have said, Frederick, he was the very soul of charity.' She clutched her husband's hand tightly.

'You rid yourself of the perambulator as arranged, and at that point your movements pass beyond my ken. We know that Durrington's promised money was not forthcoming. I assume you found a new situation, probably under a new name, living, I would imagine, in constant terror of the law. After some time you plucked up the courage to approach Mr Cardew for help, and he was in a position, either then or later, to offer you work as governess to his orphaned granddaughter.'

'It was some years later,' Mrs Chasuble agreed. 'He told me at the time that his daughter was of age and his male ward already had a tutor, but that he would keep me in mind for any future positions that came up. He was as good as his word.'

'After you came to live here you would have had no reason to guess that Jack Worthing was the baby you had abandoned. His unusual arrival in Mr Cardew's custody was, I imagine, rarely discussed even among the family, and probably never with the staff. You would have known him only as Mr Cardew's ward, and after a decade you could hardly have been expected to recognise him.'

'Indeed, no. Even as an infant, he was unusually lacking in distinguishing features. After Mr Cardew's death he claimed to have re-established relations with a reprehensible younger brother, which made it all the more unlikely I should guess at his true origins. I remained ignorant of them until the day that Lady Bracknell appeared in the morning-room and recognised me from her sister's employ.' Mrs Chasuble shuddered at the recollection. 'Only when Mr Worthing heard us discussing the particulars of the case did I learn that he had been discovered in a handbag, and consequently realise who he was. Mr Cardew must have found him in the cloakroom shortly after I met him outside the station, although I gave him no clue that would have led him there.'

'In Lady Bracknell's presence you would, of course, have felt altogether too intimidated to make a full confession. You saw that the revelation of John Worthing's true identity would be quite enough to distract from the improbabilities of your story, and you felt that there was nothing to be gained from going into further detail.'

Mrs Chasuble said, 'It is true, to my great shame. I have always espoused the virtue of honesty, and enjoined it strictly upon my charges, but in the event the temptation to err from the path of absolute veracity was too great for me to resist.'

She began to weep, and her husband embraced her. He said, 'Come, come, Laetitia, you must not castigate yourself so. I fear that none of us is perfectly honest. I blush to admit that I have myself on occasion exaggerated the calls upon my time, in order to cut short an unexpected visit from a troublesome parishioner.'

Holding his wife close, he looked at us. 'What is to be done now, Mr Holmes?'

Gently, Holmes said, 'I cannot see that anything further needs to be done, Dr Chasuble. Your wife's remorse is obvious. Sergeant Durrington is dead, as are both General and Mrs Moncrieff, so there is no question of her testifying against her accomplice or making reparations to her victims. Indeed, her chief victim has, as you have pointed out, forgiven her. She has not profited from her crime, and no lasting harm has come from it. I cannot see that punishment would do any good in this instance. I only ask that I may rely on you for further information should I need it.'

The elderly couple tried to thank him, but he raised a hand to stop them.

Holmes said, 'You spoke earlier of the Magdalen, Dr Chasuble. I freely admit that my knowledge of, and for that matter my interest in, holy scripture is profoundly limited, but I do happen to recall how that particular Bible passage ends. My suggestion now, Mrs Chasuble, is that you should go and sin no more.'

CHAPTER EIGHT
THE PRISM PAPERS

'But how did you come to know the whole story, Holmes?' I asked him on the train back to London, after summarising for him all I had learned of the Cardew family's history. 'Was it all in the police records, or did some of it come from Langdale Pike?'

'I pieced it together from documents held by the police,' Holmes said. 'As they could have done themselves, had they the wit and determination.'

Outside, the shadows were lengthening as the sun sank slowly to the right of our carriage. The woodland beauty that had pleased me on the journey up to Woolton was becoming sombre and gloomy as we narrowed the distance between ourselves and the capital.

'After your departure, I headed as arranged for Scotland Yard, where our friend Gregson obtained access for me to the records room. It did not take long to track down, in the files for 1867, the original police reports of the missing baby. That was where I first saw Mrs Chasuble's maiden name in this connection, the nursemaid Prism being naturally the chief suspect. It was a surname I had encountered only once before, and its also being the name of Cecily's former governess was too great a correspondence to be ignored.

'At first I suspected that Prism and Thomas Cardew were in cahoots, and that Cardew had had her procure an infant child for reasons of his own, later rewarding her with the post of governess to his granddaughter. However, a much later and rather apologetic note, added to the Moncrieff file only two years ago, cross-references the case with another file relating to the foundling discovered by Cardew at Victoria Station. It was quite clear from this material that Thomas Cardew had made diligent efforts to trace the parents of the child he found, including communicating with the police, before adopting him as his own.

'The reason no connection was made between a child going missing and one being discovered on the same day had much to do with the disruption and confusion caused at Victoria Station by the assault upon, and subsequent death of, one Sergeant William Durrington. The police, like everybody else, realised the child's origins only decades later, when the newspaper reports began to appear proclaiming the rediscovery of the Handbag Heir.

'There was also a cross-reference to a further file of correspondence from Ernest Worthing in 1895, relating to a lost cigarette case, which appears to have been ignored as the work of a crank, but that did not seem of relevance to our current investigation.

'Having dismissed the idea that Prism had been working for Thomas Cardew, I returned to the original file, where I read the police account of the discovery of the perambulator. One fact which was not made public at the time was that the conveyance was not found empty. Inside there were several hundred handwritten pages, which turned out to be the draft manuscript for what would have been a three-volume novel.'

'How peculiar,' I observed.

'I borrowed it with Gregson's blessing,' said Holmes, producing a thick wad of papers from an inner pocket. 'It had been sitting unread in the archives for more than thirty years, so he had little reason to object.' He passed me the stack of yellowing pages, each of them inscribed in fading ink in a feminine hand.

The title page announced, 'Beata, Or a Maid's Tale'. The author's name was given as 'Felicia Lens'.

'A transparent pseudonym,' I observed.

I turned the page and read:

> High, high up, oh! so high aloft in the ancient, craggy, woody, cliffy hills of Umbria, by the purple vineyards and among the balmy olive-groves, stands a romantic hilltop town of alabaster-coloured stucco and ruddily russet terracotta roofs, its ancient stony walls the wise and silent arbiters of many romantic secrets kept by its rustic burghers and patrician noblemen over the long and lingering centuries.

I said, 'My word, I'm glad I didn't write this.'

'You will, Watson, you will,' said Holmes. 'That is,' he added placatorily when he saw my expression, 'I imagine you will reproduce it, if our current adventure merits inclusion in your memoirs. Your professional opinion is not favourable, then?'

'Certainly not. It's absolute drivel.'

Holmes nodded gravely. 'It seems the police had come to much the same conclusion. The investigating inspector had attempted to delve into the opening pages, but he appended a note to the effect that the prose was turgid, the dialogue stilted and the subject matter nauseatingly sentimental, and moreover that it appeared to have no bearing on the case. It was clear to me that this vital piece of evidence had never been properly read.'

'I should rather think not,' I said. 'Despite its authorship, I cannot see what its bearing upon the case might be. Unless… is it written in some sort of code?'

'Alas, no,' said Holmes. 'It is what it appears to be, a sincere attempt at a literary work by an enthusiastic but naïve hand. However, I could not afford to ignore it, especially since it had lain unexamined since the original abduction case.'

He smiled grimly. 'I think you know that I am not a man to shirk his duty, Watson, but I quailed. Nevertheless, there are certain techniques that I have mastered for reading at speed when urgency requires it, which allow one to absorb the salient points of a document in the briefest time possible, and this seemed like a sufficient occasion to apply these skills.

'I skimmed through the novel in about an hour, and by the end of it I had a very good idea of the story. It continues in much the same vein as you have seen for two and a half chapters before announcing the birth of the heroine, a good-hearted peasant girl living at an unspecified time during the Italian Renaissance, and named, as you might expect, Beata. For the majority of the book her experiences are predictable enough – growing up in respectable poverty, caring for her aged relatives, being captured by brigands, falling in love with the young guardsman who rescues her, being informed by his jealous sergeant that he has died in a skirmish, running away to join a circus and the like, before she is appointed, as a vaguely justified reward for her honesty, bravery and good-heartedness, to the duke's household as nursemaid to his infant grandson Candido.'

'Ah,' I said.

'"Ah," indeed. The most significant part of the narrative for our purposes arrives when Beata is suborned against her will by that same Sergeant Guglielmo, a plausible yet conniving villain since discharged by the duke for his general perfidy. To placate him, she abstracts the young lordling from his crib and leaves him in a basket at a wagon-station for the scoundrel to find.

'This development of the plot comes extremely late in the novel, and is written in a much more breathless style, and more hurried handwriting, than the rest of the manuscript. A rushed and highly implausible ending follows, in which the baby is saved, the villains receive their comeuppance, Beata is informed by the duke that her beloved is not dead after all, and she is enabled to live happily ever after.

'A more tedious confection I have never, I am pleased to say, been called upon to peruse, but you will observe how its terms are suggestive. I am sure that "Felicia Lens" began her story a fair while before she became embroiled in the plot to kidnap Ernest Moncrieff, but she finished it as a hasty confession of what she had been forced to do, together with a wistful expression of her hoped-for outcome.'

'But nobody realised what she was telling them, because it was so atrociously written.' I shook my head. 'I'm sure there's a lesson there.'

'I had, as I have said, dismissed the idea that Thomas Cardew had colluded in the kidnap, but from the manuscript it was apparent to me that there had nonetheless been a conspiracy to abduct the Moncrieff child. Clearly, however, something had happened to place the baby in Cardew's hands, rather than those of Laetitia Prism's accomplice.

'From the rank assigned by "Felicia Lens" to the wicked Guglielmo, and the record of Sergeant William Durrington's accidental death at Victoria that day, it was not difficult to decide what that something had been. I was also able to derive the major points of the reality underlying the fiction – Durrington's dismissal by Colonel Moncrieff, his plot to gain revenge, his blackmailing of the young Laetitia Prism and her reluctant capitulation.

'It remained only for me to have a discreet conversation with Merriman about where Cecily's former governess might be found now,' said Holmes. 'He was kind enough to provide me with her new name and address, and so I hurried to Woolton Rectory, rather expecting that I might be following in your footsteps.'

'Bravo, Holmes,' I said. 'If only the police had been so astute.'

He shook his head. 'To be just, it would have availed them very little. The nursemaid Prism was already their chief suspect in the kidnapping, and she had successfully hidden herself away. Durrington, meanwhile, was dead, and there was nothing then to connect either of them to Cardew, who had ended up with custody of the child.'

'No, I see. I say, though, how did you find out about Miss Prism meeting Cardew at Victoria that day?'

'That was rather a toss of the dice, I admit, but it seemed to be the only explanation that would fit the facts. For Miss Prism to end up by happenstance in the employ of the very man she had abandoned as a child would be a coincidence on a scale that beggars belief. Coincidences occur, and it would be an error to rule them out of my considerations altogether, but I always look very carefully indeed at the alternatives.

'One possibility that occurred to me was that Miss Prism had taken the position as Cecily Cardew's governess out of concern for Jack Worthing, knowing full well that he was the misplaced Moncrieff infant and wishing to observe for herself that he was living a happy life. This idea I dismissed. To do such a thing she would have to be driven by unassuageable guilt, yet she could have alleviated this by revealing his identity, anonymously if need be, at any time during his childhood rather than waiting twenty-eight years to be confronted by Lady Bracknell.

'If she was ignorant of Worthing's origins, then the apparent improbability could only be explained by the one known connection between herself and the Cardew family: that she and Thomas Cardew were at Victoria Station at around the same time on the same day in 1867, respectively abandoning the child and finding him. Given her likely state of mind, and Cardew's known character, the scene I concocted seemed the most likely.'

'And Mrs Chasuble confirmed it.'

'She was remarkably helpful, under the circumstances.'

Had she been, however? I pondered for a while. The train was approaching King's Cross now, and once again the gloomy tenements and smokestacks of the capital were springing up around us like weeds. 'I'm not sure exactly what we've learned, though, Holmes. We know what happened to Ernest Moncrieff as a baby, but as you said, there's not much use we can make of that knowledge now. I really think the information I gathered was more useful. Although Cecily's parents are believed to be deceased, her mother is of the right age to be Mrs Teville. If the rumours about Mrs Teville's daughter are in any way accurate, then Cecily might be she.'

'All data is valuable, Watson, and the more detailed our knowledge of the background to the case, the greater our chances of a full solution. I confess that none of the information we have obtained during our day's excursion is immediately applicable to the matter Lord Goring called us in to investigate. In that respect, our most useful information still comes from Langdale Pike.'

'You mean that Illingworth's a knave,' I asked, 'and that Mrs Teville has a secret? That, too, seems rather thin stuff to me, Holmes.'

'We also know that Bunbury is a fiction, and we may guess that our dead man intended by the name to send some message to the Moncrieffs. That is, if it were his real name it would be a very great coincidence, and I have already given you my view of those. I told Gregson as much when I saw him.'

'Do you think Bunbury had blackmail in mind?' I wondered, thinking of the unfortunate young Laetitia Prism. 'It would be a crude way of signalling that he knew of Algernon's past and was willing to make it public.'

'It is a distinct possibility,' said Holmes, 'and one which we could do worse than to put before one or other of the brothers.'

'But all the family have denied knowing the name,' I pointed out, 'even Lady Bracknell. What makes you think they will change their tune now?'

'I am moderately sure that Algernon was on the verge of confiding in us yesterday, before his aunt's untimely arrival,' Holmes said. 'Let us speak to him once again, now that we know the truth.'

After our inconvenient encounter of the previous day, Holmes had set a few of his young Irregulars to track the movements of Lady Bracknell. Algernon Moncrieff's house was in Lowndes Square, a stone's throw from his brother's, making it convenient for our cab to call in at Baker Street on our way from King's Cross. Outside our house a solemn-faced girl waited to assure us that Lady Bracknell was attending a performance of Gideon Beech's new play, *Old Nick's Neophyte*, at the Aegis Theatre. Much relieved, we proceeded through the twilit evening to Lowndes Square.

We found Algernon's house to be perfectly in keeping with the other dwellings we had seen in Belgravia, though larger and more imposing than Ernest's, and more lavishly furnished than the Saviles', both of which it otherwise much resembled architecturally. We were met by a grave butler who informed us that Mr Moncrieff was presently alone and would be glad to receive us.

'Your name is Lane, is it not?' Holmes asked the man as he led us upstairs. 'You were Mr Moncrieff's manservant formerly, I believe?'

'Yes, sir,' said Lane. I knew that this was relatively unusual, as it is normally the wife's privilege to choose the servants for the matrimonial home. There was no reason why Cecily should not have decided to retain and promote Lane, of course, but I wondered whether it might instead indicate some unusual sway of servant over master – based, perhaps, on a long familiarity with the latter's secrets. Now that the idea of blackmail had been put into my head, I was seeing it everywhere.

Holmes wisely chose not to probe into this area, instead asking, 'How have you found the transition to a married household, Lane? It must have taken some adjustment.'

Lane paused to consider, though the steady pace of his progression along the corridor did not waver. He said, 'My chief concern at the time was for the quality of the wine cellar, sir. Mr Moncrieff's cellar at Half-Moon Street was excellent. Fortunately, he has been assiduous in maintaining his bachelor standards in that respect.'

'I am sure you have advised him knowledgeably, Lane.'

'I do my best to give satisfaction, sir.' The noise of enthusiastic but rather poor piano-playing had been growing as we progressed, and Lane now opened the door to a drawing room where Algernon was entertaining himself *fortissimo* on a Steinway grand.

He stopped as Lane announced us. 'Did you hear what I was playing?' he asked us, a little out of breath.

I had not recognised the piece. 'We were hardly in a position not to,' I equivocated.

Algernon said, 'Technical perfection in musicianship is overrated, don't you think? The true virtuoso is one who can infuse the music with feeling and move his audience to tears without the tedious business of playing well.'

Holmes, who was a highly able violinist both technically and temperamentally, looked pained. 'As an approach I suppose it has the merit of novelty,' he said.

Algernon beamed. 'Not in the least. It is what every third-rate musician aspires to. The novelty lies in the fact that I have found a way to justify it. You may leave us, Lane.'

'Yes, sir.'

'Mr Moncrieff,' said Holmes heavily as Lane closed the door behind him, 'we know who Bunbury was. Not the dead body, but the original Bunbury.'

'Ah.' Algernon's smile became a little less beatific. 'Then you know, I suppose, that Bunbury had no origin to speak of. He sprang into life fully formed, forever on the cusp of leaving it.'

'We understand that he was an alibi,' I said. 'A pretence to cover up your youthful indiscretions.'

'My dear Dr Watson, to cover up an indiscretion is a contradiction in terms. Discretion lies precisely in the act of concealment.'

'So you admit your dissembling?' Holmes asked.

'Certainly I do. And remarkably successful dissembling it was, too. Bunbury himself may have been an obvious hoax, but what did Bunbury obscure? I don't suppose you've been able to find that out,' he concluded, a little defiantly.

'I have no doubt that I could, given time,' said Holmes. 'But it is not my priority at present.'

'I'm pleased to hear it. I would hate to think of my past possessing priority for anybody but myself.'

Holmes sighed, already tired of Algernon's word games. He said, 'Do you have any idea why the dead man should have given his name as Bunbury, Mr Moncrieff?'

'None whatsoever. Certainly it is something that I never did. Although I must say, you seem in rather a hurry to dismiss the idea that his name really was Bunbury.'

'Not as much of a hurry as you've been yourself,' I pointed out, a little indignantly.

'That was before Holmes pointed out to me the true extent of the Bunbury genealogy,' Algernon said imperturbably. 'He has quite opened my eyes. It would be delightful to be visited by a real Bunbury, after visiting an imaginary one so often.'

Doggedly, Holmes said, 'It seems far more likely, however, that the dead man used the name Bunbury to show you that he knew of its significance, and to suggest to you that he knew more about the covert habits of your past. Has anyone been dropping hints to that effect recently, Mr Moncrieff?'

Abruptly, Algernon sighed and sat down heavily on the piano stool. He rang a bell, and Lane reappeared.

'Lane, some food for our guests, please. Cook's madeira cake, I think, and some scones and jam. And some of those little almond biscuits, if we have them.'

'Yes, sir,' said Lane. 'How many plates shall I bring?'

Algernon raised his eyebrows hospitably at us. Holmes frowned at him and I shook my head mutely. 'Just the one plate then, Lane,' he concluded cheerfully.

'He understands you well,' Holmes observed.

'Oh, I am not so very complicated a fellow,' Algernon said lightly.

'Are you now prepared to tell us who has been applying pressure on you, and to what end?' Holmes asked.

Algernon took a cigarette from a silver case. He offered one to each of us, lit them, drew in the smoke from his own and exhaled heavily.

He said, 'Since you ask, a thoroughly unpleasant chap

approached me in the street a few weeks ago. He was nobody I had seen before. His face was one I should certainly have remembered if I had. He mentioned certain events in my past which he felt I might not wish to be made known to my wife, my family or the world at large.'

'Good heavens,' I exclaimed.

Algernon continued, 'He was not mistaken on that score, but the course of action he suggested to me was quite out of the question. He said that, to protect themselves from the truth, my relatives should be persuaded to invest large sums in a particular business venture.'

Holmes asked, 'What was the venture?'

Algernon looked pained. 'Something connected with transport, I think. As my wife, my aunt and any number of London's honest tradesmen will tell you, I have no head for anything relating to business or money. That is why marrying Cecily was such a stroke of fortune. She brought to our marriage not only a substantial accumulation of capital, but also a clear head for niceties that escape me, like the precise distinction between debit and credit. Financial matters are always better left to women, don't you think? They have the determination and grasp of detail that men lack.'

Holmes was looking argumentative, so I said diplomatically, 'My own late wife was very prudent in matters of housekeeping.' Lane re-entered, bringing with him a footman who carried plates of the cakes and biscuits Algernon had requested.

Taking a large slice of madeira cake and nibbling at it, Algernon continued, 'For that very reason, the idea of my persuading Cecily, let alone Aunt Augusta, who naturally holds a similar position in my uncle's household, to make any investment on my own recommendation, is perfectly ludicrous.'

'Did you make any effort to do so?' Holmes asked.

'I may have mentioned to Cecily that I had had an investment tip from a friend, but she replied that she had taken, through our agent, the advice of the best stockbrokers in the City, that our investment portfolio was tied up in funds certain to yield satisfactory medium- and long-term returns, and that I wasn't to worry my handsome head about it. All of which was perfectly correct and sensible of her, and to be commended. Having met my aunt, you will appreciate that I could hardly expect any greater success with her.'

I said, 'But weren't you worried that this blackmailer fellow would tell them what he knew?'

Algernon shrugged. 'I only worry about things I can control, like my meals and my buttonholes. Expending worry on such a matter would have been a tedious waste of my energy. The question was quite out of my hands.'

Holmes asked, 'Did the disagreeable gentleman give a name?'

'He told me that his name was Broadwater, but I see no compelling reason to believe him. He was a hulking fellow, with the look of a brawler or a prize fighter. He had a broken nose and a cauliflower ear, and a scar above his right eye.'

I exchanged a look with Holmes. The body on the flagstones had had none of these conspicuous attributes, but the man whom we had seen lurking in the bushes of Belgrave Square on the night of Bunbury's death matched the description neatly.

Holmes cleared his throat and said, 'When you heard that the supposed Mr Bunbury had called at your brother's house, did you connect him with this Mr Broadwater?'

'Well, not in any inextricable way, but naturally the possibility occurred to me. My first inkling that he was there was when Cecily and Lord Illingworth found his body in the garden, and the first I heard of his name was when you mentioned it yourself. It gave me quite a start. My first thought was that he was a practical joker, but falling to one's death in another man's garden would suggest a commitment to satire deplorably lacking in most modern comedians. After that, I did somewhat assume that he had been sent by Broadwater or his employers to further persuade me.'

'So you were honestly unaware of his presence in the library? You did not hear Merriman mention his name to your brother?'

'I really was listening to the music, I'm afraid,' said Algernon with a smile. 'The quartet must have been unfamiliar with my theory of musicianship, because they played with considerable skill.'

'And you did not enter the library that evening?'

'Certainly not.'

'I am sorry to press you, Mr Moncrieff, but a common response to blackmail is to at least consider an attempt to make away with the extortionist. Have I your word that this is not what happened in this case?'

Algernon opened his mouth to reply, but from the doorway Cecily said, 'Oh, Algy, my dearest, has somebody been blackmailing you as well?'

Holmes and I looked on in surprise as the young Mrs Moncrieff bustled into the room and crossed to stand in solidarity with her husband. Abandoning his insouciance of earlier, Algernon held her hand and told her, with apparent sincerity, 'Yes, my own. It has been perfectly devastating. You cannot envisage how much I've been longing to tell you.'

'My poor sweet darling,' Cecily replied. 'I can only imagine how you've suffered. We shall face this together, as we face everything. I am quite determined of that.'

'You said "as well",' Holmes pointed out, a little affronted. 'Are you being blackmailed too, Mrs Moncrieff?'

Cecily gave her gay little laugh. She said, 'Oh, I have had the most absurd letter, delivered by a messenger a fortnight ago. I am quite sure that it is nothing.'

I said, 'Perhaps you should tell us even so, Mrs Moncrieff. Given what we have found out from your husband, it may be more important than you realise.'

'Well, if you think so,' she said. 'The letter was extremely serious in tone, so you can imagine how frivolously I took it. I am entirely ignorant of my family history,' she continued, 'having been cautioned against excessive curiosity by my governess from a tender age. From the evidence of my maiden name I presume that the late Thomas Cardew was my paternal grandfather, but I'm aware that other arrangements are possible. Beyond that I know only that my parents are deceased, and that I was brought up by Grandfather and later by Uncle Ernest.'

I caught Holmes's eye, and he twitched his head in an almost undetectable negative. If Cecily's guardians had not seen fit to disclose to her the accepted story of her origins, then it was not for us to overrule their decision, especially when we had reason to believe it might be false. Besides, the fact that Cecily herself raised the subject suggested that it had a bearing on the matter in hand.

She said, 'So, when I saw that the letter addressed me as "Dear daughter", I felt it betrayed a most discourteous lack of research.'

'Good Lord!' I declared.

'The letter-writer claimed to be familiar with the details of my origin, having been intimately involved with them in the capacity of a parent, and believed that they might prove of interest to society in general, and to Algy and Aunt Augusta in particular. Lady Bracknell is notoriously protective of her family's marital connections.'

'That's nonsense!' insisted Algernon. 'Aunt Augusta is terribly fond of you.'

'As am I of her, darling, but she has an unfortunate habit of letting practicalities stand in the way of sentiment.'

'No power on earth could separate me from you, my dearest,' Algernon assured her. 'Not even Aunt Augusta.'

'Algy, you have never been able to stand up to her. I don't believe you've ever even tried.'

'But she has never tried to separate you from me.'

'Well, that is very sweet of you, dearest boy, but I regard the question as untested for the moment.'

Holmes cleared his throat and said, 'Forgive my indelicacy, Mrs Moncrieff, but what were the facts that the letter-writer believed that you would not want known? You may, of course, rely on my discretion and that of Dr Watson.'

'There was a most disappointing lack of detail in that respect, Mr Holmes. I think they assumed I would be familiar with the matters they alluded to, which shows a very poor judgement of character.'

Holmes said, 'You say "they". Did the writer not describe themselves as your mother or father?'

'No,' said Cecily. 'In that limited respect they preserved their anonymity perfectly.'

'You could not identify the handwriting as feminine or masculine?'

'Oh, the letter was typewritten,' Cecily informed us.

'I see. Well, we may perhaps deduce something of the sender's circumstances from that, if not their sex. I will be able to tell more if you have kept the letter.'

'I'm afraid that I burned it, Mr Holmes,' Cecily admitted. 'It seemed the thing to do, although I replied first.'

Holmes raised an eyebrow. 'Was a return address supplied?'

'No, the messenger promised to return an hour later.'

'And in what terms did you reply?'

'One of the few specific points in the letter was that money would be instrumental in settling the situation. Algy and I have rather a lot of money, Mr Holmes, as you may know. Still, as an orphan my sentimental attachments are important to me, and I was reluctant to part with it in such a cause. Nevertheless, I replied saying that I thought the writer's suggestion might be accommodated. I have heard nothing since.'

Holmes frowned. 'That is curious. One would expect a blackmailer to treat such a positive response with more dispatch.'

From the doorway, Ernest Moncrieff's voice exclaimed, 'Good heavens, Cecily! You don't mean to say that you are being blackmailed as well?'

'As well?' repeated Holmes, somewhat incredulously this time.

CHAPTER NINE
THE PREVALENCE OF BLACKMAIL

I looked around for Gwendolen Moncrieff, to see whether she too would admit that she was being forced to buy another's silence, but it seemed that Ernest had arrived alone.

Algernon said, 'You are always most welcome in our house, Ernest, but I do expect that when a fellow arrives in a room he should be announced. A simple announcement hardly seems too much to ask. It prepares one fully for such pleasure as may lie ahead, of whatever degree, and gives one time to adopt an appropriate posture. What on earth have you done with Lane?'

'I sent him down to the cellar for some of that excellent champagne of yours, of course,' said Ernest. 'I expect he'll extract a bottle or two for himself and the other servants while he's down there. It's a price I'm willing to pay.'

'Did he not mention that I had company, old boy? Really, Lane is becoming very lax in passing on necessary information.'

'Mr Moncrieff,' said Holmes with exaggerated patience. 'That is, Mr Ernest Moncrieff. Should I take your earlier comment as implying that you, like your brother and sister-in-law, have recently been subject to attempted blackmail?'

Ernest fingered his moustache dubiously. 'Well, if you want to call it that. It is a rather alarming word to use.'

'It is a rather alarming crime. Has somebody demanded money in return for their silence regarding particular facts that might be embarrassing to you?'

'Oh, if you put it that way, then I suppose so. I have been getting letters.'

'Typewritten ones,' Holmes asked, 'sent by an anonymous messenger?'

'No, not at all. They are handwritten, in a masculine fist of distressing crudity, and arrive through the post, giving the address of a post office box. So far they have merely been threatening, with the suggestion that the threats may miraculously dissolve in the presence of money. Why are these fellows always so obsessed with money?'

'Always?' I asked.

'Oh, there was a time when I used to get letters from cranks almost every day. I thought they had got tired of it at last. I'm not sure whether you recall the case, Mr Holmes, but I was for a time notorious under the tiresome name of the "Handbag Heir", having been found as an infant in such a receptacle in the—'

He was clearly easing himself into a familiar flow, but Holmes interrupted sternly. 'What specific threats are made in the letters?'

Ernest tutted. 'Well, as I have said, the fellow is clearly a lunatic. His first letter informed me, if you please, that I am not Ernest Moncrieff!'

'My dear fellow,' Algernon said, 'I shall be quite exasperated if that is the case. I have already gone to the inconvenience of telling everybody we know that you are my brother, despite all earlier protestations to the contrary. We were best men at one another's weddings on the clear understanding that we were brothers. It would be perfectly absurd to have to announce that I was mistaken after all this time.'

'Don't be fatuous, Algy,' Ernest snapped. 'The man is either insane or a liar. His story is that he and I were exchanged when we were babies, that I was purloined from my handbag at Victoria Station and replaced by another child. Or rather, I suppose, that he was. It's all most confusing.'

Holmes said, 'I have recently looked into the matter of your early abduction, Mr Moncrieff. I found no suggestion of any such substitution.'

Ernest sighed. 'It seemed fantastically unlikely to me as well. Since all the chief events of my life have been fantastically unlikely, though, my judgement may be unreliable on that point. In any case, the chap was giving me warning that he intended to press his legal claim to the identity of Ernest Moncrieff, and thus to the Moncrieff fortune.'

Algernon shook his head in amusement. 'Dear me. Does Gwendolen know about this development?'

'No, Algy, Gwendolen does not know about this development, and I don't wish you to tell her. If a man can't keep secrets from his own wife, who can he keep them from?'

'What was your response to this communication?' Holmes asked Ernest.

'I wrote back at once, of course, explaining that there is no longer any Moncrieff fortune, my dear brother as the supposed heir having spent it all long before I saw a penny of it. We are both quite reliant upon our wives and upon the Cardew estate.'

'And what was the reply?' Holmes asked. 'You mentioned letters in the plural.'

'The second took a more admonitory tone,' Ernest admitted. 'It suggested that, since the author and I had, as previously mentioned, been exchanged during infancy, he was the son of a general whereas I was the son of the common criminal whom society has deemed to be his father. In this capacity, he suggested, it would be difficult to maintain my marriage to Gwendolen or my relations with her family, which shows a certain shrewdness where my mother-in-law's character is concerned. He implied that reparations for the wrongs I had done him might assist with his discretion in these matters, and that instructions on this point would follow.'

'When did this exchange occur?' Holmes asked.

'Oh, the week before last, I think.'

'Did you keep the letters?'

'No, they went onto the fire.'

Holmes looked exasperated at the family's lax record-keeping practices. 'Did you at least remember the address of the post office box?'

Ernest shrugged. 'I suppose that might have been astute of me. But I was expecting to hear from him again in any case.'

Holmes leaned back, steepling his fingers. 'And do you think that you did?'

'I beg your pardon?'

'The man who died at your house. Might he have come there to demand those reparations?'

Ernest looked thoughtful. 'Well, I suppose he might. But my fellow claims to be the real Ernest Moncrieff. Why would he give the name Bunbury? Bunbury was Algy's pretence, not mine. I always thought the business perfectly absurd.'

'Forgive me, Mr Moncrieff,' said Holmes, 'but do you stand by all your previous statements about the deceased? That you never met him, failed to catch his name, ignored his presence in the hope that he would go away, and in any case did not go up to the library to see him?'

'It is all perfectly true,' said Ernest. 'I haven't lied to you at all, except to exaggerate my unfamiliarity with the name Bunbury.'

'That was very foolish of you,' Algernon suggested idly. 'A lie is always preferable to the truth, as it may be shaped to be whatever one wishes. However hard one tries, the truth remains obstinately unmalleable.'

'I suppose you think that's clever, Algy,' Ernest said savagely.

'No, it is merely true. Which is a disappointment, naturally.'

Holmes shook his head, and I could tell that he was exercised, as he would say, by this succession of revelations. He said, 'I suppose we must conclude that the dead man was connected with one or more of these attempts at blackmail, but which one I cannot at this moment say. Nor can I see how they relate to one another. The approaches they make are all markedly different, but three nearly simultaneous blackmail attempts upon the same family are a coincidence I simply refuse to allow. Two, perhaps, but not three.'

At Ernest's request, Algernon and Cecily retold their stories. Considering them, Ernest concluded, 'I must say, I think you're exaggerating their similarity, Holmes. Algy's fellow sounds ugly enough to be a professional, but Cecily's and mine are obviously two cranks with different fixations.'

'There is no truth, then, in the idea that one of Cecily's parents might have survived?'

'None that I know of. I was always told that my poor foster-sister Violet and her husband had died. Of course, I was barely eleven at the time.'

'Did you meet the husband, Mr Moncrieff?' Holmes asked him.

'Ah, no. The marriage happened elsewhere. Thomas, her father, was invited, certainly, but I was too young. It does seem unnecessarily confusing if one of Cecily's parents somehow survived. It seems very inconsistent for a wife to survive an accident that carries away her husband, or vice versa.'

'To lose both parents may be described as a misfortune,' Algernon agreed airily. 'To lose one smacks of half-heartedness.'

I was shocked anew by the callousness of this, but I remembered that Algernon, like so many of the principals in this affair, was an orphan. 'You seem remarkably nonchalant, Mr Moncrieff,' I suggested, 'given that your brother believes that your blackmailer is the only serious one.'

Algy frowned. 'I admit I'm concerned by the things the impudent fellow seems to know, none of which I have the slightest intention of telling any of you. Not even you, Cecily.'

'Oh, I quite understand, dearest,' said Cecily. 'A married couple with no secrets would have very little left to offer one another. Perfect marital bliss arises from an absolute ignorance of one's spouse's character.'

'But,' Algernon went on, 'it seems to me that actually revealing anything is the last thing the fellow will do. The threat to do so is all that gives him any hold over me, but if he carries it out, it ceases to be a threat. To exercise his control is to lose it. If I refuse to cooperate, he really has no recourse at all.'

'That is an unusually clearheaded view of blackmail,' Holmes replied, his tones suggesting a somewhat increased respect for the feckless young man. 'Unfortunately, it neglects the possibility that a professional blackmailer might engineer your downfall as an object lesson for his other victims.'

Algernon paled. 'I must confess that that hadn't occurred to me. Still, what else could I have done?'

'You were in an unenviable position—' Holmes began, but at that moment Lane appeared in the door and with great loudness announced the arrival of Lady Bracknell.

By unspoken consent, everybody dropped the subject of blackmail at once.

'Good evening, Aunt Augusta!' said Algernon cheerfully,

leaping to his feet from the posture he had immediately adopted upon a chaise longue.

'Aunt Augusta,' said Cecily, kissing her cheek. 'We thought you were at the theatre.'

'Now, Cecily,' said Lady Bracknell, 'you know that I never linger beyond the interval. By then one has seen and been seen by everybody necessary.'

Tentatively, Ernest suggested, 'I believe it is customary to stay to see the actors, Aunt Augusta.'

'Certainly not,' his aunt declared. 'It would give them ideas quite above themselves. I have come here looking for Gwendolen, but it appears that she is not with you.'

Ernest replied, 'No, she—' but Lady Bracknell was not stopping for an answer.

She asked, 'And what, pray, is the opinionated Mr Holmes doing here?'

'Seeking new opinions, Lady Bracknell,' Holmes replied. 'It seems that the ones I held before are thoroughly antiquated.'

'In opinion as in art, antiquity is no guarantee of decency,' said Lady Bracknell. 'But I fear you are being trivial, sir.' She brought her lorgnette to bear on him once again. 'It seems that you have ignored my advice to desist from this impertinent inquiry into my son-in-law's affairs and to adopt a more becoming occupation.'

'The Church holds little appeal for me, I fear,' Holmes drawled, 'and I am less interested in stamps than in the letters which come attached to them.'

Hastily, Cecily asked, 'How was the theatre, Aunt Augusta? Until the interval, I mean.'

'It was tedious in the extreme,' Her Ladyship replied. 'I was with young Lady Angmering, and since her children were born she will talk of nothing but her dogs. Had I stayed I should have had no recourse but to listen to the play. As it was, I was obliged to forgo my custom of tea at Brown's after the theatre.'

'It sounds fascinating,' Ernest said quickly. 'You must sit down and tell us absolutely nothing about it. Mr Holmes and Dr Watson were just leaving, I believe.'

'Presently,' said Holmes. 'Lady Bracknell, I pray that you will indulge me. Have you by any chance been approached recently by anybody who seemed to know more about you or your family than you might have expected, who might perhaps have implied that this unusual degree of knowledge might merit some pecuniary reward?'

The silence which followed this question was like that which I imagine might precede an avalanche. My readers will know that I am not a timorous man, but I found myself fighting an urge to flee.

Finally, Lady Bracknell said, in a voice like the chilly whisper of sliding snow, 'I do not know what you are insinuating, Mr Holmes, but I know that I do not care for it. My family has no secrets that are not inscribed in the society columns and set down on the pages of *Debrett's*. We are fortunate enough, sir, to live in an age of surfaces, wherein a favourable appearance is the outward sign of private rectitude, and a pleasing demeanour an infallible indication of upright character. My own flaws, if such they are, and those of my relatives, which I regret are many, are altogether apparent to those who know us, and in that respect we are in perfect earnest.' Her tones were gathering both speed and volume now. 'We do not disguise or misrepresent ourselves, Mr Holmes, as I understand to be *your* opprobrious habit, and neither do we insinuate or inveigle ourselves into other persons' houses with the intention of deceiving them into damaging admissions.' Her voice had built now into a roar which echoed from the walls as if from the surrounding mountaintops. 'And if, sir, you have any such intention here, then I can promise you that you will meet with no success!'

Holmes bowed deeply. 'So it would seem,' he said. 'Good evening to you, Lady Bracknell.'

I let out a long and unsteady breath as we made our escape out into Lowndes Square, and waited for my nerves to subside before I spoke.

It was remarkable to consider the trepidation Lady Bracknell's force of personality inspired. I wondered whether it was the result of breeding: generations of genteel deference on the part of my middle-class ancestors, as opposed to generations of her ancestors' absolute expectation of entitlement to that deference. Perhaps, as Holmes had playfully suggested, the rich were indeed different by heredity... except that Lady Bracknell seemed to strike equal terror into the hearts of her own relatives.

'What an extraordinary family,' I observed at last. 'And what an extraordinary scene.'

'It was indeed,' agreed Holmes. Night had fallen while we were within, and the lamps had been lit, casting their buttery glow across the pavement and the trees clustered at the centre of the square. 'But as Ernest pointed out, unusual events appear to dog the Moncrieffs' steps.'

'So they do,' I said. 'It felt strangely artificial, somehow. The way they each entered in succession, with Lady Bracknell arriving at the climactic moment...'

'As if it were concocted for our benefit? Well, perhaps,' Holmes mused, 'though such extravagance of language and manner seems to be the norm in their set. Certainly, Lady Bracknell evinced little interest in the art of acting. We can do little but accept what has happened tonight at face value – for the moment, at least. We may, as Her Ladyship observes, live in an age of surfaces, but I for one am perennially curious about what lies beneath them.'

Holmes flagged down a cab and instructed the cabman to return us to Baker Street. On the way we smoked in silence and pondered the case. At least, I pondered. Holmes, I assumed, was doing the same, but I had never learned the trick of reading his thoughts from his expression as he had mine.

As he remained silent, however, I eventually revealed the fruits of my contemplations. I said, 'You know, Holmes, it needn't have been any of the Moncrieffs who killed Bunbury, or Lady Goring either. If Cecily is really being blackmailed by one of her parents, then Mrs Teville is the obvious suspect for both crimes. She's of an age to be Violet Cardew, she's rumoured to have an abandoned daughter, and she evidently takes an interest in the family. If Bunbury represented one of the other blackmailers, Ernest's or Algernon's, and if there is indeed no connection between them – well, then she might have pushed him off the balcony by way of eliminating a business rival, if she were ruthless enough.'

Holmes looked at me with a modicum of respect. 'That's not an entirely foolish idea, Watson. Although we should be wary of jumping to the conclusion that, simply because Mrs Teville could be Violet Cardew, she therefore must be. Furthermore,' he said, dashing my pride a little further, 'we saw no actual evidence of blackmail. With all the letters destroyed, we have only the word of Algernon, Cecily and Ernest that they were approached at all. In Algernon's case, it would surely be remarkable for this Mr Broadwater to hold more detailed information about him than the compendious Langdale Pike.'

Rather stubbornly, I said, 'It would surely be natural, if one received insinuations of that kind, to want to destroy the physical evidence.'

'Oh, I do not deny it, Watson.' He took a deep pull on his pipe, exhaling the blue-grey smoke to join the comfortable fug filling the inside of the cab. He replied, 'Indeed, the possibility remains that that is what happened to the late Bunbury himself.'

'We have nothing specific to connect him to any one of these supposed blackmail attempts, though,' I pointed out. 'Only the name he used.'

'True. Indeed, if blackmail is actually so prevalent among these people's circle as we have been led to believe this evening, it is quite possible that other guests at the ball might have been among the victims. Any of them, not merely the Moncrieffs, might have thought they recognised in Bunbury their own tormentor, or his representative.'

'Not *any* of them,' I said. 'We know from the maid's testimony that the murderer was a woman. That is,' I added, seeing Holmes's raised eyebrow, 'we know that Bunbury was talking to a lady on the balcony. I suppose she might not have been the same person who killed him.'

'Quite right, Watson.' Holmes was always a stickler for precision. 'Still, I think your first instinct was correct. This was not a man's crime.'

'Why do you say that?' I asked.

'Consider, Watson. You are a man of the lower, very likely the criminal, classes, having wormed your way into a rich man's house under an assumed name, with expectations of extracting money from him. What is your state of mind?'

I thought about this for a moment. 'Well, resolute, I suppose. Determined. Prepared to follow my scheme through to the bitter end.'

'Really? Well, perhaps you would be, my dear fellow. A lesser man, though... I fear he might be nervous, frightened even. He would know that he risked violence against his person simply by being there. I think we can take it that he would be feeling cautious, at least. And yet our Bunbury helpfully positioned himself with his back to the balustrade, and was pitched over it with a single push.'

'You mean that he supposed he had nothing to fear from the person to whom he was talking?'

'Indeed. Which would imply that that person was either a friend, which is improbable, or someone he considered unlikely to present a physical threat.'

I nodded. 'Bunbury was no very impressive specimen, but he would probably have felt confident of overpowering a woman.'

'Or he might simply not have expected violence from such a quarter. I would propose that you yourself would not expect it from a pretty young woman, such as Cecily or Gwendolen Moncrieff... or Mabel Goring.'

'I really cannot imagine Lady Goring having any guilty secrets for a blackmailer to exploit,' I protested. 'The poor girl seems the very soul of honesty.'

We had arrived now at our destination. Holmes gave me a satirical look as he paid the cabman. 'Then you believe, like Lady Bracknell, that a person's probity can be read plainly in their outward look and manner, as their guilt might be written upon their palm? I cannot concede that, Watson. We have both known handsome, well-spoken murderers, and brutal-looking louts who proved to be as gentle as lambs.'

'Well, of course we have,' I grumbled, opening the front door. 'But surely you accept that one can judge a person's character by talking to them?'

'That would depend entirely on how good they are at dissembling, Watson. It is a skill in which people with secrets tend to be practised.'

'Unless they themselves are innocent of the secret, like Cecily,' I objected as we climbed the stairs.

'But by the same token, Mabel Goring may have a family

secret that might be to her discredit were it known, but for which she bears no responsibility. Although I grant you that in that case, her husband or brother might have made for more promising prey.'

'I cannot believe that that girl is a killer, Holmes, and that's that,' I declared, stomping into our sitting room.

'I am delighted to hear it,' observed Lord Goring coldly. He was waiting for us in my favourite armchair, reading a newspaper and sipping a cup of Mrs Hudson's tea. 'It is always gratifying to know the esteem in which one's wife is held.'

'Lord Goring,' I stammered, once again disconcerted by the full and chilling force of an aristocrat's authority. 'I'm sorry – I was merely—'

'Pray don't trouble yourself, Dr Watson,' the viscount sighed. 'It is perfectly understandable under the circumstances. A friend of my family, Lord Henry Wotton, is wont to observe that the one thing worse than being talked about is not being talked about. After the past few days I feel quite confident in declaring the converse to be true.'

Urgently, Holmes asked, 'What brings you here, Lord Goring? Has there been some development in the case?'

'I think you could say that, Mr Holmes.'

'Not a fatal one, I hope? It has been my experience that a single murder will frequently bring more deaths, as the killer attempts to avoid the consequences of his crime.'

'Nothing so dramatic, mercifully,' Lord Goring drawled. 'The police have released Lady Goring, though they do not tell me why. I presume that it is some belated effect of Robert's or my father's demands. Certainly both have been petitioning the commissioner with a fervency which would have put the fear of heaven into me.'

'More likely Inspector Gregson has new evidence,' Holmes observed, his excitement evident in his voice. 'I last saw him at lunchtime, when he felt quite justified still in keeping Lady Goring incarcerated. My investigations since then have taken their own peripatetic path, so if he has attempted to communicate further with me, I should expect the message to be awaiting us here.'

I glanced around but saw no such missive. It would not have been unknown, though, for our clearsighted landlady to tidy away such a note in the presence of a visitor whom she knew it might concern.

Holmes concluded, 'Gregson would not have let Lady Goring go without some information that appeared to vindicate her.'

'*Appeared* to, Holmes?' Lord Goring looked excessively annoyed.

'Evidence can be susceptible to multiple interpretations, my lord,' Holmes replied steadily. 'If some evidence for Lady Goring's innocence were to prove flawed, that would not mean that she were guilty, merely that her innocence was unproven.'

'Well, in any case, it is no longer your affair,' Goring told us both firmly. 'My one concern has been to place Lady Goring beyond suspicion, and that end has been achieved.'

'Not through our efforts, I am afraid,' Holmes noted.

Magnanimously, His Lordship said, 'Regardless of whether this has been your doing, you have earned my gratitude for your endeavours, and you have earned your payment.' He cleared his throat, annoyed at the embarrassment of having to discuss such matters. 'What sum do I owe you?'

'Forgive me, my lord,' objected Holmes, 'but I cannot regard the matter as settled. I must consult with Inspector Gregson to find out what his new view of the case is, and how it fits with what we have discovered today. I am certainly in no position to make any definitive statement about the identity of the murderer.'

'Forgive *me*, Mr Holmes,' said Lord Goring icily, 'but I did not engage you to identify the murderer. I engaged you to establish the innocence of my wife. As that is now done, your services are no longer required.'

'And I explained to you that I would instead make it my business to establish the truth,' said Holmes. 'That business has not changed. Further, I have been cooperating with Inspector Gregson in this matter, and the crime of murder is within his purview and jurisdiction. It is not within yours.'

Lord Goring considered this in chilly silence for a moment, then gave a little laugh. 'Very well. I promised to pay you to investigate, and so I shall. Now I am offering in addition to pay you for *not* investigating, surely an easier and more agreeable occupation.' He smiled his charming smile. 'Will you take on this new commission, Mr Holmes?'

Holmes's voice was as wintry as Goring's had been a moment before. 'I seem to be making a habit of being invited by the nobility to desist from my legitimate investigations. At least you are good enough not to suggest alternative hobbies with which to occupy my time.'

'So you refuse?' His Lordship stood, his face frighteningly impassive. He was, I supposed, unused to having his wishes defied by those whom he paid. 'Mr Holmes, I am not without influence, both that which comes from wealth and family and that which comes through friends and connections. I might make your life distinctly less comfortable, should you refuse to cooperate. Noble bachelors and other illustrious clients would cease calling upon you, and you would find the police a great deal less cooperative than has been their wont.'

Holmes's voice was perfectly calm as he replied, 'I choose the cases I take on, Lord Goring, and the death at Number 149 Belgrave Square now occupies my full attention. I will be working on it until, at least, Inspector Gregson no longer requires my services, and very possibly beyond that point if it continues to interest me. Your money is a matter of absolute indifference to me.'

'Nevertheless,' Goring snapped, 'I shall continue to offer it. If against my protestations you insist on honouring your commitment, then I shall honour mine. As it is I who engaged you in this case, Mr Holmes, you will continue to keep me apprised of your discoveries, or you shall reap the consequences. Good evening, sir – and Dr Watson.' And so saying, he left.

Calmly, Holmes crossed to the mantelpiece and began to fill his pipe.

'What extraordinary behaviour,' I observed, not for the first time that night. 'For him to take no further interest in the case is understandable, but urging you to let it alone seems quite excessive.'

'Indeed, Watson, indeed. Once again I am offered money in return for my silence. The transaction appears to be a fashionable one, though I am sure that I have never asked for such a thing.' I saw that beneath his tranquil surface my friend was, once again, quite angry at the insult that had been done to his professional integrity.

'What will you do?' I asked.

'Do? I shall do nothing different from what I had in mind already. It is too late to expect to hear more from Inspector Gregson tonight, but we may visit him in the morning and request an explanation of his changed view of Lady Goring's guilt. In the meantime, as I told Lord Goring, I cannot do otherwise than continue my investigations. If I am needed urgently, you may find me at one of the following,' he said, and reeled off a list of locations, none of them familiar to me.

'Are those all public houses?' I asked.

'They are. Ones that I know to be frequented by retired military men of non-commissioned rank.' He considered. 'They are rather rough places. Possibly a disguise may be in order.'

'Should I come with you?' I asked.

'No, Watson, I will be better able to blend in alone. I promise I have no intention of becoming embroiled in any brawls. You will be of more benefit to me in the morning, fresh and rested. Get a good night's sleep, and we will reconvene at breakfast.'

CHAPTER TEN
LORD ILLINGWORTH'S SECRET

I did get a good night's sleep, but not at once. I saw Holmes off on his errand – which is to say, I saw off a tanned and weather-beaten itinerant labourer, carrying a stout ashplant and a knapsack, in whom only one who knew Holmes as well as I could have detected any degree of resemblance to my friend – then bathed and readied myself for bed.

It was past midnight and I was enjoying a final tot of whisky with a novel before turning in. Following Holmes's comments about Mr H.G. Wells's *The Time Machine*, which I remembered enjoying, I had settled down with his latest book, *The Invisible Man*, when I heard a knocking from the hallway. Mrs Hudson having long since retired, I wrapped my dressing gown about myself and went downstairs.

I had not expected Holmes to return so early, but perhaps he had already discovered whatever information he sought in London's less salubrious taverns. He had a key, of course, but it was not unknown for him to leave it behind in his own clothes when he left on such incognito outings. In areas outside those problems wherewith his mind was fully engaged, he could be surprisingly absent-minded.

When I answered the door, however, the insistent knocker was not Holmes. It was a woman, wearing a hooded cloak against the chill of the night. She stepped inside at once and removed it, surrendering it to my astonished hands.

'Lady Goring!' I hissed, wary of waking Mrs Hudson. 'What are you doing here, alone and so late? It is most improper.'

'Oh, please don't be dreary, Dr Watson!' Mabel Goring smiled. 'Your reputation is perfectly safe. You are too honourable, and I too unadventurous, for any impropriety whatsoever.' Beneath the cloak she wore a jacket and sturdy boots, and a light dress that could have afforded little protection against the chilly night air.

I said, 'But if my landlady should find you here...'

'Then we shall tell her that I came to consult with Mr Holmes, and in his absence am speaking to you instead, which is thoroughly respectable and has the merit of being the truth.' Though her tone was cheerful, her pretty face was marred by lines of worry and she looked terribly tired. 'Mr Holmes *is* absent, I suppose?'

'You'd better come up,' was all I could think to say. Before closing the door I cast a nervous glance around the street outside, but saw nothing of note except the coach in which Lady Goring had presumably arrived, waiting a little further along Baker Street.

I settled her in front of the fire and offered her a warming brandy, which she declined.

'Does Lord Goring know you're here?' I asked, thinking again of the irregularity of the situation. While I had no doubt that her motives in appearing here were as innocent as she had told me, her presence in my rooms, unchaperoned, so late at night, made it easier to believe that in the past she could have behaved in an indiscreet way that might have interested a blackmailer. I peered out of the window, and this time saw a figure detach itself from the shadow of a doorway further down the road and stride away in the opposite direction from the coach.

She said, 'Oh, he believes I'm asleep at Robert's house.' As she said this, I realised with fresh unease that what I had taken for an unseasonal, flimsy summer dress was actually her nightdress. 'I pleaded nervous exhaustion this evening, and told them all that I wanted to be left alone. Robert and Gertrude have gone to a reception at the Bohemian Embassy, but poor Arthur was so attentive I eventually had to send him home. At least little Baby Arthur will see his papa tonight, if not his mama.'

'But won't the servants tell them you've been out?' I asked.

'Oh, nearly all of Robert's servants are old friends of mine,' she said. 'Only the housekeeper and coachman know, and they won't give me away.'

I asked her whether she had been treated kindly by the police.

'I can't complain of their accommodation,' she replied. 'They kept me in a perfectly comfortable interview room all yesterday, and the constable assigned to me was most attentive. I was remanded to Holloway Prison overnight, but they brought me back in time for breakfast. I cannot recommend the sleeping arrangements, but I was not there for long.'

I shuddered at the thought of the accommodations at Holloway, though I had no doubt that Lady Goring had been given the best of them. My respect for her fortitude was growing, nonetheless. 'Did they give you any indication of why they released you?'

'Only that some new evidence suggests I am not the guilty party,' she replied. 'Poor Inspector Gregson was apologetic and quite embarrassed.'

'He mentioned no further particulars?' I asked. I knew that I sounded like Holmes, questioning a young woman in this way about such upsetting experiences, but I knew too that this was information he would demand from me as soon as I told him of Mabel's visit. Besides, after our conversation in the hall I was duty-bound to treat this as a professional consultation, insofar as my role as Holmes's companion could be considered a professional one.

'Nothing at all,' she said. 'But that's exactly why I am here. Whatever this new evidence is, I fear it may be unreliable. I hope that I am wrong, but I do not think I am.'

The late hour and the whisky had been conspiring to make me feel rather sleepy, but this remark chased all thoughts of slumber from my brain. 'Why would you say that, without knowing any of the details?' I asked.

She looked at me with exceptional candour in her periwinkle eyes. 'Dr Watson, I ask you to believe that I'm entirely innocent of this crime.'

'I have no doubt of it,' I declared. That, at least, was not something Holmes would have said without firm evidence to that effect.

'Nevertheless, I am worried that the police may now be following the wrong path. And I am sorry to say that my family may be leading them along it.'

Her pretty face looked troubled now. She said, 'I heard my husband and brother talking at the house, after Inspector Gregson released me. They were too cautious to say anything in my presence, but I was in the conservatory while they were smoking in the garden, and I could hear them well enough. I heard Robert remark, "She was telling the truth, then. Thank God for that." And Arthur replied, "As I told you, her word may be relied upon, at least when it is to her own advantage." Their voices sounded distant, with none of the warmth they usually show when they discuss me.

'I could not believe that Robert would have doubted me, especially about such a matter, but I couldn't imagine who else they might have be speaking about, so I stayed to listen. I heard Robert say, "We can only hope that Gregson will stay convinced. I've seen the man's record. He is exceptionally tenacious." And Arthur said, "Gregson is not the one who concerns me most. Holmes is. I never would have involved him had I known."'

'What do you think he meant by that?' I asked her.

'I can't imagine. Since I'm not guilty, there's nothing Arthur could have *known* that would make him think I was! But then I heard Robert say, "*Can* he be paid off?" and Arthur reply, "His reputation suggests not, but I had better try. The last thing we want now is his stumbling upon something that casts it all into doubt again."'

'"Stumbling"?' I repeated, quite indignant on Holmes's behalf. My friend's approach was a painstaking one. He considered, probed, scrutinised and deduced. It was true that luck occasionally played a part in his investigations, as it might in anyone's endeavours, but the term 'stumbling' made his investigations sound clumsy and aimless.

Mabel was frowning at my indignation. 'That did not strike me as the most significant part of my husband's statement, Dr Watson.'

'Well, no, I suppose not,' I agreed, slightly abashed. 'What do you think it all means?'

She said, 'I don't understand all of it, but I'm worried that Arthur and Robert have contrived to have someone plant false evidence to exonerate me. They would have had the best of intentions, of course. Both of them want nothing more than to protect me. But if it could lead to another innocent person being arrested, perhaps even tried and convicted? I could never sleep easily if I were to allow that. I have little enough reason to trust the police, but I have faith that Mr Holmes will find out the truth.'

'That is very brave of you,' I said with sincere admiration. 'But do you really believe that Sir Robert and Lord Goring would do such a thing? I admit I know neither of them well, but your brother, at least, has a reputation for absolute rectitude.'

She said, 'Oh, he is a very good man! And so is my husband, though his virtues may be better known to me than to the world at large. But no man's rectitude is absolute, no matter what his reputation may say. A short time ago – two years ago, in fact, for it was the very day that Arthur proposed to me – Robert was offered a Cabinet position by the prime minister, and he turned it down.'

'But he served in the Cabinet before the last election,' I recalled, confused.

'That is correct. He changed his mind the same day. I only know of his initial refusal because Lord Caversham, Arthur's father, asked me to use my influence to persuade him. Of course, I was rather distracted at the time, but I was not quite so wrapped up in myself, or in Lord Goring, that I failed to notice a strange atmosphere in the house that day. I believe that Robert was ashamed of something that he had done, and that Gertrude was censorious of him, and that that was why he declined the position. Gertrude is a very moral person, and she has high expectations of others. Indeed, I believe she married Robert because nobody else could measure up to her ideals of integrity.

'Of course, it can't have been anything very reprehensible that Robert had done, as she soon overcame her objections, but that is why I do not believe that anybody, Robert included, is incapable of doing wrong. It is a good thing, too, for only the imperfect are capable of the virtue of forgiveness. The ideal is the enemy of the human, and I would far rather be the second than the first.

'So yes, falsifying evidence would be a terrible thing to do. But if anything would lead Robert or Arthur to do such a thing, it would be their affection for me. At least...' she added hesitantly, '...so I should have said, before I overheard them in the garden. I suppose they must be under a great deal of strain because of me, to have sounded so.'

'I see,' I said. 'And I have your permission to tell all of this to Holmes? You are not concerned for your brother and husband if these facts became known?'

'It was to tell Mr Holmes that I came,' she reminded me. 'I am lucky to be surrounded by good men: Arthur and Robert, and now you and Mr Holmes. I know that you will not wish them to suffer for their kindness, but neither will you stand by and see an innocent person convicted. I believe that Mr Holmes is clever enough, and you kind enough, to square that circle.'

'So you wish Holmes to continue investigating,' I concluded. 'As a matter of fact, your husband did call earlier this evening, and tried to persuade him to desist. Holmes was no more amenable to persuasion than Lord Goring expected. Indeed, he is out seeking more information about the case at this very moment.' I recalled that, in fact, I had very little idea of what, exactly, Holmes was hoping to discover.

'I'm so pleased to hear it,' Lady Goring beamed. 'In that case, I had better be going back to Grosvenor Square. Gertrude will be back from the reception soon, and she may wish to look in on me when she returns.'

She stood, and I did likewise, ready to show her out. But something else had occurred to me. 'One moment, please, Lady Goring,' I said, sounding to myself like Holmes again. 'Can I take it that the testimony you gave in my presence yesterday morning was all accurate? There's nothing you wish to retract or amend?'

Mabel paused, considering. 'Most of it was,' she said at last.

'Everything material, anyway. I wasn't quite frank about my reasons for going up to the library.'

'I see.' I tried to sound stern. 'And those were?'

She sighed. 'I was concerned for a dear friend. I had seen how Lord Illingworth was behaving towards Cecily, and it upset me. I dare say you have heard of his history?'

'I have indeed,' I said, recalling Langdale Pike's characterisation of the man as a habitual philanderer. 'How was he behaving?'

'In a manner I would describe as excessively fond. Of course, Cecily is a sweet girl and many people are excessively fond of her. I am myself. But when a man of Lord Illingworth's reputation is seeking time alone with a young wife, particularly one whose husband is so ineffectual and self-absorbed as dear Algy, it is a worry. I went to the library to consider what I should do about it: whether to talk to Cecily, or to Algy, or even to Lord Illingworth, or simply to let the matter slide. Cecily is a grown woman, after all, soon to be a mother, and should perhaps be trusted to make her own decisions. I'm sure that she would say so, at least.'

'And what conclusion did you come to?' I asked.

'I have not reached it yet,' she admitted. 'What would you do, Dr Watson?'

'I'd confront the fellow and threaten to thrash him to within an inch of his life,' I averred. 'Not that that's an option for you, I realise, but you may call upon my services if need be.'

I showed her to the door, where she resumed her voluminous cloak. Her coachman came in response to her wave, and Lady Goring left, apparently unobserved. The coach was unmarked, and in her cloak Her Ladyship would have gone unrecognised. Any unpleasantness that our watcher in the shadows might stir up about the visit would, I hoped, attach to me alone.

I retired to bed, slept well as I have said, and awoke to find

Holmes still absent. He returned as I was eating Mrs Hudson's kippers, drinking my coffee and reading the *Morning Chronicle*. I was unsurprised to see Sir Robert Chiltern's name prominently featured, that being a frequent enough occurrence, but the reason was a surprising one. It seemed that he had given a speech in the Commons the previous afternoon opposing the government's latest bill to regulate financial irregularities.

Though heaven knows I am no avid follower of politics, Sir Robert's involvement in our case had caused me to note the circumstances concerning the bill, which he had been widely expected to favour. The regulations it would introduce were to limit the proliferation of a certain kind of fraudulent reinvestment scheme, the details of which I was unable fully to follow, and it had been supposed that he would pledge the Opposition's support for these measures. His reputation for fiscal prudence and probity had virtually dictated it, and the newspaper professed itself much surprised at the feebleness of his arguments against it. Even so, without his backing the bill was expected to founder.

I realised that at the time the speech was given, his sister must have still been in custody, and I supposed that this aberrant behaviour could be accounted for by the very natural distraction such a state of affairs might cause. It seemed peculiar to me, though, that in such a situation Chiltern had not excused himself and allowed some deputy to make the speech in his stead.

Politics has never been my area of interest, however, and I had already moved on to a consideration of the criminal stories when Holmes returned, grimy, tired and footsore, having tramped between a dozen different public houses situated across London. He tossed aside his stick and knapsack, retired to his bedroom, and emerged ten minutes later in his own clothes, looking not only well-scrubbed but somehow also radiantly refreshed.

'My dear fellow,' he said, 'I have made what may prove to be a breakthrough in the case. I may have an identity for Mr Bunbury. Time will tell, or rather Major Roderick Nepcote will. He is meeting us at ten o'clock at the police mortuary.'

Surprising though this statement was, I was bursting with eagerness to tell Holmes what I had learned from Mabel Goring, and he acquiesced to listen. I told him of her visit, not forgetting the presence of the sinister observer; of Lady Goring's suspicions of Lord Illingworth and his possible designs on Cecily; and also of her misgivings about her menfolk, including her idea that Lord Goring might have some less than honest reason for warning Holmes away from the case.

'That point, at least, did not require much mental exertion to deduce,' Holmes observed drily, helping himself to a kipper.

'But don't you see, Holmes?' I asked excitedly, for I had given this matter some consideration overnight, and had arrived at a conclusion that I hoped was worthy of Holmes himself. 'Lady Goring believed that the conversation she overheard related to herself, but she had no proof of that. Her brother and husband spoke of a "she" whose word had proved reliable, and was somehow connected with Lady Goring's release. What if they were talking about someone else entirely? Lord Goring, at least, knows Mrs Teville, and perhaps knows more than he has told us. If she is a career blackmailer, and not merely an opportunistic one, then she might be able to apply her sinister pressure to others – perhaps even to Inspector Gregson, or someone else at Scotland Yard. And her price for that might be your removal from the case!'

Holmes considered this for a moment. 'An adventurous leap, Watson,' he concluded eventually, 'but made with some deftness of footing. You are coming on. As you say, it seems clear that Goring and Chiltern were discussing someone other than Lady Goring, and we have already suspected the hand of a female criminal in this case. I would remind you, though, that we have no direct evidence against Mrs Teville, not even that of her identity. It would also be unusual for a blackmailer to victimise someone personally connected to them at a later stage in their career. One might imagine Violet Cardew beginning by blackmailing her daughter out of desperation and then, having discovered a taste or a talent for it, proceeding to apply the technique to others, but the reverse would be more surprising.'

He added, 'I also have grave trouble seeing Tobias Gregson acting so intemperately as to incur the attentions of a blackmailer. But hark!' he said, before I could reply. 'I hear his most constabulary tread upon the stair. Pray, not a word of this to the inspector for the moment, Watson, though I shall have to confess our appointment in the mortuary. I should much prefer to be certain of my facts before I share them.'

Precisely as he finished the sentence, Mrs Hudson ushered in Inspector Gregson, who for once was beaming with pride. 'Well, gentlemen,' he said, 'the case is as good as solved. There are a few details yet to be cleared up, and we haven't made our arrest just now, but it's perfectly clear to me who did it, and it's only a matter of time before I get my hands on him.'

'Him?' I repeated in surprise.

Gregson replied, 'Oh, the lady on the balcony is a red herring, Dr Watson. Or a midnight-blue one, perhaps,' he added, tickled by his own witticism.

'Please tell us from the beginning, Inspector,' Holmes requested. 'The doctor and I are entirely agog.'

'Well, gentlemen, I can tell you in confidence that we're now seeking Lord Illingworth in connection with the murder of the unknown person going by the name of Bunbury. His Lordship may be trusted in the diplomatic service, but between you and me, he is not the sort of man who I would wish introduced to my daughter. It seems he has rather a habit of getting girls into trouble, and not just servants either.'

'While that is certainly reprehensible, it does not mean that he is capable of murder,' Holmes observed. 'The offences are quite different.'

'I'll grant you that, but it does not encourage me to give him the benefit of the doubt. But let me tell you what we've really found out. We've been getting statements from the last few guests we didn't manage to talk to on the night, to find out what they have to say. Some of them have been elusive, and the last two we needed to speak to were Lord Illingworth and Mrs Teville.'

'They know each other,' I observed, remembering the sturdy diplomat speaking to the lady with the fan. 'It was Illingworth who helped Mrs Teville leave, despite your constables' best efforts.'

'So I gather, but by the lady's account he was just being gentlemanly. She says they don't know each other well – in fact, I think she rather dislikes him. She also corroborated much of what we already knew about the times guests arrived and left, and what they were wearing. She had nothing in particular to say about Bunbury, and she hadn't been near the library. She did, though, see what happened to Lady Goring's shawl.'

'Mrs Teville saw her take it off, then, as she said?' I asked, with relief but also some suspicion.

'Just as she said,' Gregson confirmed. 'That's why we let Her Ladyship go yesterday. Not the constabulary's finest hour, perhaps, but I still maintain that I did as I must under the circumstances.'

'You may rest assured of that, Inspector,' Holmes confirmed. 'It was your duty at the time.'

'Well, regardless of that,' said Gregson, trying his best to give an impression of indifference to Holmes's approval, 'Mrs Teville told us that she saw Lady Goring remove the shawl in the music room. She was sitting close to the fire, it seems – Lady Goring, that is – near where Mrs Cecily Moncrieff was sitting with Lord Illingworth. Mrs Teville's view was that Lord Illingworth was monopolising Mrs Moncrieff, and that Lady Goring was remaining nearby out of concern for the young lady, on the grounds of his scandalous reputation. Mrs Teville understands that her own reputation might not make her an entirely trusted chaperone in such circumstances.'

That fitted with Mabel's own account, although as I had only received her permission to share it with Holmes, I did not tell Gregson so.

Holmes asked, 'Did you learn of Lord Illingworth's notoriety from Mrs Teville, Inspector?'

'No, again she corroborated what we knew already. I have my ear to the ground, Mr Holmes, and there isn't much that gets past me.' Gregson paused to gather his thoughts, then continued, 'Mrs Teville remembers noticing at the time that the brooch was pinned to the shawl. She says she was concerned in case some servant saw it, or one of the musicians, and found the temptation a bit too much for them. She was going to take it when she left and give it back to Lady Goring. But then she saw Lord Illingworth doing the same, so she supposed that it would find its way back to her. He may be a reprobate, but he's a wealthy man and she didn't take him for a thief.'

Holmes asked, 'So Lady Goring preceded Lord Illingworth from the room?'

'According to Mrs Teville, Cecily Moncrieff left first, and Lady Goring followed shortly afterwards. Lord Illingworth remained for a few minutes, then gathered up the shawl and went. A few more guests arrived, then Mrs Teville left some time later.'

'And what do you believe happened next?' Holmes asked.

'My guess is that Illingworth tore the brooch away from the shawl deliberately, so he could incriminate Lady Goring afterwards. He was in the music room when Merriman mentioned Bunbury's presence. He must have been worried when he saw Lady Goring go up to the second floor ahead of him, but when she came down again within a few minutes he realised that she had only served to strengthen the story of her guilt. He went upstairs to the room, found Bunbury already outside on the balcony, gave the man the brooch, and then pushed him over.'

'Why, then, did Mabel Goring not mention having seen Bunbury when she entered the library?'

'He might have gone out onto the balcony while he was waiting, if he had found the door unlocked,' Gregson said. 'Or he might have panicked when she arrived, tried to hide behind the curtain, and found it ajar then. Either way, it would make Her Ladyship's testimony an honest one. She would have been unaware of his presence there.'

'And the woman who was seen on the balcony with Bunbury?' asked Holmes.

Gregson said, 'Ah, well, we only have the maid Dora Steyne's word for that. My guess is that Dora is in Lord Illingworth's pay, or else suborned somehow. He's a persuasive man, especially where the female sex is concerned.'

'I see. From what you told us the day before yesterday, Dora Steyne's room is at the top of the house, overlooking the garden.'

'It is indeed,' said Gregson. 'From there it would be much easier to toss that shawl into the tree, where it would be seen, in furtherance of the plan to implicate Lady Goring in the crime.'

Holmes had already given Gregson a brief account of his ballistics experiment at the Moncrieff house, and Gregson had responded with a stern lecture about the sanctity of police evidence, before shaking his head and making a note to send a constable round to collect the shawl. My friend asked now, 'Has Dora confirmed your suspicions?'

Gregson replied, 'We brought her in this morning and my men are questioning her. If she's guilty we will know soon enough. But, of course, another servant might have thrown the shawl, or Illingworth could have made his way up to the servants' quarters and done it himself.'

'Though either option would mean we might trust Dora's testimony once again,' Holmes noted, 'as far as we did previously, at least. It seems to me that all you have at this stage is supposition, Inspector. Certainly the fact that the shawl was in Illingworth's possession is suggestive, but Mrs Teville might have been quite correct in supposing that he would hand it back to its owner. Lady Goring might then have put it back on, and the murder taken place in exactly the way you previously supposed.'

'If that was all we had you would be right,' Gregson continued rather smugly. 'None of what I have told you proves anything as far as it goes. But it was enough to make us even keener to interview Lord Illingworth. I went to his house in St James's Square and had a stern word with his manservant and secretary, and they admitted he hasn't been back home since the day after the Moncrieffs' ball, with no word to either of them about where he might be found.'

Holmes raised an eyebrow. 'That is certainly interesting,' he confessed. 'We saw him that day, at a distance in the street, and he certainly seemed somewhat distracted. Perhaps, though, such behaviour is not so very unusual for a man of Illingworth's habits. There are doubtless other places where he might choose to stay.'

'Well, that was what his secretary said, though not at first. When I mentioned murder, though, he was quick enough to tell me that this has happened often enough before. Still, with Mrs Teville's testimony it sufficed to justify us searching His

Lordship's townhouse, and his study particularly. And what do you suppose we found there?'

'You know that I dislike supposition, Inspector.' A trace of a smile played about Holmes's lips. 'But were I to oblige, I would suppose that you found evidence that Lord Illingworth has been blackmailing his daughter, Cecily Moncrieff.'

'Good Lord!' I exclaimed, quite astonished.

For his part, Gregson looked crestfallen, and somewhat petulant at having his thunder stolen. 'How did you know?' he asked.

'I did not *know*, Inspector. At your insistence, I supposed. Lord Illingworth has a history of irregular paternity, and you said that he was showing particular attention to Cecily.' He did not mention that we had known this ourselves before his arrival; nor, I noticed, did he mention our own theory of a female master criminal, which would surely have cast some doubt upon Illingworth's guilt. 'Watson and I discovered yesterday that, while Cecily's mother is believed dead, her father's identity is known only by vague rumour even to her closest friends – a fact we would have told you already,' he added in response to Gregson's indignant expression, 'had you not been so eager to recount your own activities.

'We also learned that Cecily is being blackmailed by someone addressing her as "daughter". It is not difficult to put these pieces together to make a coherent picture. Since it would be the height of foolishness for Illingworth to retain a copy of his own typewritten letter to Cecily, I surmise that he kept her reply to him, out of a misplaced, and I have to say quite twisted, sense of sentiment. From what we know, though, he does appear to be somewhat fond of the young woman.'

Gregson scratched his head a little resentfully. 'Well, your guess is on the money, Mr Holmes. What we found, in one of his desk drawers, with very little effort made to hide it, was this.'

He took from his pocket a much-folded letter, which he handed over. Holmes read it aloud.

Dear mother or father, if such you are, which I must inform you I consider doubtful,

If the warnings I have been given about the behaviour of young children are true, then to feign death to avoid parental responsibility shows admirable delicacy of feeling on your part, but I cannot but feel that the time for such demonstrations of sentiment passed some years ago.

After nearly twenty years' absence, I would expect less formal manners from a parent than for them to introduce themselves to me by correspondence alone, yet rather better ones than to do so only with veiled hints of shameful secrets and the price of silence.

Given my advanced years, I see no reason to establish communication between us now. Even if you are indeed my flesh and blood, I have in my husband and his connections all the family I need, and in my aunt-in-law, if I am scrupulously honest, perhaps somewhat more.

You allude to the wealth that it is my good fortune to enjoy. Allow me to reassure you that it is a very good fortune indeed, and that I enjoy it enormously. If it is necessary to avoid such communication then what you suggest can be arranged, but this must be a unique transaction, with no further correspondence ensuing.

The letter was wisely unsigned, but it had been written in a prettily rounded feminine hand, on headed notepaper bearing the Lowndes Square address of Algernon and Cecily Moncrieff.

Holmes said, 'I assume that the Moncrieff family have not yet been made aware of this development. I would urge that, unless it becomes unavoidable, they should not be told the identity of Cecily's blackmailer. I cannot imagine that it would do any of them any good to know, and it would be likely to cause unnecessary distress.'

Gregson nodded. 'Very much my own thoughts on the matter. Although it may become impossible to avoid it, of course.'

'I admit, Gregson, that I retain some doubts as to how this constitutes a case for murder against Lord Illingworth. Given the circumstances of the death, I would be surprised if the murderer were a man like the earl, larger than Bunbury and physically fit. If we allow that Illingworth was able to place the victim at his ease, however, so that he was sufficiently off his guard to be pushed over the balustrade, and even if we further accept that the earl is so unscrupulous as to make it appear that Mabel Goring was to blame for the crime, what did he gain by killing Bunbury?'

'That's not easy to say until we know who Bunbury was. But everything about the way the fellow turned up at the house, including the name he used, suggest that he was there with blackmail on his mind as well. If Illingworth thought he was a rival, he might have tried to kill him.'

'Or he might simply have bought him, if he is as wealthy as we are told.'

'If he's as wealthy as all that,' Gregson countered, 'why blackmail his own daughter in the first place?'

'That is a significant point,' Holmes conceded. 'Did your search of the house unearth any evidence of recent debt or insolvency?'

'There were any number of unpaid bills, but I gather that that is to be expected for the gentlemen of that set.' Gregson looked disapproving, as well he might. 'If it becomes material, we may have to talk to his bankers. But there is another possibility, if the victim really was a blackmailer. Illingworth is obviously a man with a lot of secrets. Maybe this Bunbury was trying to blackmail him as well as the Moncrieffs. Maybe that was why Illingworth killed him.'

'Based on everything we know,' Holmes acknowledged, 'that is a more promising line of inquiry. Nevertheless, at present there is no case for Lord Illingworth to answer, for the murder at least.'

'Well, when we find him we'll hold him for blackmail until we have the evidence we need,' Gregson vowed. 'One way or the other, we'll get him.'

CHAPTER ELEVEN
AN EDUCATED GARDENER

Mentioning our appointment with Major Nepcote at the police mortuary, Holmes invited Gregson to join us, but the inspector was bound for Lord Illingworth's St James's Square townhouse, to speak to the remainder of the earl's servants. He promised to meet us later at Scotland Yard.

In the cab to the Yard, Holmes made me cognisant of his nocturnal exploits. He had, it seemed, spent a peripatetic night trawling a list of insalubrious taverns where the landlords were surly, the beer tasteless and the floors liberally scattered with sawdust, but where the clientele might include men who had served as common soldiers in the regiment commanded by Ernest and Algernon's father during the 1860s. He had found a number of them, a few of whom had remembered William Durrington, the former sergeant who had compromised Letitia Prism's loyalty to Colonel Moncrieff, though mostly they seemed to feel little fondness for the man.

In his character as a wandering labourer with a nebulously defined family connection to the Durringtons, and applying some lubrication in the form of rounds of drinks, Holmes had been able to extract from them some reminiscences. They had confirmed Mrs Chasuble's suspicion that Durrington had been cashiered for selling drugs to the troops. However, the conjecture that Ernest Moncrieff senior had dealt with the matter himself was seemingly incorrect.

'In fact, the popular view is that the colonel was a peaceable man, who avoided confrontation wherever he could,' Holmes told me.

Evidently, Durrington's pusillanimous commander had passed the distasteful duty on to some more junior officer, who had dealt with it more ruthlessly than he would have been able to. Durrington had believed, possibly correctly, that his commanding officer was sufficiently susceptible that he could have persuaded him to keep him on, had he only been given the opportunity. His grudge against the colonel came about not because the latter had discharged him personally, but because he had been afraid to do so.

Despite this, the general opinion among Holmes's informants, which some gave more forthrightly than others given Holmes's purported relationship to him, had been that the late sergeant had got his just desserts.

'This was to be expected, of course,' Holmes noted.

'I should think so!' I exclaimed.

'Of course, that is the moral view of the matter. But what I mean is that any who might have been more sympathetic to Durrington's illicit activities would have been those who benefitted from them, if opium can be considered a benefit. Nobody who was a devotee of the poppy in 1867 can reasonably be expected to be alive now and sufficiently compos mentis to defend their supplier to us, and so the survivors are censorious.'

With careful interrogation, however, Holmes had been able to identify one person who might have been more kindly disposed towards Durrington, the man had who served as his corporal before Durrington's dismissal. Some of Holmes's informants suspected that this man, one Charlie Findon, had been, if not actively involved in Durrington's drug-running scheme, then at least turning a blind eye to his activities in return for a modest share of the proceeds.

Holmes had eventually found Findon in a far less reputable establishment in Whitechapel, a filthy den of thieves and vagabonds where tasteless beer would have been a godsend and the floor was strewn with much less savoury substances than sawdust. Despite his sordid surroundings, Findon had reached his mid-fifties in rude health, having never partaken of the substances his sergeant peddled then or since. After his initial suspicions were eased through the application of gin, he was inclined to be garrulous on the subject of his old boss to the man claiming to be Durrington's distant relation.

His recollection of the sergeant's disgrace was not substantially different from that of his former comrades, except that in his view Durrington had been harshly treated for his crime.

'What he told me was, "The way I seen it, he done old Monkey-face a favour,"' Holmes said, giving an effortlessly convincing imitation of the man's hoarse cockney accent. Holmes had gathered by now from Findon's former comrades that 'Monkey-face' was the regiment's nickname for Colonel Moncrieff. '"That old coot done his stint out in India when he was just a captain or what-have-you, and now he was sitting pretty back home he wasn't in no rush to go nowhere else. Thing is, there's some blokes what enlist what wants some argy-bargy, and coves like them lot don't take well to sitting idle on their backsides all day. The sarge had the what's-what to get 'em settled back down. After he'd gone they all got antsy for want of the treacle, and ended up rowing and scrapping like the very Devil. Old Monkey-face had some bigger headaches then than a few pipe-hungry dossers."'

According to Findon, Durrington had greatly resented his expulsion from the regiment, and had heaped imprecations on the colonel's head for not doing him the courtesy of dismissing him in person. Findon had, in fact, ceased to have much to do with his former sergeant soon afterwards, partly because of his growing obsession with this topic, and partly because of Durrington's jealousy and anger after Findon was given his stripes and charge of Durrington's old platoon.

One point which Findon recalled, though, Holmes had found of particular interest. "'Sarge had a kid,' he told me. "Wrong side of the sheets, mind, 'cause old Bill Durrington never got his self spliced. But he was fond of the little bleeder even so. Thing is, the lad got whelped round the same time as old Monkey-face's grub, didn't he? Same ages, near enough. So Bill gets to thinking to himself, he thinks, 'How come Young Monkey-face gets a nursery to his self with all the wooden toys he can slobber over and a dollymop to push him about the place, when my Timmy and his ma doss down in a mucky lumber with three other petticoats and their nippers? How's that fair, then?' He got quite jawsome on that score, did Bill.'"

I said to Holmes, 'Well, presumably if Durrington had given the mother of his child a reasonable share of his wages—'

'Doubtless, Watson, doubtless, but I fear the late Sergeant Durrington is beyond profiting from your practical wisdom now. The pertinent point is that, according to Findon at least, the difference between the circumstances of his son Timothy and those of Colonel Moncrieff's son Ernest struck Durrington as profoundly unjust. Hence, we must assume, the extension of his grudge from the father to his blameless child.'

'And hence Ernest's abduction. I say, Holmes!' I realised suddenly. 'One of the blackmailers was claiming that Ernest had been swapped with another child during the kidnapping.

Do you think it's possible that Durrington substituted Timothy for Ernest?'

'It seems unlikely. If that were Durrington's intention, why would he make elaborate plans involving handbags and railway termini when he could simply have met Laetitia Prism while she was walking with the child and effected the exchange? No, I believe he simply intended to hold the Moncrieff child for ransom, as he told her at the time. One might generously imagine that he intended to use the ransom money for the benefit of his own son, but given his character it seems doubtful.'

'So what did happen to the child?' I asked. 'Durrington's son, I mean. He'd be Ernest Moncrieff's age now. Still, I mean.'

'A most apposite question, Watson, and one which I took it upon myself to seek an answer to.'

It had taken Holmes considerable effort, a deal more gin, and in the end the sum of ten shillings to pry from Charlie Findon the name and former residence of the mother of Durrington's child – one Jane Bramber, long since deceased – and then some tedious further conversation in inns and on street corners to identify a living relative, a cousin of hers. This man, when Holmes intercepted him leaving for an early shift at the docks that morning, had been able to inform Holmes of the younger Durrington's current position.

Holmes smiled. 'Timothy Durrington,' he told me, 'is employed as an undergardener at the London home of Major and Mrs Nepcote, where he may well have encountered the current generation of the Moncrieff family. Further enquiries, the last of which I made before returning for breakfast this morning, told me that the man has not been seen since the afternoon preceding the Moncrieffs' ball, and may expect a dismissal when he does return. My strong suspicion is that he will not.'

'You think that he was Bunbury,' I realised. 'That's why you asked Major Nepcote to meet us at the mortuary. Wouldn't somebody at the house have recognised him, though?'

'It could have been awkward had he run into either of the Nepcotes, but otherwise, I think not. Few people of that class look closely at servants, particularly outdoor servants, and even those with a glancing familiarity with one are unlikely to think of him when presented with a man in a suit. Much of our recognition of faces depends upon the context in which we see them.'

Holmes's account had eaten up most of the distance from Baker Street to Westminster, where the New Scotland Yard buildings stood. As we approached, I regarded the structure, designed by Norman Shaw some ten years before. It had always seemed oddly whimsical to me, its continental red-and-white-striped brickwork and its peculiar corner turrets unsuited to a building with such a practical, and even grim, purpose.

As we drew up outside, I saw a carriage waiting, and surmised that the major was there already. As Holmes and I disembarked, however, a shrill voice cried, 'Dr Watson! Such a relief to see so familiar and so comforting a face at such a distressing occasion!' and to my dismay the small but dapper figure of Roderick Nepcote was followed out of the carriage by his young wife.

Inside, Holmes gave our names to the sergeant on duty with his usual offhand urgency, and he, the major and I were led down to the mortuary, accompanied, despite all the protests I or the policemen in attendance could muster, by the voluble Mrs Nepcote. Any hope I might have had that Holmes's presence might have absorbed some of her interest faded quickly as she clutched at my arm, protesting her trepidation at her forthcoming, entirely voluntary ordeal, praising my bravery and my generosity in agreeing to see her through it, and occasionally complimenting me on the firmness of my biceps.

'Oh, but that's him!' she shrieked when, after we had been

shown into the cellar where the police surgeons did their work, the body of Bunbury was brought out and partially unshrouded for us. 'That's Durrington! Oh, what a terrible thing to happen, and to such a harmless man! I swear, Dr Watson, he would never have hurt a fly! Oh, what a tragedy, and how perplexing that he should have been at Mr Moncrieff's house that night, and giving the name Bunbury, I understand…? How entirely inexplicable, and how awful!' She continued in this vein for some time.

Although it was clear that she was acting out a scene, and with considerable relish, her husband, the major, was ignoring her while he peered with interest at the body, and Holmes evidently considered her noise an unwelcome and possibly malicious distraction. Though I was reluctant, chivalry required me to play my part. I patted her arm and muttered soothing words while struggling to hear what Holmes and Major Nepcote were discussing. Though I would have much appreciated an opportunity to examine the body's head wound in mortuary conditions rather than the uncongenial environment of Ernest Moncrieff's lawn, I was eventually forced, to my considerable frustration, to take the lady outside and find her somewhere to sit down.

'So terrible,' she repeated for perhaps the fifth time, 'to think that he was lying there in the garden for heaven knows how long before dear Lord Illingworth and little Cecily Moncrieff discovered him. And how strange to think that he was waiting in the library while we were enjoying ourselves without a thought of him. What *was* his business there, I wonder, with Mr Ernest Moncrieff? I cannot fathom what it might have been. Do you know, Dr Watson?'

'No, madam, I do not,' I said shortly, although by now I had a fairly clear idea. I would not give this well-fed vulture more than the bare minimum demanded by propriety. Then it occurred to me that I could at least use this opportunity to confirm what Mrs Nepcote could tell us of the evening's events. 'You knew he was in the library, then?'

She looked at me, her dry eyes wide. 'Oh, not at the time, Doctor, of course, but the police were so interested in that room when I spoke to them, and he fell to the ground beneath that balcony. Where else could he have been?'

'Did you see where he fell?'

'Oh, only through the window from the ballroom. I had no idea it was poor Durrington, of course.' I had no doubt that she had tried to get the best look at the body that she could, but I could well believe that a woman such as she had failed to recognise a junior servant from a distance in the moonlight.

I asked, 'But had you realised that... the victim was upstairs in the library when you told the police that you saw Lady Goring enter?'

'Well, I suppose I knew it from the fact that they asked. They asked me about the room, you see, not about dear Lady Goring. Oh, Dr Watson, I hope they do not suspect her of the murder – for it was murder, was it not?'

'I'm afraid that question is beyond my medical expertise,' I equivocated. A point struck me. 'Did you see whether she was wearing her shawl when she went upstairs?'

'She wasn't, I'm sure of it. I remember thinking at the time that she should be careful about taking it off, with that beautiful spider's-web brooch pinned to it. It would have been a dreadful pity for that to have been misplaced.'

So said Mrs Nepcote, but by now, between her false hysterics, her insinuations and her angling for information, I was unsure whether anything she said was to be trusted at all.

Rather gleefully, she added, 'I wonder whether Mr Holmes will discover the murderer? Oh, this is so shocking, Dr Watson, so very horrific. Of course, I suppose the two of you must have met very many murderers in your adventures. You must be used to the lengths to which they will go to protect themselves. I am sure that it is a great credit to your friendship that Mr Holmes is alive at all, after defying so many homicidal persons. It must be a great worry to you,' she added enigmatically, 'to consider that one day your protection may fail.'

I mumbled something about Holmes being more than capable of looking after himself, but at that point my friend mercifully emerged, bringing Mrs Nepcote's ineffectual husband with him. I looked to Holmes for information, and he nodded. 'Major Nepcote is also assured of the body's identity. Evidently, the late Bunbury was Timothy Durrington.'

Politely, he asked the Nepcotes if they would mind waiting while we found Inspector Gregson, speaking discreetly to the sergeant at the desk to ensure that the couple did not leave without us.

'We must search Durrington's personal effects,' he told me quietly as we headed for Gregson's office, 'and before anybody else has an opportunity to tamper with them, assuming that that has not happened already.'

I said, 'Do you think the Nepcotes would do such a thing? Just now Mrs Nepcote delivered what might have been a warning to desist our investigations, but honestly I cannot tell what weight to give to any of her utterances.'

Holmes said, 'I, too, find it irritatingly difficult to predict what the Nepcotes might do, or indeed what their servants might have done in their absence. They may be entirely blameless in this matter, since employing a hereditary enemy of one of their acquaintances would be a minor coincidence compared with some others we have encountered in this case. Or it may be that Ernest Moncrieff was not the only person whom Durrington was attempting to blackmail. I would prefer to resolve the matter as soon as possible, in any case.'

We found Gregson in his office, having evidently found little of further interest at Lord Illingworth's house. He was, however, deep in conversation with Constable Northbrook, the policeman who had been guarding the door at the Moncrieffs' house when we first arrived there, which the two of them broke off as Holmes and I arrived.

'Tell Mr Holmes and Dr Watson what you've just told me, Northbrook,' the inspector suggested after greeting us.

'Yes, sir,' said Constable Northbrook. He informed us that he had been interviewing Dora Steyne, the maid at the Moncrieffs' house who had claimed to have seen a woman on the balcony, speaking to the man we now knew was Durrington. Since her arrest the maid had stuck determinedly to her story, until the constable let her know that the police had evidence against Lord Illingworth, and suggested that the peer was very probably on the run.

She had changed her tune quickly enough then, and confessed that, just as Gregson had suspected, she had been given Lady Goring's shawl by the earl, and had thrown it down from the window of her room to hang in the tree opposite the balcony. Northbrook's first inclination had been to place a disagreeable construction on the maid's relationship with His Lordship, but Dora was resolute that nothing more had occurred between them than a simple act of bribery.

'This looks like the evidence we've been wanting, gentlemen,' Gregson concluded. 'Illingworth was involved in the murder plot, right enough.'

'It is evidence of underhand behaviour on his part,' Holmes allowed, 'and given the undoubted presence of the brooch and part of the shawl in the deceased's hand, it is quite suggestive.'

'And best of all, we can discount the girl's testimony about seeing Lady Goring on the balcony,' I added.

'Actually, Dr Watson, sorry, sir, but we can't,' the constable informed me apologetically. 'Dora's been straight with us about the business with the shawl, and she expects to be dismissed without a character reference after what she's done, so she's got no reason to lie to us now. But she insists on her testimony about the woman on the balcony. She says she knows what she saw.'

'Was it while she was disposing of the shawl that Dora saw this woman?' Holmes asked sharply.

'That's right, sir,' Northbrook reported. 'She went up there about half past ten, just like she said, except she didn't tell us why. Lord Illingworth had just given her her orders – he'd bought her off on a previous visit to the house. That's why Dora got so scared later on, when we asked her if the woman she saw was wearing a shawl – she didn't know if she'd be giving something away if she said no.'

'She noticed that the shawl was torn, of course?'

'Yes, sir, she mentioned that particular. She took it up the stairs to her room that she shares with another of the maids, opened the window, and saw the bloke and the woman down on the balcony, but they were talking and didn't notice her. So she threw the item into the tree, shut the window, and got on with her duties as quick as she could.'

What did it mean that the shawl had been put in place before Durrington was even murdered, I wondered? It suggested a callous degree of forethought, at least, and a willingness to take risks. How would it have looked if something had gone wrong and the murder had not taken place as planned?

'But how do you explain this, Gregson,' Holmes wondered, 'if Lord Illingworth was the murderer? The lady's presence on the balcony hardly seems to support that theory, unless you propose that the earl changed into a blue satin ballgown for the purpose of committing the crime.'

Gregson sighed at the pleasantry. 'We need hardly go that far,' he said. 'We know that Cecily Moncrieff is friendly with Lord Illingworth, ignorant as she is of his true relationship with her, and that he's encouraged her in that. I don't suggest that any blame lies with her, but it might be that His Lordship suggested she step into the library and have a word with Bunbury, as a way of scouting out the territory, so to speak. She and Mabel Goring are both blonde, similar in height and build, and you said yourself that her teal dress might be mistaken for a dark blue one in the moonlight.'

'I said that it could be, were it not for her condition. If she had been seen from behind then perhaps, but from Dora's window above, her outline would have been quite clear.'

'Besides, Cecily Moncrieff swore that Durrington was a stranger to her,' I reminded him. 'I feel sure that she would have never been so blasé about the death of a man to whom she had spoken.'

'Well, what we feel isn't evidence, Dr Watson, and it's a good thing too, most of the time. But who is this Durrington?'

'Durrington is Major and Mrs Nepcote's undergardener,' Holmes replied coolly. 'He is also the son of the man who conspired with the Moncrieffs' nursemaid to abduct the child Ernest in 1867, but you know him best as the late Mr Bunbury.'

Gregson whistled. 'It sounds like there are some matters you haven't apprised me of, Mr Holmes.'

'It was to do so that we came here, but time has become somewhat pressing,' Holmes said. Efficiently, and with admirable economy, he sketched out what he had learned from police records of Sergeant William Durrington and his legacy, omitting to say by whom we had had the information confirmed. He went on to describe the letters received by Ernest Moncrieff, that we had every reason now to believe had come from Timothy Durrington. He added that Major and Mrs Nepcote had been kind enough to identify their servant's body, and that they were awaiting us in the lobby and doubtless growing rather restive, while their servants had ample opportunity to hide Durrington's personal effects.

He said, 'In my experience, blackmailers almost invariably keep written records of their victims and the evidence they hold against them. Their power relies upon the ability to prove wrongdoing on the part of another. Paper records are almost as important in their profession as in yours, Gregson.'

I said, 'But if the fellow was a gardener, would he be able to read and write?'

'It would be unusual, but hardly unheard of. It is an important question, certainly, since Ernest Moncrieff's blackmailer was either literate enough to pen a letter and to read its reply, or had a close confederate who was.'

Gregson took a moment to absorb this. 'And you will be wanting to search the place for this blackmail material?'

'It would be most irregular to do so on our own,' Holmes agreed demurely. He spoiled the effect by adding, 'And since we were in the building, it seemed only polite to invite you along.'

The inspector said irritably, 'I can send a man with you, but I cannot spare the time myself. This Durrington fellow's dead, but Lord Illingworth's alive and at liberty. Knowing who his victim was will be invaluable, of course, and I'm glad you have found it out for us, but searching the Nepcotes' house at the moment seems like a distraction to me.'

Holmes said, 'I believe that Durrington's recent activities may be most relevant to the question of why he was killed, and therefore of who killed him.'

'Oh, it must be done, of course,' Gregson agreed. 'Northbrook, you'd better go along with Mr Holmes and Dr Watson.'

Constable Northbrook looked delighted to have been assigned the duty, and to have the opportunity to observe Holmes's work. The three of us joined Mrs Nepcote, who was twittering with impatience, and her stoical husband, the major. The lady at once set about attempting to forestall our mission, her first objection being that she had been a keen observer of her gardener's private life and knew it to be a blameless one, into which she could countenance no such prurient intrusion. She then insisted that the feelings of the other servants, who had not yet been told of his death and would be distraught about it, must be respected; and finally, that she had not expected visitors that day and that it would take some time to set the house, which was always scrupulously immaculate, in order. Holmes sternly overrode her absurd protests, with Northbrook's deferential but equally firm support, and at length we set off in the Nepcotes' carriage.

The constable rode above with the coachman, leaving Holmes and myself little alternative but to travel inside with the couple and listen to Mrs Nepcote's interminable monologue, which ranged freely from the horror of her employee's untimely and violent death to the menu for her dinner party with the Marchioness of Ferring on the next Saturday but one.

Major and Mrs Nepcote lived, inevitably, in Belgravia. In its size and grandeur, its pale stone and its porticoed entrance, there was little to choose between their address in Eaton Square and Ernest Moncrieff's house a few streets away. The Nepcotes did, however, possess a considerably bigger garden than the one in which their servant had met his end, with rose beds and herbaceous borders laid out neatly in a concentric pattern, justifying, if not strictly necessitating, their engagement of both a gardener and an undergardener.

During the journey Northbrook had been speaking with the coachman, whose name was Highdown. 'He was quite chatty, sirs,' he told us. 'Said Durrington was friendly enough, but he tended to keep himself to himself. Spent most of his evenings off, and most of his wages, taking classes at the Working Men's College. Highdown says he wanted to better himself.'

'It's a more admirable ambition than becoming a blackmailer,' I observed.

'Yet one of the first things he would have learned, if he were not already able, would be how to read and write,' noted Holmes. 'This is very useful information, Northbrook.' The constable blushed.

Beyond the garden was the mews containing the stables and coach house. The groom and coachman shared a long room built across the very rear of the building, while the two gardeners had smaller garrets facing the house.

It was in Durrington's tiny room that we started our search. The undergardener had slept on a pallet, his clothes hung from a rail or folded in a tiny chest of drawers that was, along with the pallet and an elderly wicker chair, his only furniture.

The three of us stood at the door, gazing in at the cramped space. The room seemed clean enough, and in the winter I imagined that it might feel rather snug, assuming that there were no draughts. Living above horses always tends to provide a comfortable warmth.

Even so, the fact that Ernest Moncrieff and his wife now enjoyed the full benefit of a luxurious townhouse, a few hundred yards from this tiny box of a room in which Timothy Durrington had lived out his private existence, starkly illustrated the disparity which Durrington's father had observed between the two boys' circumstances.

'Well, it doesn't look like this will take us long,' Northbrook observed.

'We should search the rest of the mews, at least,' I said, knowing that the senior gardener and groom, and probably any other of the servants who had so wished, would have had every opportunity to purloin their colleague's property while their employers were with us at Scotland Yard. For now, the other inhabitants of the mews were being given cups of tea in the kitchen; we had been introduced to them briefly as we arrived. 'Perhaps also the house,' I added doubtfully. I could not imagine the major, or more pertinently his wife, readily giving their permission for such an intrusion, nor Gregson, as things stood at the moment, treating the issue of a warrant as a priority.

'The house is a long shot, Watson,' said Holmes. 'The probability is that the material we seek will be in this room, or failing that, elsewhere in this outbuilding. To a gardener, the house is foreign territory to which he would not routinely have access.'

'That's true, sir,' Northbrook agreed. 'My uncle's a gardener for a family in Surrey, and he only gets asked into the house for the servants' Christmas dinner, and one time after my auntie died. Been there twelve years, he has, and only set foot inside those thirteen times.'

Suggesting firmly that we observe his work from the doorway so as not to disturb the scene, Holmes proceeded to inspect every inch of Timothy Durrington's garret, from the wooden beams of the ceiling to the bare boards of the floor.

He first checked the pockets in the various items of clothing, which were empty, and the bedclothes, which were likewise unproductive. He moved on to the chest of drawers, in one of which he found a box of pencils and a sheaf of papers.

The top sheet, though blank, bore the impressions of recent writing having imprinted a sheet above it, and Holmes was able, by careful, light shading of the pencil, to reconstruct the wording. It proved to be nothing more interesting than a written order to a market gardener for seedlings and fertiliser.

The rest of the pile held nothing of an incriminating nature, though Holmes turned up some competently executed landscape drawings, some notes on the history of music and some French vocabulary. 'A man of eclectic interests,' he observed. 'And not altogether practical ones. Durrington would have done more to further himself had he studied botany or horticulture, to which his experience would be relevant.'

'The coachman said he wanted to better himself, not further himself,' Northbrook observed diffidently. I understood his nervousness at finding himself correcting Sherlock Holmes, but my friend acknowledged the point with a thoughtful nod. However deceived Durrington might have been about his true birth, it seemed that he had little interest in making himself more useful as a gardener. Instead, he had been making attempts, however crude, to cultivate the character of a gentleman.

Holmes swiftly exhausted the overt possibilities of the room, and moved on to considering its hidden spaces. 'It is reasonable,' he said, 'to suppose that Durrington was aware of the risk he took, in going to blackmail Ernest Moncrieff in person. Were Moncrieff to be uncooperative, he stood a real chance of being arrested, and this room searched. In that case he would hardly want his records recovered, yet it seems unlikely that he would be willing to destroy them. Ergo, we will find them in the best hiding place he was able to contrive.'

The drawers were easily removed from the small chest, but there was nothing hidden behind them. The linings of the clothes, when slit open, held no secrets, and although there was a small hole in the pallet from which the straw was leaking, enlarging it with a penknife and rummaging vigorously amongst the stuffing uncovered nothing of interest. Through careful probing Holmes discovered a loose floorboard, but when the constable helped him pry it up the floor cavity was equally bereft of useful items.

'He must have hidden it somewhere else,' I noted, rather redundantly.

The room of the senior gardener, Heene, was better furnished, but, when searched, had nothing more to interest us than Durrington's. Nor did the larger room that the groom shared with Highdown, the coachman. When we went downstairs it quickly became clear that both the stable and the coach house were bare rooms, with little in them beyond the usual clutter of such places. I suggested the carriage itself, but Holmes had already satisfied himself during our journey that it contained nothing of interest. 'It was hardly to be supposed that it would,' said Holmes. 'He would have placed his dossier somewhere where it would remain reliably at hand.'

Frustrated, we trooped outside and stood contemplating the beautifully tended flower beds, evidence of Durrington's skill in his job, if not his devotion to it.

'Do you suppose one of the others has taken it, then?' I asked. 'The other gardener, or the groom?'

'Or Highdown,' the policeman pointed out. 'There's nothing to say it was taken while the coach was out, rather than before.'

'If any of them took it, the question of where it is hidden remains much the same as it did before,' said Holmes. 'On the other hand, any thief need not have been one of the servants who sleeps in this building. A set of keys will be kept in the house.'

'Durrington might have posted it to himself at his post office box,' I suggested. 'Or given it to a friend among the household staff for safekeeping.'

'Or a friend who lives somewhere else altogether,' Northbrook noted gloomily. 'Someone he met at the college, maybe.'

The three of us stared morosely across the garden to the house, then Holmes laughed suddenly and slapped his forehead. 'What an imbecile I am!' he cried. 'The answer is so obvious a child could have seen it. Northbrook, please step into the kitchen and ask Mr Heene to join us.'

'Do you think he has it?' I asked as the constable went about this errand. 'The other gardener, I mean?'

Holmes sighed. 'Watson, if you were a gardener and wanted to hide something, where would you think of putting it?'

I frowned. 'Well, I suppose—' I began, and was probably about to say something terribly foolish when Northbrook returned with the senior gardener.

'Ah, Heene,' Holmes said affably. 'Would you tell us, please, where in the garden Durrington was working immediately before his recent disappearance?'

I saw the realisation enter Constable Northbrook's eyes just as it must have done mine.

Five minutes later, after much complaining, Heene was digging up the herbaceous border that Durrington had laid down during his final afternoon at his job. He was watched by the three of us, Major and Mrs Nepcote, and, through various windows, by most of the house's complement of servants.

'Durrington would have known exactly where he buried it,' Holmes was explaining, 'and could have retrieved it with minimal fuss. We do not have the luxury of that knowledge.'

'But this is no good for the plants, sir,' Heene told Holmes. 'No good at all.'

'For God's sake, Heene, we can buy more damned plants,' snapped Major Nepcote, with sudden and quite uncharacteristic vehemence. 'Durrington's dead, and we can't buy him back.

Now stop complaining and put your back into it.' It was the first time I had been able to imagine the mild old gentleman as a commander of men.

After a minute or so more of begrudging digging, Heene's spade hit an obstruction. He took up a trowel, bent down, and carefully uncovered a large package wrapped in oilcloth. It was larger than Durrington's sheet of papers, perhaps the size of a photograph album or scrapbook.

The gardener passed it to Holmes, who seized it with a cry. He cut the string with some secateurs that lay to hand, and hastily unwrapped it.

CHAPTER TWELVE
THE REMINISCENCES OF A BUTLER

Northbrook commandeered a room for us in the main house, from which the servants and, despite Mrs Nepcote's repeated attempts to join us on various pretexts, our hosts, were strictly barred. The worthy policeman even arranged for the kitchen to provide us with sandwiches, which we ate distractedly while Holmes and I inspected with him the contents of Timothy Durrington's dossier.

The package, as I had guessed, contained a scrapbook, one that had never been expensive and the cloth binding of which was now threadbare with age. Peeling from its earliest pages were yellowing, faded cuttings from columns of newsprint dealing with the abduction of the Moncrieff baby in 1867.

'Durrington couldn't have collected these,' I realised. 'He was a baby himself at the time. And Sergeant Durrington was dead when they were published.'

'The mother then, perhaps,' said Holmes. 'This Jane Bramber. Conceivably she assembled these papers as a record of the effect Timothy's father had had on the world. If so, the boy must have inherited it when she died, which my tavern acquaintances tell me occurred when he was ten. The album is of an age with its earliest clippings.'

The newspaper stories contained few details that Holmes and I were not already familiar with, and nothing that challenged the facts of the case. The guilty nursemaid was mentioned, but not named as Laetitia Prism, and there was, as we expected, no reference at all to Thomas Cardew. A wholly separate item drew attention to the sad death of Sergeant William Durrington at Victoria Station, but made no connection between the accident and the Moncrieffs' loss.

'I say, though, Holmes,' I remarked. 'This report says that Durrington's wife and infant son were with him at the time of the accident. Well, I suppose it was easier for them to refer to her as his wife.' It seemed that Jane Bramber had taken young Timothy Durrington to visit relatives in Brighton, and that the child's father had met them at the station. Reading between the lines, the journalist seemed to imply that a fellow passenger had made some lewd comment about Miss Bramber, and that this had provoked the brawl in which Sergeant Durrington had fallen to his death beneath an oncoming train. 'Was that detail mentioned in the police reports?'

'It was not.' Holmes was frowning. 'I suppose she may not have wished to make herself known to the police, especially if she knew that her mate had been present with criminal intentions. It does, I suppose, explain why Durrington wished Ernest deposited at Victoria rather than handed over to him elsewhere. I imagine Jane was there to help conceal the abduction from the public eye.'

'But doesn't that support the idea that Sergeant Durrington intended to swap the children?'

'Hardly, Watson, hardly. A man carrying a single infant would be conspicuous, but a man and a woman carrying twins would seem less remarkable. If the scheme had been aimed towards exchanging the children, which I still doubt, it would have made more sense to do so later, once the ransom had been paid. Leaving young Durrington in a handbag at Victoria Station would have provided no guarantee that he would be mistaken for and brought up as Colonel and Mrs Moncrieff's son, as the story of Ernest Worthing amply demonstrates.'

'It looks as if Timothy Durrington believed it, though, Mr Holmes,' Northbrook noted. While we were speaking he had leafed forward in the scrapbook, to its more recent contents. These were mostly newspaper stories from 1895 about the rediscovery of Ernest Worthing's identity, and the subsequent reports of his engagement and marriage. These were meticulously dated, in a crude but careful hand which we took to be Durrington's own.

As I have said, the story of Ernest Worthing had provoked a great deal of interest from the press at the time, and it seemed that Durrington had collected every report that he could find. As the pages turned, though, an eccentric interpretation of these events began to appear. At first this manifested in nothing more than occasional appearances of question marks, in Durrington's hand, next to the name 'Ernest Moncrieff'. Then a rather shoddy retrospective piece relating to the 1867 abduction was underlined and annotated with various comments calling attention to facts missing from this retelling of the story.

At the end of this excerpt, the biblically confused sentence, 'Happily now, however, after many years wandering in the wilderness, the Moncrieff family's prodigal son has at last been restored,' had been heavily underlined and surrounded with a positive galaxy of question marks.

On the next page, in a society column mentioning the wedding, the name 'Ernest Moncrieff' was crossed out neatly and 'Timothy Durrington' written in its place. From this point, this amendment had been applied consistently.

Some of the articles included photographs: of Ernest, of Algernon and of the late General Moncrieff, among others.

While resemblances within families are rarely straightforward, it was noticeable that Ernest had been passed over by the close similarity that his brother bore to their father. Durrington, on the other hand, had coincidentally shared their slight stature and their darker hair, a fact commented upon with great emphasis in the annotations.

'It seems quite clear,' said Holmes, 'that Durrington developed an *idée fixe* about Ernest Moncrieff's identity that was in itself irrational and quite independent of any truth in the matter. He believed quite sincerely that the babies were swapped, that the man now acknowledged as Ernest Moncrieff had been born to Jane Bramber as Timothy Durrington, and that he himself was General Moncrieff's son, Ernest. Small wonder that he dreamed of exchanging his humble position with Ernest's exalted one.'

Something occurred to me. 'I say, though,' I said again. 'He seems only to have been interested in Ernest.' Algernon and Cecily were mentioned, I realised, only in articles dealing primarily with Ernest's own life. Though their story, that of a man marrying his famous long-lost brother's ward, had also been of interest to the newspapers at the time, none of the column inches devoted to it had been collected by Durrington. 'There isn't even a report of Algernon and Cecily's wedding.'

'Very true, unless there is a second dossier which we have not found. It would appear that Timothy inherited his father's specific ire against Ernest, rather than a grudge against the Moncrieff family at large.'

'But that does not explain why he would have used the name Bunbury,' I pointed out. 'That related to Algernon's shameful secret, not to Ernest at all.'

Turning the page again, we found the letter which Ernest had told us he had written to his blackmailer, objecting in jocular and evidently unconcerned terms to the idea that he was not himself, and warning Durrington that the Moncrieff family fortune was no longer available to be inherited.

'Headed notepaper from his club,' Holmes observed. 'He must have written it there to avoid the eagle eye of Mrs Moncrieff.'

On the page after that was the final item in the scrapbook. It was, again, a letter written on printed notepaper, the heading this time bearing Ernest Moncrieff's own address. The letter was unsigned, and the author had taken steps to disguise their handwriting by printing the words neatly in capital letters:

149 Belgrave Square
London

    Dear Sir,

    Present yourself at this address at 10.15 p.m. on Monday week, to speak to Mr Ernest Moncrieff about a matter to your mutual advantage. Come to the tradesmen's entrance, and give the name 'Bunbury'.

    If you fail to appear there will be no further opportunities for communication with the Moncrieff family.

'This paper is of notably fine quality,' Holmes observed briskly. 'As I have not had the honour of any written communication from the Moncrieffs, I cannot be positive that it is genuine, but neither, I presume, could Durrington. The writing is, I think, female, but the writer has made it deliberately difficult to be certain.'

'Is it Gwendolen?' I asked.

Holmes nodded gravely. 'As the mistress of the house, she is undoubtedly a likely candidate. On the other hand, there is a chance that the paper is a forgery. Though it would make no difference to Durrington, it would tell us whether the writer of the note had access to the genuine article.'

'It wasn't Gwendolen on the balcony, anyway,' I recalled. 'She was wearing a powder-blue gown that evening. Unless she changed, but as the hostess she would hardly have had the opportunity. Holmes... whoever sent this note may well be the murderer.'

'The point had not escaped me, Watson,' he replied drily. 'Whoever it was, they knew that Bunbury would be present and had every opportunity to plan his death.'

'It was a strange venue to choose,' I mused, thinking of Holmes's comments about Lord Arthur Savile a few days earlier. 'Why not ask to meet him somewhere deserted, where he might be made away with in secret?'

'That we cannot know at present, unless it was with the specific intention of making Mabel Goring out to be a murderer.'

'But surely the real killer's Lord Illingworth, like Inspector Gregson's been saying?' asked Northbrook. 'The inspector reckoned he wanted to bump off a blackmailer. Well, we know now that Durrington *was* a blackmailer. And even if that is a woman's handwriting, Illingworth finds it easy enough to get women to do his bidding. Dora Steyne lives and works in the house – she could easily have got hold of the notepaper.'

'I cannot rule it out,' said Holmes, 'but it leaves open a number of questions. Notably, the name Bunbury remains unexplained, though at a further remove. We now know that Durrington gave it because the note asked him to, but why the writer chose it we have no idea.'

'We know the identities of Cecily's blackmailer and of

Ernest's,' I mused, 'but not Algernon's. That is to say, it doesn't look like Durrington. Was it Illingworth?'

'There was nothing at his house to suggest it was,' Northbrook admitted.

'I have an idea regarding that point,' Holmes told us, 'though it is one that concerns me greatly. This case may have ramifications that go some way beyond those we have appreciated so far. And if so, then I fear that Lord Illingworth is but a cog in a larger and more dangerous machine. I propose that you, Northbrook, convey this important evidence to Inspector Gregson with all dispatch.' Closing Durrington's scrapbook, Holmes wrapped it carefully in the oilcloth and retied the package. 'Meanwhile, Watson and I shall endeavour to determine where the Moncrieffs keep their notepaper, and whether this is a specimen of it.'

We bade farewell to Major Nepcote and his wife, who by now was quite frantic with frustrated interest in what we had found out, and would doubtless spread her own imagined version of it throughout her acquaintance by the end of the afternoon, and stepped out into the cool spring sunshine.

'Constable Northbrook,' said Holmes, 'we know that Durrington was operating a post office box. We do not have the number, but it seems likely that it would have been either in a post office near to here, or near to somewhere else he frequented, such as the Working Men's College. You have his description. Could you see what you may find out?'

Northbrook promised that he would try, and set off to find a cab to carry him and Durrington's scrapbook back to Scotland Yard.

From Eaton Square, Belgrave Square was but a short walk along Belgrave Place, and it was scarcely more than five minutes before we were approaching Number 149.

As we neared the house, a figure emerged from Number 148,

the house belonging to Mrs Winterbourne, and I recognised it as Mrs Teville. She wore a coat over a fashionable dress in what, once again, looked like an attempt to recapture her lost youth. Over it was thrown the mink stole she had worn to the ball, unless it was another one; in full daylight it looked rather less pale and faded.

'Mr Holmes, Dr Watson,' she exclaimed. 'I see your helpfulness to the police has not yet exhausted itself. Are you here to see dear Mr Moncrieff?'

'If he is at home,' Holmes replied, rather shortly.

Feeling a need to moderate my friend's brusqueness, I added, 'The police are grateful for your testimony regarding the night of the ball, Mrs Teville. You may have helped prevent a grave injustice.'

'You are too kind,' she replied. 'I merely answered the inspector's questions honestly.'

'Nevertheless,' said Holmes, gazing at her with greater alertness, 'you may have prevented suspicion from wrongly falling on an innocent young wife.'

I realised that he had carefully left possible the implication that it was Cecily Moncrieff whom she had protected – assuming, of course, that she had not heard about Mabel Goring's arrest. I watched for any signs of concern for the safety of the woman who might be her daughter, but saw no untoward reaction.

I also searched her face for any family resemblance to Cecily Moncrieff, but her make-up disguised the contours of her visage too effectively.

Mrs Teville noticed my attention and averted her eyes coyly. 'I hoped to visit dear Mrs Winterbourne, but I find that she is elsewhere. There is a solidarity between us widows, you know. We see the world in a way which other women cannot. Perhaps between widowers there is a similar freemasonry, Dr Watson? I am right that your poor wife is deceased, am I not?'

To my consternation, I realised that one of our potential suspects was flirting with me. Stiffly, I replied, 'I have that misfortune, madam.'

'It is harder for a man than for a woman, I think,' Mrs Teville speculated. 'We women must learn resilience early in life, whereas a man is often helpless without a woman to protect him.'

I have to confess that I felt a pang at this. The loss of Mary had been a hard blow to bear, and even five years later I remembered feeling for a while as if I could barely stand upright without her. Of course, during that time Holmes, the other chief support in my life, had also been absent and assumed to be dead.

'Such has not been my experience,' my friend told the widow firmly, whether in response to my distress or not I could not say. 'The bachelor existence seems to me an eminently satisfactory state, and I would exchange it for no other.'

'And I am sure that the housekeeper Dr Watson mentions so often yet so briefly in his stories plays her part in that, Mr Holmes. A woman need not be a man's social equal to be indispensable.'

I said, 'I should find widowerhood to be more supportable, I think, had Mary given me an heir. Has fortune favoured you with children, Mrs Teville?'

It was an ungallant ploy, perhaps, but the woman had shown little enough regard for my feelings. Her eyes narrowed and the enticing smile fell from her lips. Shortly, she said, 'Sadly it has not. Perhaps one day I shall marry again,' she added, defying me to make any comment about her age.

I said, 'If that is your hope, then I hope you achieve it. Like Holmes, I find a single man's existence to my preference for now.'

'Then I wish you every joy of it,' said Mrs Teville neutrally, and passed on her way down the street.

Holmes knocked on the door of Number 149 and Merriman the butler showed us up to the drawing room, where we found the missing Mrs Winterbourne being entertained by Gwendolen Moncrieff. They sat over tea, Gwendolen brisk and golden-haired and talkative, and Mrs Winterbourne dark in her widow's weeds but no less cheerful in her speech.

'Mr Holmes,' said Gwendolen, smiling sternly as she greeted us, 'I understand that you have been making some most offensive insinuations to my mother.' I recalled suddenly that this young woman was the only one of the younger Moncrieffs who was not, to our knowledge, being blackmailed. 'Mama dislikes insinuations almost as much as she dislikes categorical statements. I must ask you not to do such a thing again, or at least not in my absence. I very much hope next time to witness her reaction.'

'I can make no promises on that score, Mrs Moncrieff,' said Holmes. 'Since what Lady Bracknell unfortunately mistook for an insinuation was a simple statement of fact, I am unable to foresee how she may interpret any observation of mine in any future conversation.'

Mrs Winterbourne laughed unkindly. 'One does not have a *conversation* with Lady Bracknell, Mr Holmes. You might as well say that a person coughing at a concert is in conversation with the orchestra. At most one can hope to punctuate, never to divert, the inexorable movement of the whole.'

Gwendolen frowned. 'I do not think that you should speak of my mother in that way, Mrs Winterbourne. Mama does not care for it when people say true things about her.'

'Whether she cares for the things that she hears depends on her opinion of the speaker, not on theirs of her,' said Mrs Winterbourne carelessly. 'Others' opinions of Lady Bracknell affect her no more than that of a single blade of grass affects a hurricane.'

Much though I agreed with Mrs Winterbourne's view, expressing it so bluntly to Lady Bracknell's daughter seemed to me a trifle ungallant. Had the widow been a man I would certainly have remonstrated with her, but since the situation was one of a lady commenting on another lady to a third, I felt rather unclear as to where my chivalrous duties lay.

'How poetically you express yourself, Mrs Winterbourne,' Gwendolen observed placidly. 'I suppose you have had a great deal of practice during your various courtships.'

'I say, that's rather below the belt,' I began, then stopped in embarrassment at my appalling turn of phrase.

Mrs Winterbourne laughed at my discomfiture. 'How delightful to see a gentleman so familiar with the Queensberry Rules! But Mrs Moncrieff and I are old friends, Dr Watson. I don't think we have any need to trouble the dear marquess.'

'I had no idea that you and that nobleman were acquainted, Mrs Winterbourne,' Gwendolen calmly replied. 'Although he has been widowed a short while, I am told his recent decline has been entirely mental. He might live many years yet, so I fear he is unlikely to be the kind of gentleman whose admiration you would wish to cultivate.'

Now thoroughly out of my depth, I looked to Holmes for assistance. He was standing by the writing desk which sat open by the window. As I glanced at him, away from our hostess and her guest, who were now entirely preoccupied with one another, I saw that the writing desk held a small pile of pieces of paper. Holmes had purloined a single sheet, which he now folded and pocketed.

Oblivious, Mrs Winterbourne laughed again, this time in genuine amusement. 'You are quite keeping up the family tradition of crushing repartee, Mrs Moncrieff. I do not think, though, that you have quite matched your mother's mastery of indifference to the import of others' remarks.'

Gwendolen said, 'I am pleased to see how your own conversation has improved since the foolish prattling of our schooldays, Mrs Winterbourne. I notice, for instance, that your consonants are considerably better enunciated.'

'Holmes,' I said urgently, 'I think perhaps we'd better leave.'

'Of course, Watson,' Holmes replied, as genially as if the conversational temperature in the room were many degrees warmer. 'It has been most pleasing to renew our acquaintance, Mrs Moncrieff, Mrs Winterbourne.'

Not for the first time, I hurried from the room, and from the Moncrieffs' house, disconcerted and discomfited. Holmes, however, showed no unease at all.

'The notepaper is identical,' he told me, as soon as we were outside the house. 'Any of the house's visitors or occupants could have abstracted it from the bureau as readily as I.'

He showed me the sheet as we strolled along the square away from Number 149. 'There is no name in the heading. A household's notepaper is normally printed in several variations – versions bearing the names of the master and mistress of the house, and of any family members residing with them, and some which carry no name but the address alone. Paper like this is intended for guests who wish to write a letter while at the house.'

I said, 'But surely Gwendolen might have used the generic paper instead of her own?'

Holmes nodded. 'She would hardly have identified herself in writing to a blackmailer.'

'But for all we know, Cecily might have written it,' I observed, 'or a guest like Mrs Winterbourne, or a servant like Dora.' Indeed, this case had been full of women, from the redoubtable Lady Bracknell to her younger relatives and their widowed friends; not to mention Mrs Nepcote, who, while not widowed, was surely likely to become so at an eminently remarriageable age.

'Not all servants are literate, even the indoor kind,' Holmes reminded me absently. 'But once again we have more information than before, and that never goes amiss. And now, I think, to Lowndes Square, as we are in the area.'

'Are we to talk to Cecily next?' I asked, but Holmes smiled enigmatically and set off at a stride towards the west exit from the square.

Again, the walk to Algernon and Cecily's house from Ernest and Gwendolen's took us less than ten minutes. Holmes's knock was answered once more by Algernon's solemn-faced butler, Lane.

'Mr and Mrs Moncrieff are at home, gentlemen,' he told us. 'Shall I show you up?'

'Not today, Lane, thank you,' Holmes said breezily. 'It is you who we have come to see. May we step into your pantry, perhaps?'

Lane frowned in elaborate concern. 'Really, sir, I think I should inform Mr Moncrieff that you are here. I am sure there is nothing that I can tell you that he would not.'

Holmes said, 'Oh, I am perfectly certain that that is untrue, Lane. Will you admit us, or shall we stand here conversing loudly until we attract attention from the rest of the household?'

Lane looked behind him in alarm. 'This is most irregular, sir,' he observed. 'But it seems you leave me no choice.'

He took us through to his pantry, a snug room where the family silverware was kept under lock and key in glass-fronted cabinets. As is often the case, the room also functioned as Lane's sitting room, and curtains concealed a further area in which he presumably slept. We settled ourselves in the three stiff-backed chairs that stood by the tiny fireplace.

Though the butlers in such distinguished households are practised paragons of imperturbability, I thought that Lane's studied gravity concealed a certain nervousness at having the world's most famous detective so unexpectedly occupying his private space. Although I had no idea why we were there, I tried to reassure him with a friendly smile, which he regarded with unblinking disdain.

Lane cleared his throat. 'Mr Holmes, I would appreciate knowing what this visit concerns.'

'You have been with your master for some time, haven't you?' Holmes asked him.

The butler replied, 'Not so very long, sir. As you know, Mr Moncrieff is a relatively young gentleman. I entered his service when he came up to town from Oxford, some five years ago. Before that I was in the employment of a Mr Brooklands.'

'But I imagine he has confided in you a great deal during that time. Especially, perhaps, before his marriage.'

Lane said, 'In my experience, confiding in their manservants is often the habit of young bachelor gentlemen.'

'It is perhaps rash of them,' suggested Holmes.

'I have heard others in my profession express that opinion,' Lane said gravely, 'often with detailed examples. It is essential, however, for a young gentleman to find someone whom he can trust absolutely, and we are privileged to assist him in the process of elimination.'

'And have you been discreet with Mr Moncrieff's confidences, Lane?' my friend asked.

Lane hesitated. 'Before I answer that question, sir, I should like to know which answer is likely to cause me the lesser distress in the future.'

Holmes smiled thinly. 'Your candour does you credit, Lane.'

'I find it preferable to honesty, sir.'

'Mr Moncrieff, on the other hand, has apparently served himself less well. At least, he has been approached by somebody who claims to hold information that could discredit him. And since the knowledge among his circle that he was in the habit of concealing his youthful exploits under the guise of visits to his invalid friend Mr Bunbury has done little towards that end, we must assume that there is something more disreputable to be found in the detail of those affairs.'

'I believe that might be a safe assumption,' Lane said guardedly.

'Allow me to assure you that my present interest is not in those details,' Holmes told him. 'I would not wish to tax your loyalties, Lane.'

'I fear they could scarcely bear any increase in taxation, sir.'

Holmes said, 'While Mr Moncrieff's exploits presumably involved other individuals not of his circle, a man with the wit to invent the Bunbury alibi would also have the basic common sense to conceal his identity from such individuals. Only somebody close to him would be in a position to know both what he had been doing and that it was he who had been doing it.'

'Regrettably, sir, your argument is unassailable,' Lane agreed ruefully.

'So, Lane, pray tell me the answer to my question. An honest one, if you please.'

Carefully, Lane said, 'There are, as you surmise, certain parties who have been in receipt of information from certain quarters about Mr Moncrieff's former activities.'

'Those quarters being these ones?' Holmes gestured around us at Lane's abode.

'Yes, sir.'

'I shall require more particulars,' my friend said. 'The whole story, if you please.'

Lane sighed. 'I apologise in advance for the dullness of this reminiscence, but I was once married. The occurrence arose from a series of misunderstandings between a young person, myself, and ultimately her father, brothers and uncles. It was not an outcome in which I found any great satisfaction, and I took steps to ensure that its consequences for me would be as limited as possible.'

'I understand your meaning, Lane,' Holmes said, 'although I can hardly congratulate you on it.'

'No, sir. Despite what one sometimes hears, it was not an occasion for congratulation. However, I believe that the young person involved, and the still younger person who ultimately eventuated, have since been well looked after by their vigilant relatives. As you might suppose, I would be most reluctant to disrupt that cheerful family situation in any way. So you may imagine my dismay when, some months ago, I was approached by a party who seemed keen to make them aware of my identity and whereabouts.'

'This person already knew of this family, and their connection with you?' Holmes asked.

'Yes, sir. Another individual, who knew me at the time, had recently visited the house as a coachman, having gained employment in that capacity with Sir Clapham Woods, and recognised me. I believe it is from him that this party had gained his information.'

'Did the party have a name?' Holmes asked. 'Could you describe him?'

'He gave his name as Mr Broadwater.' Briefly, Lane outlined the scarred, broken-nosed, cauliflower-eared appearance of a man clearly matching the bruiser Algernon knew by that name. 'He told me that, if I wanted my former connections to persist in their happy state of ignorance, I should let him know any regrettable secrets I might be aware of from Mr Moncrieff's past. Fortunately, I had a considerable stock of them to hand.'

I found myself unable to stay silent any longer. I burst out, 'You mean that you betrayed your employer's confidence to escape being forced to support the wife and child you abandoned?'

The butler nodded gravely. 'In a nutshell, sir.'

'I see,' I said, rather lamely. 'Well, that's despicable behaviour, Lane.'

'So I have been led to believe, sir.'

He turned his attention back to Holmes, who asked patiently, 'Did you have the impression that this Mr Broadwater was acting alone?'

'Since you mention it, sir, I am certain that he was no more the chief instigator of the affair than I was its chief object. He referred more than once to a principal to whom he was answerable.'

'And did you ever meet him?' Holmes asked, with the lightest of emphasis on the final word.

Lane corrected him at once. 'Her, sir. Broadwater always referred to his principal using feminine terms. I regret to say that that was all that I was able to learn.'

'So there is a woman behind all this!' I said excitedly.

'So it would seem, Watson. Well, Lane,' said Holmes. 'What you have told me puts me in rather a difficult position, doesn't it? I should inform your employer of your disloyalty. Indeed, since the information you supplied was used for criminal purposes, I should inform the police. Why are you smiling, Lane? This is a serious matter.'

Lane did his best to look grave again. He said, 'I am sorry, sir. In my experience, sir, when gentlemen tell servants what they *should* do, it is invariably because their intention is to do otherwise.'

'I see.' I could see that Holmes was trying not to smile himself now. 'Well, Lane, given your employer's character I can see how you might have reached that conclusion, but I wouldn't rely on it. In this instance, you are fortunate enough to be correct. I am still working out the possible consequences of this whole affair, but I may need to call upon your help further before it is over. I presume that I may rely upon your cooperation?'

'I shall do my best, as always, to give satisfaction,' Lane replied gloomily.

With our permission, he showed us out through the servants' entrance so that we would not accidentally bump into Algernon or Cecily. As we were leaving, I asked, 'I say, Lane, do you know Durrington, Major Nepcote's gardener?'

'I seldom associate with my employer's brother's friends' gardeners, sir,' said Lane. 'But if we should happen to meet, I shall certainly remember you to him.'

We walked to the Knightsbridge Road, where we hailed a cab to return us to Baker Street. As we passed from the grandeur of Belgravia back through the antique opulence of Mayfair and into the shabbier gentility of our own district of Marylebone, I asked Holmes, 'Do you think it's the same woman as the one who wrote that note to Durrington? The woman on the balcony? Could one person be behind all of this?'

'Perhaps,' is all he would say, and I could see that he was deep in contemplation.

We arrived at our rooms in Baker Street to find Inspector Gregson pacing impatiently back and forth across the sitting room. He bristled with suppressed excitement, which upon our appearance burst forth into full expression.

'He's confessed!' he cried, brandishing several sheets of typewritten paper at us.

CHAPTER THIRTEEN
A WOMAN OF SOME IMPORTANCE

'Lord Illingworth?' Holmes asked at once.

'None other,' confirmed Gregson. 'This is an admission of guilt, or as good as one, signed in his own hand and posted to Scotland Yard on the day he went missing.'

'So you still do not have him in custody?'

'No.' Gregson drooped slightly. 'I'm sorry to say we are nowhere close to it. But this is the last of the evidence we needed to confirm his guilt.'

Holmes took the letter from Gregson and examined it minutely, fingering it, sniffing it and holding it up to the light. He pronounced that it had been typed upon a high-quality brand of paper favoured by the civil and diplomatic service, using a nearly new Remington Number Six machine.

'We had come to that conclusion ourselves,' Gregson replied irritably. 'Of course, the first thing we did after reading it was to put it next to the samples we took from Illingworth's study. The paper stock and the typewriting both match.'

Holmes said, 'The letters on the right-hand centre of the keyboard have been struck with some force. Is that in line with Lord Illingworth's habits?'

Gregson looked even more irritated. 'We can check that, of course.'

Holmes said, 'It is no great matter. It might indicate intensity of emotion, or merely a need for haste. You say it was posted on Tuesday?'

Gregson nodded. 'We assume that he wrote it following the ball at the Moncrieffs', and posted it before absconding later that day.'

Holmes nodded gravely. 'He posted it, I would estimate, at a little after half past one o'clock, at the post office at the corner of Piccadilly and Albermarle Street, while wearing a pinstripe suit and a navy ulster.' Knowing that my friend had come by this knowledge by nothing more miraculous than simple observation, and indeed that I could have told him the same myself, I was amused by the expression of astonishment and awe that crossed Gregson's face.

Aloud, however, the inspector simply said, 'But what do you make of the substance, Mr Holmes?'

Holmes read it aloud. It was more a statement than a letter, and it opened abruptly.

The life that I have led is one that would be judged wicked in the eyes of the world, were they ever to be granted the opportunity to behold it. To deny it would be both futile and tiresome, and while I am frequently the former, I have striven never to become the latter.

Such a Puritanical verdict would be equally tiresome, however, for moral generalities and other old-fashioned theories hold little interest for me. The only disgrace is to betray one's own ideals, and mine are the joy, the beauty and the colour to be found in an unfettered life. It follows, then, that the only sin of which I could be guilty is to be dismal, ugly or drab.

I fear that I must now confess that I have been all three.

When I speak of my indifference towards the judgement of others, I refer of course to human society at large. Society in its more elevated sense, that enlightened echelon of English public life that my peers and I occupy, is another matter entirely. Their opinion of me has a very practical effect upon my freedom to live the life of which I speak.

It is indeed true that my acquaintances consider me very wicked, but in Society a reputation for wickedness is the cause of fascination, not of revulsion, for reputation is a sketch, a mere cartoon of reality. What might be shocking if we saw it in bright colour or solid form, given full and vivid life by the skill of the painter or sculptor, appears harmless when rendered in mere lines of pencil, by however great an artist. Think of Leonardo's drawings of anatomical dissections, and compare their attenuated fascination with the ghastly effect of even a glimpse of the hideous reality.

'I have to say this does not read very like a confession, Gregson,' Holmes noted, interrupting himself, 'despite the allusion to some offence of a nature so aesthetic as to elude me entirely. Does he eventually mention the murder?'

Gregson sighed. 'I suggest that you carry on reading,' he said. Holmes continued.

I know my reputation well. It is barely exaggerated, and in places falls far short of the reality. I have taken my pleasures where I chose, heedless of the injury to others. I have worked my will upon women who were beautiful, brilliant and blameless, and on exceptional occasions all three. I have publicly disowned my dalliances and their consequences, though privately I believe I have been generous enough to settle at least some of the grievances so incurred.

Of none of this am I ashamed, nor do I apologise for it.

A few episodes reached a less satisfactory conclusion, however, and recent events have conspired to return one of these in particular to my mind.

I met Violet Cardew more than twenty years ago. Unmarried at twenty-two, she was quite the prettiest trinket I had seen, and I was determined to make her my plaything. I was but twenty-five myself, and had no expectations of the peerage into which I would come some thirteen years later, but even so I was well practised in making myself agreeable to women. It took some work to achieve, but eventually Violet was persuaded to elope with me.

I have generally found my conquests among a rank beneath my own in society, but Violet was different, not merely a beauty but an heiress. She was the daughter of Thomas Cardew, a man of good family who, though he lacked the title of nobility, was exceedingly well endowed with a far more essential social lubricant. Cardew had a male ward also, some years younger, but it was understood that his fortune would go to his flesh and blood.

I suppose that rather than running away with me, I might have prevailed upon her to enter a more traditional arrangement, but why would I have done so? I had no need for Cardew's money, my mother gave me all the support I needed, and the encumbrance of a wife was not one that I sought then any more than I do now.

It was some time, therefore, before the subject of matrimony was broached between us. As the months passed, however, the topic became more pressing, until she issued me with an ultimatum. She insisted that her child should be acknowledged as mine, and she herself regarded by the world as my wife, even if the arrangements were made belatedly. I felt no such compunction, preferring our affairs to continue as they were, and I told her so in no uncertain terms.

It was an ugly act, and its consequences were dismal and drab. Though she had threatened to return to her father, Violet was too proud to turn to him for help, and too ashamed to turn elsewhere. After the child was born she took her own life, and the infant was sent to live with its grandfather and adoptive uncle.

As I am sure the police have by now established, that child was Cecily Cardew, with whom I was taking the air last fateful night, and her uncle was our host, Ernest Moncrieff, known at the time as Jack Worthing.

'Ah,' commented Holmes. 'Finally, His Lordship approaches the point.'

With Thomas Cardew dead, neither of them suspects my past connection with the family, and nor I believe does anybody else, even the many-eyed Lady Bracknell.

I realised that young Cecily was my daughter, of course, as soon as I began to hear reports of Ernest Moncrieff's remarkable history, and on my return to London from the embassy in Vienna I began to ingratiate myself with the family, hoping for regular communication with her. I suffered a grave disappointment a few years ago: another child of mine, of whom I became fond later in his life, and whom I offered a place at my side, thanks to the pernicious influence of his mother left me for a Puritan wife, taking both of them away with him to America. I hoped to avoid such a disappointment with Cecily, especially since it seems she is carrying my grandchild.

Even so, I was cautious, very cautious, about dropping any hint that I might have known her parents.

The reasons for this should be clear. As I have said, my expectations in the next world are of no interest to me. Society is the only divinity I recognise, and its opprobrium the only judgement I fear. I understood from an early age that, if I confined my attentions to women of lower rank, I would be considered deliciously wicked without attracting any but the most trivial condemnation from my peers.

For Violet's sake, however, I broke with this prudent habit and dallied for once with a woman of some importance. She was a respected young woman of nearly my own class, and unlike most of my mistresses I did not merely ruin, but destroyed her.

If this were known, my reputation would no longer be a thrilling thing, but one of horror. The foreign would become familiar; the sketch would be made grisly flesh. I would keep my title, to be sure, and the wealth to which I am now accustomed, but I did well enough without those. Rather, the respect of my equals, my position in Society, would be denied to me. I would no longer be tolerated except at its very fringes. I should become an outcast, as unwelcome as a fallen woman or a misbegotten child.

At this I could no longer keep silent. 'What a contemptible specimen!' I exclaimed, outraged by the immorality and selfishness espoused in Illingworth's testament. 'Such hypocrisy, after he himself ruined those women and fathered those children!'

Holmes nodded. 'I quite understand the strength of

your sentiment, Watson, and naturally I too deplore the earl's behaviour. Yet I fear that in branding him a hypocrite you are misjudging him. The attitudes he speaks of here are those of society, not his own. Whatever else we may say of this tract, the writer displays considerable clarity regarding his own character.'

'That is hardly the point,' I complained.

'Perhaps not, Watson. Perhaps not, indeed. Shall we continue?'

This fear is why I have listened most earnestly, and reciprocated by zealously assenting to every proposition put to me, when approached by a person who knew of my history with the Cardew family. There can be few crimes more dismal, ugly and drab than blackmail, for it is the one crime in which the victims are as much to blame as the perpetrators.

At this person's bidding (or rather, that of her intermediary, for to my knowledge I have never met her, nor have I learned anything more of her than that she is of the female sex) I have invested all but a fraction of my own wealth in a body named the Peruvian Railway Company, and moreover have used the weight of my superior experience and wisdom to persuade many of my acquaintance to ruin themselves in the same project. Where they have been resistant, I have passed on via my liaison such damaging information as I know of them, so that they too may fall victim to his employer's extortion.

Now those wells, too, have started to run dry and I have been pressed into worse acts, ones which I would never have considered in my days as a carefree rake. Whatever I was then, even in the case of Violet, I had never been tempted to become involved in murder. Had I been, I should of course have succumbed at once, for that is the proper way to treat temptations, but, despite everything else, such urges do not belong to my nature. It is not a matter of conscience, but merely of temperament.

Nevertheless, when I took Cecily into the garden last night I knew that she would be faced with the sight of a dead body, for I had a hand in placing it there. You may think this reckless, given her condition, and perhaps it was. Perhaps I showed it to her out of curiosity, to see how much she had inherited of my own amused detachment from the travails of the world. If she had proven as weak and tender-hearted as her mother, why then perhaps I should not have wished for a grandchild by her.

Or perhaps I only hoped that I might afford myself the paternal opportunity of comforting her in her distress. There was precious little else I could do to wring any satisfaction from the situation.

I do not apologise for this either, since Cecily acquitted herself admirably. What I do regret is that I have allowed the fiends who have tormented me to entangle her in their poisoned web, and that I even went so far as to do their work for them, writing to her in my capacity as an anonymous parent, though it ended any chance of ever calling myself a father to her, with the end of gaining her fortune also for their sordid fraud.

Reflecting on this unworthy act has brought me experience of a wholly new sensation. I speak of that white-faced winnower of self-regard that men call shame.

I have, you may be sure, made enquiries into the identity of the woman at the centre of this web, who has so neatly trapped me and parcelled me up to consume at her leisure, but she has concealed herself too well. She has confederates in Vienna, for it was there that I was first approached some six months ago. I believe she is a lady, with a status acquired perhaps by marriage, but beyond that I remain, as she intends, entirely ignorant.

It may be that she is someone from my past, seeking her revenge. I have known great bitterness expressed by those who loved me once, especially those since burdened with children.

Whoever she is, now that she has left me trussed up ready for the police she will not sit idly on her silken strands. My usefulness to her is largely spent, and exposing me will be no great sacrifice. My role in Violet's death will be known, and so will Cecily's parentage. Poor girl, who grew up with the benefit of neither parent and has done nothing to deserve the disgrace that will be heaped upon her.

Well, nothing can be done about it now. Cecily knows already that her parent is false, and soon she will learn that a man whom she has thought a friend has betrayed her. That she will come to hate me is inevitable, and my only comfort shall be that I shall not be here to suffer it.

I assure the police that there is nothing to be gained by searching for me, not even the opportunity to hold me to account for my past misdeeds. A return to the past is only sought by the guilty and the hopelessly nostalgic. They are the irredeemable seeking the impossible.

Time is a river, ever flowing onward, and for me that river is at its end. If you remember me, remember me as a man who tried everything except humility, and who succeeded in everything except nobility.

Illingworth

'It sounds as if he's drowned himself in the Thames,' I said callously, remembering that when we had last seen the earl he had been heading towards the Embankment, and hoping that it was true. The contempt shown for others in Illingworth's account, especially women and the children and grandchild of his own blood, had given me a violent loathing for the man. Although he could hardly have jumped from the Embankment in broad daylight without exciting the attention of witnesses, it seemed very possible that he had remained there until dusk, or walked along the bank until he reached some more secluded spot for suicide.

'That is what he would prefer us to think,' said Gregson. 'He will be hiding out somewhere in the countryside, or perhaps lying low at the docks trying to buy passage abroad.'

'I incline to Watson's view of the matter,' Holmes observed. 'The account seems excessively direct. It does not read like the work of a man who hopes to evade justice by earthly means.'

'But what of the effect on our case, Mr Holmes?' Gregson asked. 'Illingworth admits that he had a part in Timothy Durrington's murder, even if he stops short of saying that he did the deed himself.'

'That part seems hedged around with qualification,' Holmes replied. 'He speaks of being "involved" in murder, and of having "a hand" in the corpse's presence in the garden. There is not the wholehearted candour with which he speaks of his career as a seducer.'

'Well, a man can't be arrested for seduction,' objected Gregson. 'Not unless he makes a promise to marry the woman, and it doesn't sound like His Lordship made a habit of that.'

'Yet his words on the murder incriminate him quite sufficiently to be arrested. My conclusion is that he participated in a conspiracy to murder, but was not himself the murderer.'

I wondered whether it was necessarily true that Illingworth was being wholly candid in his account. The earl had first been approached by his blackmailers in Vienna, and had re-established communication with Cecily on his return. Had his mysterious tormentors instructed him to cultivate her acquaintance? Or had they perhaps merely given him the information he needed and trusted in his character for the rest? The incident with his natural son would have suggested his likely inclination in the matter.

'To me it looks as if he is angling for revenge,' said Gregson. 'He makes it sound as if this blackmailing female conceived the plot to kill Durrington, so that even if we catch him, he knows we will be going after her as well. Who knows whether it is true?'

'In that case,' Holmes said, 'the document's evidential value would be worthless. If he invented this woman's involvement in a murder plot, why not invent the plot itself?'

'But Durrington *was* murdered,' Gregson objected.

'Yet you contend that this account of the murder is unreliable. It is true that Illingworth might be a vindictive liar who is willing to risk gaol or the gallows to bring his blackmailer down, but I think it a remote contingency. I think it more likely that this is Illingworth's last testament, and perhaps the most honest statement of his life.'

'Well, either way we need to find him,' said Gregson. 'It has been two days already.'

'Then dredge the Thames,' said Holmes shortly. 'Did Constable Northbrook have any success, incidentally, in tracking down the post office box Durrington kept?'

'Oh, we found it,' Gregson said. 'It was held at the nearest office to the Working Men's College, but it was empty. The postmaster recognised Durrington's description, but he says there has been no post for him for two weeks.'

'A pity. It was a remote contingency, but one worth checking. Well, Inspector, if you need us tomorrow, Watson and I will be in search of the sinister spider woman of whom the earl writes so colourfully.'

'Well, I think you're wasting your time, and you think I'm

wasting mine,' said Gregson dolefully as he picked up his hat. 'Time will tell who is in the right, I suppose.'

He bade us good night and left, leaving Holmes and me alone.

Mrs Hudson bustled back in once the inspector was gone, bringing us tea and some letters that had arrived for us during the day. I leafed idly through missives from friends, professional colleagues and an overenthusiastic reader pointing out some inaccuracies regarding Sikh nomenclature which he claimed to have found in *The Sign of the Four*, before opening one which – though I should perhaps have been expecting it – made me gasp in affronted incredulity.

It was a single sheet of notepaper onto which words of newsprint, cut from a newspaper, had been stuck with glue. It read:

DR WATSON

WE KNOW WHO VISITED YOU LAST NIGHT, AND WHY

IT IS NOTHING TO US BUT RICH RESPECTABLE

ELDERLY PATIENTS MAY BE LESS TOLERANT

IF YOU COOPERATE THEY NEED NEVER KNOW

WHILE YOU AWAIT OUR INSTRUCTIONS YOU

SHOULD CONSIDER WHAT FUNDS YOU HAVE TO USE

ALSO WHAT INFORMATION YOU CAN GIVE ON

MR SHERLOCK HOLMES

It was signed, improbably enough, 'A FRIEND'.

'The sheer effrontery of this!' I exclaimed, enraged, as I passed the letter to Holmes for his consideration. He seized on it with a cry of joy, delighted to have material evidence of the blackmailer in his hands.

'Great heavens,' he said, raising an eyebrow. 'They wish to

discover *my* guilty secrets? But my dear fellow, you have been publishing them for all to read in the popular press for some time now. If they can find anything more to my discredit than the peccadilloes with which you regularly entertain your readers, they are welcome to try.'

Two minutes later, after scrutinising the note intently with his magnifying glass, he passed it back to me with a grunt of disappointment. 'The words are clipped from widely available London newspapers – the very editions that mentioned our involvement in Lord Arthur Savile's arrest, if I am not mistaken – and the paper and gum are such as any cheap stationer in the capital might sell. The scissors used were somewhat blunt, but beyond that I can detect no trace of individuality. Of course, since you have advertised my deductive methods to the reading public across the nation, we can expect a similar caution to be applied to all threatening missives sent to this address in future. Have you the envelope?'

I passed it to him, and he perused it with equal care before setting it aside. 'The handwriting is the same as that of the letter to Durrington,' he observed. 'Observe the "B"s of "221B Baker Street". The curls continue to the left of the upright at the top and bottom, in a way that matches those of "BUNBURY". Seeing this I am more confident that the hand is a female one.'

'But do you think that she, or they, really know who visited me?' I asked. 'It could well have been Broadwater who observed my visitor's arrival, but Lady Goring had taken care to be anonymous. He could not also have been watching Sir Robert Chiltern's house, but another of their confederates could have been. If that person noted the time when she left and returned, they could easily put two and two together. If Lady Goring becomes embroiled in a sordid scandal I shall never forgive myself!' I declared. I added ruefully, 'And neither, I am sure, will Lord Goring.'

'It is possible,' Holmes admitted, 'but I do not believe so. This note is not a subtle one. It does not hint, but states its case and purpose bluntly. If our blackmailers knew that Lady Goring was your visitor, they would have said so. They would have had no trouble finding her name in newsprint, as it is rarely out of the society pages. That would have made for a much more compelling threat, given your well-known tenderness towards the weaker sex. That does not mean that they are not taking steps to find out the identity of your visitor, but this is, I think, a bow drawn at a venture.'

'Damn the woman!' I swore, meaning, of course, the malicious letter-writer rather than Mabel Goring. 'However are we to bring her to justice, Holmes?' I wondered. 'She takes such pains to be avoid being known to anyone. Unless we find this Broadwater fellow and follow him, I can't see how we can track her down.'

'Broadwater would surely be too canny for such tricks, Watson,' Holmes said, 'and we have no way of knowing when he is next likely to appear. But even setting aside Lord Illingworth's speculations, by now we have a great deal of information about this woman, her techniques and motives.

'She is utterly without compunction, both in whom she makes her victim and in how far she will then degrade them. She operates through at least one intermediary in London, and others in Vienna. She coerces her victims into revealing compromising information about others, who can then be blackmailed in turn, extending the network of those bound to her. And she peremptorily invited Algernon Moncrieff and others to invest in a dubious enterprise for which we now have a name.'

He lapsed once again into silence, staring into the embers of the fire as he drew slowly on his pipe, and after a while I gave up the idea of eliciting anything more from him and went to bed.

In the morning I emerged to find him sitting in exactly the same position, the fire and the pipe long since cold.

Mrs Hudson's breakfast seemed to invigorate him, however, and shortly he was remarking, 'The Peruvian Railway Company is not a name with which I am familiar, I confess. As a rule, matters of business are not among those in which I interest myself. However, I know somebody who will be able to advise us on the matter.'

Sitting at the bureau, he dashed off a quick note, then opened the window and summoned one of the Irregulars from the street outside.

'Alfie, take this to an MP named Mr Kelvil, at the House of Commons, and wait for an answer,' he told the scruffy lad who answered his summons. The boy wore a threadbare jacket and an ancient rugby cap that, as far as I could tell, had once belonged to a member of the Harrow First XV. 'If you have any trouble getting in to see him, tell the policeman on duty that Sherlock Holmes sent you, and that I may be found at Wormwood Scrubs Prison for the next few hours.'

'Cor!' said the child, much impressed by his mission, and scampered off.

'I remember Kelvil,' I said. 'You helped him in that matter of the missing memorandum.' It had not been a very interesting case. The MP was a dull but sincere little man who was the antithesis of Lord Illingworth in every way. He believed in purity in all walks of life, and in public works to alleviate the lot of the poor. He and his wife had eight children, whom he cared for deeply.

Holmes said, 'He is known as an opponent of political corruption almost as dogged as Sir Robert Chiltern, and has the advantage over him of having, so far as I am aware, no relative involved in this case.'

I asked, 'Why not simply ask your brother?' Mycroft Holmes had made it his business for decades to keep abreast of every disturbance in the smooth functioning of the political, civil and commercial life of the Empire, on no less an authority than that of its Empress. Something like a fraudulent railway scheme might bulk relatively small amongst his other priorities, but it would surely not have escaped his attention.

Holmes said, 'There are a number of reputations at stake in this case, Watson, not least your own and Lady Goring's, and while the disgrace that it might bring on some of the other victims may be better deserved, I would prefer not to do our blackmailer's work for her. The involvement of Lord Illingworth, a senior diplomat, means that Mycroft surely already has his eye on the case. Merely asking the question might give him the information he needs to deduce something to the discredit of some person of importance to the realm.'

'Why, who else do you suppose this woman has compromised?' I wondered. 'Is Gregson, after all, another of her victims?' Yet that seemed unlikely, as she would surely have tried to use the inspector's connection with us to her advantage.

'I would prefer not to pre-empt what Mr Kelvil has to tell us, Watson,' said Holmes. 'Suffice it to say that I would not wish to bring the matter to the attention of an official with Mycroft's reach and influence. My relationship with Mr Kelvil was merely professional, and I can trust him to supply the information we need without asking inconveniently perceptive questions.'

'Yes, I see.' I tried to recall the other point that had puzzled me, but which our conversation had driven from my mind.

Then I had it. 'But Holmes, why on earth are we going to Wormwood Scrubs?'

'Ah!' Holmes seized his coat and hat from the stand beside the door. He said, 'Because that is where they are keeping Lord

Arthur Savile until his trial, and it is Lord Arthur Savile who holds the next piece of this most intriguing puzzle.' At once he was effervescent with energy, his excitement in the case suddenly irrepressible. 'Come, Watson! The game is afoot, and we must hound it to its very extinction!'

CHAPTER FOURTEEN
LORD ARTHUR SAVILE'S PUNISHMENT

Wormwood Scrubs being out on the westernmost fringes of the city, we caught an Underground train from Baker Street to the Uxbridge Road, and thence the West London Railway took us out of the city past brickworks, claypits and farms to the recently rebuilt station that served the new prison. All along the way, Holmes was positively chafing with impatience.

The gaol was a modern one, designed upon fashionable principles of rehabilitation in preference to punishment, and its gatehouse, in red brick and Portland stone, held busts of the penal reformers John Howard and Elizabeth Fry. They presented a sympathetic, humane face to the world compared to London's other, danker and more squalid houses of correction.

It was, for all that, a prison, and the chill I invariably feel when the gates of such a place slam shut and are locked behind me did not fail to revisit me there.

We were escorted through the grounds to an interview room with a view of the inner courtyard, where the inmates were permitted to exercise. A few moments passed, during which Holmes continued to fidget abominably, and then Lord Arthur Savile was ushered into our presence.

His Lordship greeted us affably enough. As a prisoner awaiting trial, and a person of status at that, he was permitted a certain latitude in the terms of his confinement. It was quite clear that he was not being kept with the other inmates. He wore his own clothes, and offered us Turkish cigarettes from a silver case. He was in all discernible ways the same agreeable, handsome, shiftless nobleman whom we had taken into custody a few days previously.

'The Peruvian Railway Company?' he said, when that business concern was mentioned. 'Yes, as it happens I have heard of it. I have staked most of my fortune on it, for all the good it is liable to do me. Why do you ask?'

Holmes asked him, 'On whose advice did you invest there?'

'Oh, a fellow I met,' said Savile lightly, but his face had taken on an equally familiar look of alarm. 'He said it sounded like an excellent scheme and when I looked into it, it sounded all right, so I started moving my money there.'

Holmes stared at Lord Arthur in silence for a while, as the sun streamed in through the narrow barred window of the interview room. At length he said, 'She can no longer harm you, you know.'

The aristocrat looked startled.

Holmes continued, 'The worst has already happened. Your crime is known. Unless I have gravely misjudged you, there is nothing in your past that is worse than murder.'

Lord Arthur frowned ferociously. 'I suppose you are right,' he reluctantly agreed, 'but it is confoundedly hard to think about it in that way. I have been scared of her for so long, you see. When you came into my house talking about Podgers' death, I was certain she had sent you.'

'So I recall,' said Holmes. 'You said, "So she's been talking, then." I foolishly assumed that you were referring to your wife.'

'No, Sybil's a perfect angel, thank heaven, and she has never known anything to tell. She has been surprisingly understanding about this business, though.'

'I will grant you that is surprising,' said Holmes carefully.

Lord Arthur shrugged. 'She knows me well, and understands that I could not have behaved differently under the circumstances, though she is naturally distressed by the end to which it has led me. Her delicacy of feeling does her great credit.'

Holmes cleared his throat. 'I have no doubt that Lady Arthur is an excellent woman, but our interest today is in another matter. If you see fit to cooperate with us I shall ensure that the fact is taken into account at your trial, although I make no guarantees as to the outcome.'

'As far as that goes, if the choice is to be between a life in prison and execution, then I think either outcome equally abominable,' said Savile gravely. 'I would almost prefer the option that would leave Sybil free to marry again if she wishes. But I shall help you anyway, Mr Holmes. Why should I not? We all owe you for your public service, even if, on this occasion, it hasn't been to my benefit.'

Holmes inclined his head in acknowledgement. 'That is generous of you, under the circumstances. Now, what can you tell me about the woman who has been threatening you?'

Savile took a long, shuddering breath. 'She first spoke to me sometime around two years ago. She had found out somehow about Podgers – don't ask me how, for I have never told a soul. I suppose I have quite often talked about cheiromancy, though, in a general sort of way. I have mentioned that I feel grateful that it delivered Sybil to me—'

'How so?' I interrupted, frowning.

Holmes sighed in mild exasperation, though whether at Savile's eccentricity or my slowness I could not tell. 'Lord Arthur believes that, had he not been forewarned of his own proclivity to murder, he might have committed the crime at a time not of his own choosing, and thereby forfeited Lady Arthur's affections.'

'Well, quite,' Savile confirmed, oblivious to Holmes's scepticism. 'And, you know, I have had ten years of happy marriage, even were it to end tomorrow. Had I not murdered Podgers in good time, the horrible possibility would have hung over me that I might have killed somebody important to me instead, like Sybil or the children. No, it was far better to get the distasteful business over and done with.'

'I see,' I said, though Savile's logic still seemed to me perfectly preposterous. In my view his best chance at the trial would be a plea of insanity. I might even be persuaded to testify in support of it.

'I suppose that somebody with sufficient interest in my money might have noticed me mentioning palmistry in that sort of way, and made the connection with what everyone believed to be Podgers' suicide,' said Lord Arthur. 'Now I think back, though, I am not sure that she knew it for certain at all. She certainly didn't give me a marvellously detailed account like yours, Mr Holmes. I suppose it was more a shot across the bows, as it were.'

Holmes said, 'So she hinted that she knew you had killed Podgers, and you were sufficiently alarmed to confirm it?'

'I suppose I was,' said Lord Arthur ruefully. 'Now that I think about it, she might have been hinting at all sorts of things to different people, just to see what their response was. She's the sort of woman who might pass that sort of thing off as a joke if it didn't hit home.'

'Do you mean that you knew her personally?' I started to say, but Holmes waved a hand to silence me.

He asked, 'What did she ask of you, once you had confirmed your secret?'

'Well, to bet my shirt on this railway company, as I have done. After that she started asking me whether any of my friends had any disreputable secrets, but I told her I didn't have a notion. Why would I, after all? None of them knew mine.'

Holmes nodded. 'And what was her response when she realised that she had bled you dry and you could be of no further use to her?'

'By then our communication was no longer direct. Her man told me that she was disappointed in me, and passed on her increasingly dire threats to expose me. What could I do, though? I had nothing more to give her. That was why I assumed that your arrival was her doing.'

'None but my own, I'm afraid,' said Holmes.

'I say, though, Holmes,' I put in. 'There *was* that woman who passed Herr Winckelkopf's ledger to the police. You don't suppose…?'

Holmes shook his head. 'I think not. The incriminating records in that book would have represented much richer capital to the person we are dealing with. She would not have relinquished them to crush a single victim. I think that the police's interest at a time when Lord Arthur was expecting to be exposed was, after all, a coincidence.'

'My arrest plays very well into her hands, though,' Savile pointed out with surprising shrewdness. 'If any of her other victims should start having second thoughts, all she need say is, "Look what happened to Lord Arthur Savile."'

I said, 'She could say that of any scandal, surely. Her victim would have no way of knowing whether it was anything to do with her.'

'Ah, but in Lord Arthur's case there would be records of his investment in the railway company to back it up,' Holmes pointed out. 'I fear that he is correct. As I was observing to you this morning, our work risks advancing this perfidious scheme, whether or not it is occurring at Mrs Cheveley's behest.'

'At whose behest?' I asked. I was bemused, although the name did sound somewhat familiar.

Lord Arthur, however, seemed quite astonished. 'I don't believe I told you her name, Mr Holmes.'

Holmes nodded. 'As we have been speaking for so long without it coming up, I guessed that you were feeling some residual compunction on that score. I thought I would spare you the trouble.'

'He might have saved us a great deal of trouble if he'd used it on Monday,' I complained. I had remembered, however, where I knew the name from. 'But Holmes, is this that woman who Pike was telling us about? The one who—'

'Your blackmailer was Mrs Cheveley, then?' Holmes asked, ignoring me again.

Lord Arthur said, 'That is right. I was introduced to her at a party of Lady Markby's. She was a perfectly captivating woman, or might have seemed so, had I not had Sybil to spare me all thought of others. She had only recently arrived in London society, and she disappeared from it sometime afterwards.'

'Realising that a criminal career is better conducted from the shadows, no doubt. Have you any idea where she might be found now?'

Savile shook his head glumly. 'For the most part I have been dealing with a rather hideous fellow who works for her. I have enquired after her among my friends from time to time, without giving the true reason, but nobody claims to know her any more. She came here from abroad, Vienna I believe, and it is assumed she has gone back there.'

'I think not,' said Holmes. 'I think not, indeed. Thank you, Lord Arthur, I believe you have been of inestimable help to us.'

The guard took His Lordship back to his cell, and we were conducted from the interview room, along brick corridors and through locked iron doors, back to the faux-medieval gateway which led us once again, with no little relief in my case, into the outside world.

As we hurried back across the common to St Quintin Park and Wormwood Scrubs Station, Holmes exclaimed, 'As I surmised, Lord Illingworth's guess was wrong. It was not some old flame of his who was tormenting him, but one of Lord Goring's.'

'She does not appear to have tormented Goring himself, though,' I observed. 'But how did you know that our mysterious lady blackmailer was this Mrs Cheveley?'

Holmes looked up from his clay pipe, which he had been filling with swift fingers since we left the prison gates, with a smile. 'I did not, until Lord Arthur confirmed it. However, the assumption seemed a reasonable one. It is rare generally, and rarer still in the echelon of society we are dealing with, for a woman's name to be connected with monetary fraud and sharp business practice. The fact that Mrs Cheveley is directly known to some of our principals made the proposition seem distinctly likely, and the fact that she spent time in Vienna, where Illingworth was first approached, brought it close to a certainty.'

I said, 'But why do you suppose she wanted Durrington dead?'

My friend lit his pipe with careful deliberation, took a deep draught, and exhaled with satisfaction. Speaking just as rapidly as before, he continued. 'With one exception, we have connected every victim we have encountered to the same blackmailer. Both Algernon and Lane named Broadwater as their intermediary, while in Cecily's case Lord Illingworth himself took on that role. Illingworth, Lane and Savile were all induced to provide compromising information on their friends, and the same is now expected of you. Illingworth and Savile were obliged to invest their capital identically, and we can assume that this would also have been true of Algernon, Cecily and soon yourself. Lane presumably has no capital worth mentioning, and was valuable only for the information he held on Algernon.'

I had been following this carefully. 'Would that not be consistent with two blackmailers? One employing Broadwater to threaten Lane and later Algernon, and another, this Mrs Cheveley, blackmailing Savile, Illingworth and eventually Cecily?'

Holmes shook his head. 'Quite apart from the intimate connection between Cecily and Algernon, there are too many points of similarity. Savile and Illingworth both mentioned an intermediary, though they did not name him. Algernon said that he was encouraged to invest in a transport scheme, though he could not name it. How many blackmailers have you heard of who insist on their ill-gotten gains being paid to a company rather than a person? Besides, we know that Broadwater's employer is a female.'

I said, 'You haven't mentioned Ernest Moncrieff.'

'He is the exception I alluded to,' Holmes replied. 'We know enough to be sure that Timothy Durrington was blackmailing Ernest, if that was indeed his rather nebulous intent, for reasons uniquely his own. He made no attempt either to compromise others of Ernest's acquaintance, or to persuade him to invest his money in anything other than Timothy Durrington.

'Durrington was a free agent, blackmailing a member of the Moncrieff family on his own account rather than under Mrs Cheveley's auspices, and that she could not tolerate. His grounds for extorting money from Ernest were nonsensical, but Mrs Cheveley will have had no way of confirming that. Rather than risk losing some of the family's wealth to this interloper, she sent the invitation to lure Durrington to his death at the Moncrieffs' house, and took further advantage of the situation to place Lady

Goring under the threat of a murder charge. We know that the invitation was written by the same person as the address on the envelope to you.'

'But how did she get her hands on the writing paper?' I asked.

'A guest or servant, another of her victims, will have procured it for her. In having Durrington killed and Lady Goring suspected of the crime, she eliminated a rival and gained a potential hold over Lady Goring's relatives in one stroke. Hence, as you surmised, Lord Goring's surprising change of mind concerning my own involvement in the case.

'In any case, our villainess is one with whom our client has had past dealings, whether he is aware of it or not. Our logical course of action is to visit Lord Goring at home, and ask him to tell us everything he knows about Laura Cheveley.'

CHAPTER FIFTEEN
REVENGE OF THE SPIDER WOMAN

'I've been thinking about Lord Goring, Holmes,' I told my friend on the train from Uxbridge Road Station back to Baker Street. No station on the Underground circuit was closer to Lord Goring's house in Curzon Street, so we would be obliged to pass within a few hundred yards of home before continuing our journey.

It was a quiet time of day, and there were no other passengers within earshot. 'Is it possible that he's more deeply entangled in this than we think?' I continued. 'Mrs Cheveley is an old attachment of his, and it does sound as if she got Mabel Goring freed from gaol. Could the two of them be working together now?'

'If so, it would be foolish of him to have involved me in the first place,' Holmes pointed out. 'While it is not unknown for a criminal who believes he can deceive me to engage my services in the hope of establishing his innocence beyond doubt, it takes a particular combination of folly and arrogance to do so. Although,' he added, 'as a rational man I cannot rule out the possibility that others, more justifiably conceited, have been successful.'

'Really?' I was shocked. 'Holmes, surely you don't believe—'

Placidly he said, 'Calm yourself, Watson, I am speaking of a logical possibility merely. I do not think it probable, but if I have been successfully hoodwinked I would know nothing of it. A criminal who could achieve such a thing would be even cleverer than the late Professor Moriarty, whose genius for obfuscation I was able to penetrate, but there is nothing impossible in the idea. An athlete is only the fastest or the strongest in his field until a faster or a stronger emerges, and the same surely applies to intelligence. The criminal may yet live who can pull the wool over my eyes.'

'But Lord Goring?' I asked.

'It hardly seems likely. But I confess that the notion has crossed my mind. The viscount has, I am told, a formidable intellect. His reputation is as a philosopher as well as a dandy, surprising though the combination may be. The reason he has not made more of his talents is, as his father Lord Caversham tells any person who will listen, that he refuses to apply himself. It is, perhaps, conceivable that he has done so, but in a field where success is best secured by keeping it invisible.'

I said, 'You said yourself that our investigation is furthering Mrs Cheveley's schemes, allowing her to discard the victims she has wrung dry while acting as an object lesson to those who may still be lucrative to her. And it was Lord Goring who initiated that investigation.'

'Only into the death at the Moncrieffs', Watson. Our involvement in the Savile case predates our knowing him.'

'That's true,' I agreed. 'But since then we've found out all Illingworth's secrets, and Cecily's, and some of Algernon's.'

'In fact, we have found out virtually none of Algernon's,' Holmes admonished me, 'beyond what was apparently common knowledge. Lane was far more discreet with us than he evidently was with Mr Broadwater. And Illingworth freely confessed his secrets, which are also Cecily's, although I dare say my presence at the Moncrieffs' house may have encouraged him in that direction. I imagine he might have reacted with even more alarm had he seen us watching him on his way to the post office.

'More to the point, however, I have grave doubts about the idea that Lord Goring might work with Mrs Cheveley, so signally against the interests of his wife and her family, on the basis of an association between them that ended in estrangement many years ago.'

'Well,' I said doubtfully, 'I suppose that if Goring is part of a conspiracy, then Lady Goring was never in any real danger. Unless,' I added with a shudder, 'he actually meant to get rid of her.'

'Or unless,' Holmes drawled, 'she, too, is an accomplice.'

I began yet again to strenuously defend Mabel Goring's innocence, but then I saw from the gleam in Holmes's hooded eyes that he was deliberately baiting me, and subsided with a grunt of annoyance.

'To return to the question of motives,' Holmes said. 'We might speculate that Lord Goring harbours a grudge against Sir Robert or Lady Chiltern, incurred before or since his marriage, or a rediscovered infatuation with Mrs Cheveley for which his marital life cannot substitute. Or, perhaps the least unlikely option, he might simply be another victim she has compelled to do her bidding, now so thoroughly entwined in her web as to be complicit in spinning it. But we have no evidence of any such thing. It remains speculation merely, and speculation, as you know, is anathema to me. It is of the utmost urgency that we establish the facts of the matter, and nothing less will do.'

At Baker Street Station we were met by Alfie, the young lad with the unearned rugby cap, who was enterprisingly awaiting our return, having learned from Mrs Hudson that we were travelling by Underground. He handed Holmes a message which my friend stood immobile to read, the pedestrians on the pavement parting irritably around him while Alfie waited patiently for his endeavours to receive some appropriate pecuniary acknowledgement.

Eventually, Holmes patted his pockets and produced a shilling, which he handed to Alfie with a terse word of thanks. The urchin scurried away, and Holmes deigned to tell me what he had read.

'Mr Kelvil goes into admirable detail, Watson, and invokes technicalities which are obscure to me. His gist, however, is that the Peruvian Railway Company is exactly the kind of dubious business concern that would be outlawed by the government bill that Sir Robert Chiltern was previously believed to support, and which he apparently now opposes. It will not have escaped your notice that the evaporation of the police case against Lady Goring followed closely on the heels of Chiltern's speech in the Commons, which effectively overturned the bill.'

'Good heavens,' I said, since it had in fact eluded my attention up to that point.

Holmes looked grim. 'Whether with Lord Goring's connivance or not, Mrs Cheveley has moved on from acquiring funds by blackmail for her dubious ventures, to using it as a tool to legitimise them. She is applying an insidious pressure to the very workings of our democracy.' Holmes affected to have no interest in politics, but I knew that the law as it pertained to criminal activity was a matter of real import to him.

We took a cab to Lord Goring's house, which for a change was not immediately by Belgrave Square but in Mayfair, not very far from the house of Sir Robert and Lady Chiltern.

'Lord Goring is not at home,' the viscount's butler informed us after we had introduced ourselves. He stood in a magnificent front doorway framed by a grand portico, with pillars and a pediment.

'Then we will speak to Lady Goring,' Holmes declared.

'Lady Goring is not at home,' the butler said in identical tones. 'She is with her sister-in-law, Lady Chiltern.'

Holmes glanced up at the pillared stone of the house and sighed. He said, 'Is Lord Goring not at home in the same sense that Lady Goring is not at home?'

The butler gazed stoically at us. 'I cannot imagine what you mean, sir.'

Holmes sighed. 'Pray tell Lord Goring, in his absence, that Sherlock Holmes wishes to see him concerning Mrs Cheveley. I believe that this information will precipitate his instantaneous return.'

'Very good, sir,' the butler replied, entirely unperturbed. 'If you would please wait in the hall?' he asked, and vanished upstairs.

A few moments later, he returned and said, 'Lord Goring will see you now, gentlemen.'

'My compliments to His Lordship on his mastery of translocation,' Holmes observed urbanely. 'The Society for the Scientific Investigation of Psychical Phenomena will be most impressed.'

'Indeed, sir,' the butler agreed impassively.

He showed us to a well-appointed library, laid out well over a hundred years before in the Adam style. We found Lord Goring sitting with Sir Robert Chiltern, next to two untouched sherry glasses and a decanter. Both men wore quilted smoking jackets, Lord Goring's gloriously embroidered with Chinese dragons. 'Thank you, Phipps,' His Lordship said distractedly. Despite his finery he looked concerned, and Sir Robert was so pale that I worried for his health.

'Mr Holmes,' Lord Goring said. 'I asked you to keep me informed of your investigations, and I thank you for honouring that request. However, I cannot appreciate your insisting on entry into my home when I have given strict instructions that I am not in, in order to bandy about an embarrassment from my youth. I understand that, as a detective, you have ways of finding these things out, but I consider it bad form to bring them up when they are long ago resolved to the satisfaction of all parties. Now, what is it you have to tell me?'

'Lord Goring,' Holmes nodded pleasantly, 'I have no desire to rake over any scandal from your past. I am no Mrs Cheveley.'

Sir Robert winced. 'That name again. Whatever it is that you are insinuating, Mr Holmes, I suggest that you come straight out with it. I also have history with that woman that I have no wish to revisit.'

'And I repeat that history is not my interest here,' Holmes said patiently. 'I am speaking of current events. Mrs Cheveley is, I am convinced, the prime mover behind the death of Timothy Durrington, alias Bunbury, at the Moncrieffs' house. She is conducting a complicated criminal enterprise involving blackmail and financial fraud, in which a number of your friends are embroiled against their will and which has, I believe, recently extended to engulf the pair of you. Lord Goring, am I wide of the mark?'

Lord Goring closed his eyes and inhaled deeply. He said, 'I am afraid we will have to tell them, Robert.'

Sir Robert groaned and slumped back in his chair. 'I'll be ruined, then, at last. That damned woman will be the end of me.'

Settling into one of the comfortable leather armchairs, Holmes said, 'We will avoid that eventuality if we can, Sir Robert. Even if we cannot, the life of a public servant is one you have chosen freely, and I can imagine no greater public service than helping to place a malevolent criminal behind bars.'

'He's right, Robert,' Goring said. 'This is a greater matter than your career, or even our family. Let us by all means do what we can to limit the damage, but first let us do what is needed to cage that serpent. She has been at liberty for too long.'

Sir Robert shook his head mournfully. 'Oh, very well. But will you tell them everything, Arthur? I haven't the stomach for it.'

'Of course,' said Goring. After courteously offering us each a drink, which we declined, he drained his sherry, then poured himself another. He said, 'First, I must apologise. I know I spoke ill-advisedly when we last met. It was tactless of me, even rude.'

'Think nothing of it, Lord Goring,' Holmes replied at once. 'I have no need of any apology, merely of your account.'

'Of course,' said Goring. He sighed. 'As I suppose you have discovered, I was briefly engaged to Laura Hungerford, the woman you refer to as Mrs Cheveley. It was an act of exceptional foolishness on my part, and the only excuse I can plead is that of my youth. Though younger still, she was a dishonest person, both disloyal and deceitful. I broke off the engagement when she stole some property belonging to my cousin. Out of a chivalrous impulse that I now consider misplaced, I let it be believed that our parting was due to some fault of mine.

'Two years ago she appeared at a party at Robert's house under the name of Cheveley, and attempted to exert pressure on him of the kind you have described. There is no need for us to discuss the details, except to say that they could have ended his career immediately. Robert's party being then in government, she tried to induce him to give official sanction to an enterprise involving canals in the Argentine, which was nothing more than a base swindle. In the event, I was able to recover and destroy the… material she held, and thus salvage Robert's reputation. The episode took a great toll upon us both and on Lady Chiltern, although between us we were able to shield Robert's sister, who shortly afterwards agreed to become Lady Goring, from the knowledge of it.'

'One moment.' Holmes interrupted him. 'Sir Robert, was it on this account that you considered rejecting the offer of a position in the Cabinet?'

Sir Robert hung his head. 'It was, though I have no idea how you can know if it. I felt great shame at the way I had been compromised. Between them, Arthur and Gertrude persuaded me to rise above my past mistakes and to accept the portfolio.'

'Thank you. Lord Goring, pray proceed.'

The viscount said, 'Mrs Cheveley disappeared from society shortly afterwards, ostensibly to return to her haunts abroad, but I had my suspicions that she remained in London, to try her hand at a more systematic form of criminality. I am no detective, Holmes, but I noted certain acquaintances of mine making foolish investments which they were unable to explain satisfactorily, and politicians changing their minds in surprising ways. Some of them I have observed crafting artful, or occasionally artless, conversations aimed at discovering areas of my own life where shameful secrets might dwell. I came to recognise a pattern in such behaviour.

'When I came to you on Monday evening and requested assistance for my wife I was quite sincere, but I had also an ulterior motive. I had heard of your part in the arrest of Lord Arthur Savile earlier in the day. I know Lord Arthur only slightly, although I bought this house from him. It belonged to his late cousin, Lady Clementina Beauchamp. Though I see him but rarely, he was one of those whom I suspected of having fallen under Mrs Cheveley's influence, as was Lord Illingworth. I hoped that, by bringing you into association with the latter so soon after the former, I might set you on her trail. Nothing would give me greater pleasure than to see that woman arrested.'

Holmes said, somewhat acerbically, 'And why did you not say so at the time, my lord?'

'Primarily for fear that, if I revealed her part in the matter,

Mrs Cheveley would retaliate by placing Mabel in yet worse danger. It seemed sensible, though, to allow you to reach your own conclusions, rather than having them suggested by me. In that way you would be firmer in your convictions. I had not then realised, of course, that the two investigations would be so intimately connected.'

'And when did you realise?' Holmes asked quietly.

Lord Goring sighed. 'I received a message the morning following my wife's arrest, informing me that I might learn something to her advantage, if I attended an… assignation. It was to be at a tearoom in Shoreditch, a place that, as you may imagine, was not of a kind I would normally frequent, and I was to arrive alone and incognito. I do not believe that the last stipulation was necessary, but it evidently amused the blasted woman to see me borrowing my valet's clothes.'

Holmes leaned forward eagerly. 'She came in person?'

'For me, she did,' said Goring grimly. He evidently did not consider it a compliment. 'Our past association means something to her still, though nothing good. She has borne a grudge against me for many years, and now that resentment is extended to the whole of our family. That is why she arranged for my wife, the mother of my son, to become the chief suspect in the murder of this fellow Durrington, but it is not the whole reason. She is an intensely practical woman and her every action serves her ends, usually financial ones.

'She has hair of a very dark shade of red and her eyes are greyish-green. She wore a simple silk dress in heliotrope, a colour that has always suited her. Indeed, she had dressed as well as she ever did, and I told her so.

'"I get about so little nowadays," she replied. "I have standards to maintain, and a dressmaker who is pining away for want of my custom."

'I said, "I'm surprised you're not worried that you'll be recognised." She is a striking woman in appearance, as I hope you will have the opportunity to see for yourself.

'She said, "Oh, few people are as fascinated by me as you are, Arthur. That is their tragedy, and yours."

'I said, "I came here to learn how I may help my wife. I have no interest in trading unpleasantries with you, Mrs…?"

'She laughed gaily. "Mrs Cheveley will do very well for now. Although you could call me Laura, you know."

'"We both know that I will not, and why I will not," I said stiffly. "Let us get down to business, if you please."

'"Business is very much why we are here," said Mrs Cheveley. "Your business, and mine. Your business is to help your pretty Mabel to escape the noose, and mine is the business of others."

'"It will not come to the noose," I said, but with less certainty than I might have wished.

'"Certainly it won't," she replied. "Provided that you and Robert Chiltern do as I say in all particulars. If you do, I can arrange for testimony which will free her."'

Holmes interrupted him. 'Those were her words? "I can arrange for testimony"?' I recalled that the witness statement which had convinced Gregson to free Mabel had come from the widow Mrs Teville. I had ceased thinking of her as the blackmailer once Lord Illingworth was revealed as Cecily's treacherous parent, but the fact that she was not Violet Cardew did not mean that she was incapable of arranging the threats made to Cecily, or to others.

'Her exact words,' Lord Goring confirmed. 'She said that only she could ensure that Mabel's name was cleared.'

'Then Mrs Teville, who provided that testimony, is another of her confederates,' Holmes said. 'Either she is a victim, like Lord Illingworth, or an employee, as we assume Broadwater to be.'

I recalled that Mrs Cheveley had been at school with Gertrude Chiltern, whereas Mrs Teville I guessed to be in her mid-forties, and besides, had fairer hair than the dark red Lord Goring ascribed to his old flame. But there was also the question of Mrs Teville's secret daughter. Mrs Teville's age was difficult to guess with accuracy. If, for instance, she were in her late rather than her early forties, then she might just have a daughter of Lady Chiltern's age, and perhaps one with hair of a different colour from her own. Could that be the nature of Mrs Teville's connection with Mrs Cheveley?

As I considered this, though, I realised that there was a further alternative that we had been ignoring, and one which made perhaps more sense than any other.

As my mind raced through these conflicting possibilities, Lord Goring had been continuing. 'Mrs Cheveley insisted to me that Robert should use his political influence on her behalf. She knew a good deal more than I did myself about his forthcoming speech in the House, and what he was expected to say. She told me what he should say instead.'

With another low groan, Sir Robert Chiltern said, 'To enlarge this accursed woman's wealth I have betrayed my party and my constituents, and perjured away my good name. May God forgive me – but Gertrude, I am sure, never will.'

'You do both yourself and Gertrude an injustice, Robert,' Goring pointed out. 'You did it for Mabel's sake, not for Mrs Cheveley's. Gertrude will understand that. And there is yet time to make it right. Politicians change their minds all the time; indeed, I believe that they are well known for it. When this is over you can simply say that new facts have come to light which lead you to support the government's bill after all. You might even say that you were maliciously deceived before; that is very nearly true.'

'I admit,' said Holmes, 'that I am surprised that Mrs Cheveley so readily delivered the evidence she promised. It would fit her established habits better to keep the threat hanging over you both, at least until Lady Goring's trial.'

Lord Goring sighed. 'Oh, the threat has not disappeared, Holmes. She may yet have the testimony withdrawn. I did not know that Mrs Teville was the witness in question, but I assume she could yet state that she has been acting under duress, presumably exerted by Robert and myself as influential members of the establishment, and contradict her previous statement. The police would at least need to reopen the investigation, and who knows what evidence the vile woman might concoct to draw poor Mabel back into it?'

Holmes said, 'I assume that her conditions also included a stipulation that you call off my involvement in the case.'

'That is nearly correct,' said Lord Goring. 'In fact, she presented me with two alternatives. I chose to warn you away. I could not risk you finding something out that would appear to call Mabel's innocence into question once more. But also… I hoped that you might become suspicious. I hoped that you might investigate *me*.'

'And thus come around, once more, to an awareness of the nefarious Mrs Cheveley and her villainies?'

'That was the outcome I hoped for,' the viscount agreed.

'But,' Holmes asked, 'what was the other alternative which she presented to you?'

'If I could not pay you off and stop you investigating, I should instead retain your services and keep a close watch upon you. In this case she wished me to cultivate your society, and to seek any chinks in your armour that she might use to her advantage. You will appreciate that I was not very hopeful of success in that eventuality.'

'Yes, I see. Tell me something, though. It would seem that you have failed to discourage me from my investigation, so your part now is to find out everything you can to my disadvantage. If you were to succeed, how would you inform Mrs Cheveley of this?'

Lord Goring scowled. 'I would place a message in a particular location, which she tells me is checked twice every day, in the morning and afternoon. There is a loose brick in the wall surrounding my neighbour's garden. The location cannot easily be seen from anywhere where one is not oneself conspicuous.'

'Capital!' said Holmes. 'Apparently our friend has been studying her spycraft. I imagine life among the Viennese *demi-monde* will have afforded her numerous opportunities to acquaint herself with members of the profession. I had hoped that Lane might be our conduit, via Broadwater, but how much more satisfying it is to pass our message through a channel that she has herself created.

'So be it, then.' Holmes beamed at us. 'We must give Mrs Cheveley exactly what she has asked for.'

CHAPTER SIXTEEN
THE DISGRACE OF SHERLOCK HOLMES

When I had awakened that morning to greet Sherlock Holmes beside the remains of our long-dead fire, I had not anticipated that before the end of the day I would be sharing the bedroom of Langdale Pike's Piccadilly flat with a Scotland Yard inspector and a peer of the realm. That was, however, where Gregson, Goring and I concealed ourselves that evening, in accordance with the plan hatched by Holmes to draw the attention of the elusive Mrs Cheveley.

'Be haughty with her,' Holmes had instructed Goring as he wrote his missive. 'Lay down the law. Insist that she must consider this the full remittance of your debt to her, and that she shall have no further hold over you.'

'We cannot trust her to comply with that,' Sir Robert Chiltern had pointed out. 'She might mouth words of agreement, but they will never bind her.'

Holmes sighed. 'We do not need her bound, merely convinced. It is necessary that Lord Goring's message be believed, and he would capitulate only out of desperation. He must make it sound as if it means everything to him. I assure you, if all goes well, after tonight Mrs Cheveley will pose no further threat to you or to anybody else of your acquaintance.'

The substance of Lord Goring's message was that he had been making enquiries among Holmes's friends, and that Langdale Pike could offer her the information that she sought concerning the detective's guilty conscience. She was invited to visit Pike that evening, in his rooms near Piccadilly, and to come alone.

Such a suggestion would have scandalised any real lady, of course, but none of us expected that Mrs Cheveley would defer to such conventional scruples. Having sent Lord Goring to conceal the message in his neighbour's wall, Holmes repaired directly to Bradley's Club in St James's Street to gain Pike's belated assent to the scheme.

'Langdale is by far the most plausible acquaintance of mine to be the originator of such an offer,' Holmes explained to me. 'Mycroft is out of the question, and however hopeful her approach, Mrs Cheveley would surely be suspicious of any betrayal by you. To those who know her character little enough, Mrs Hudson might seem a better source, but I would not wish to place her in any danger, nor any of the Irregulars.'

Holmes had a detachment of his street children watching Goring's neighbour's house in shifts, and although they had been unable to loiter near the exact spot where the letter had been placed, they had seen a man matching the description of Mr Broadwater duck around the corner of the wall and then leave again shortly afterwards.

Assuming that Mrs Cheveley would have the building where Pike had his rooms similarly watched, the inspector, the viscount and I arrived via the tradesmen's entrance of a neighbouring building with an adjoining cellar. Pike met us and escorted us up to his apartment, which had an air of disinterested opulence entirely in keeping with that of the man himself.

A velvet divan stood partially atop a priceless Persian rug, and an exquisite rosewood table had acquired scuffmarks and the unmistakeable stain of a wine glass. The pictures on the walls were mostly of slender young men enacting scenes from classical myth or Christian martyrology, in what must have been a comfortably warm climate.

We had arrived some time before Pike's appointment with Mrs Cheveley was due, and Holmes was to arrive later still. Lord Goring had left Sir Robert Chiltern waiting for news at his home with his wife and sister. Ostensibly, Holmes had refused to expose a man of Chiltern's standing to such a compromising situation, but I suspected that he had doubts about the politician's behaviour in a crisis.

I broke the awkward silence while we waited by asking Pike if he had learned any more of Mrs Teville.

'A little more,' he told me. 'I believe that she is the same woman as a Mrs Erlynne, once of scandalous reputation, who enjoyed a short period of notoriety in London society some five years since. Her irregular relations with gentlemen meant that she was welcome only at the most daring or sordid fringes of society, but she redeemed herself by marrying a minor member of the nobility, evidently susceptible and now deceased. They moved abroad, of course, but the marriage salvaged a small measure of respectability for her nonetheless.'

'Was his name Teville?' Inspector Gregson asked.

'No, it was Lorton, Lord Augustus Lorton. He died two years after their marriage, which came as no great surprise to anyone familiar with his habits. Mr Teville, if he existed, is nobody who has come to my attention, but if Mrs Erlynne met him abroad he might very well not have done. My knowledge largely pertains to England, and in particular our bustling capital.'

'Have you learned any more of the identity of her supposed

daughter?' I asked, remembering my suspicions concerning the parentage of Mrs Cheveley.

Pike shook his head. 'Disappointingly, no. I have found out what little more I can from my informant the maid, but she tells me only that the young lady is highly placed in society, and is ignorant of the actual nature of the connection between them. Apparently, she considers this Mrs Erlynne, or Teville, a friend and even a protector, rather than a relative of any kind. It may be that what Mrs Teville is most eager to protect is the young lady's innocence on this matter, and that this is the threat Mrs Cheveley holds over her.'

'Or perhaps just the fact that she is this Erlynne woman, if she was so disreputable before,' Gregson suggested prosaically. 'Mrs Teville seems to enjoy her place among the finest society. She would not want to lose it.'

For my own part, I suspected that the connection between the two women was a much more direct one. Indeed, I thought it eminently possible that Mrs Teville's daughter was not only the erstwhile Mrs Cheveley, but someone whom I had actually met. Mrs Nepcote was a redhead of around the right age, and in her marriage to Major Nepcote had managed to combine social respectability with complete domestic impunity for any dubious behaviour. She had known Durrington, of course, as well as most of the other blackmail victims, and she had been by turns obstructive to Holmes's investigations and inquisitive about his personal life and mine. She would have to be a consummate actress, of course, to maintain such a vivid outward character, but a woman of Mrs Cheveley's felonious accomplishments would surely have skills of that nature to call upon.

The only real objection I could see was that it would require Lord Goring, who would know her under both identities, to have remained silent on the connection, but there might be various reasons for that. I was resolved to watch His Lordship carefully as the proceedings progressed.

As the appointed time approached, Pike hustled the three of us into his bedroom, where an indeterminate number of satin dressing gowns were strewn across a rumpled four-poster bed. He showed us the connecting door to the adjoining dressing room, which had its own separate entrance into the drawing room, and exhorted us not to open it upon any account. Then he left us to our own devices.

We sat awkwardly in a row on the wide foot of the bed, while the silence between us stretched. Lord Goring sprang up occasionally to pace back and forth, ignoring my pantomime of annoyance. Gregson, well used to waiting in his police work, remained as placid as a carven Buddha, glancing only occasionally at his watch.

Eventually, Mrs Cheveley arrived, half an hour after the appointed time. 'You are alarmingly late,' we heard Pike admonish her after the briefest of introductory greetings. 'Holmes is due at any moment.' He knew as I did that Holmes was waiting in a public house around the corner, and would be tipped off by an Irregular as soon as his quarry arrived, but his urgency lent verisimilitude to the affair. I assumed that Mrs Cheveley herself was late because she suspected a trap.

'Mr Holmes is coming here?' she asked coolly. 'That was not part of our arrangement, Mr Pike. I might begin to imagine that you have been deceiving me.' Her voice was cooler and calmer than that which I was used to hearing from Mrs Nepcote, although there was enough of the familiar about it to convince me that my theory was correct. 'I have no patience for deception, at least when it is practised by others.'

'It seemed easier to let you hear what Holmes had to say than to tell you,' Pike explained, in a bored tone of voice. 'Please, hide in my dressing room. No, I am afraid we have little time for badinage,' he added, as Mrs Cheveley began to feign a giggle, 'you must do as I ask. I promise you that what you learn tonight will be the undoing of Sherlock Holmes, should you decide to make it so. If you choose, it will give you a sway over him that will last for the rest of his career. You can be the new Napoleon of crime, a Moriarty with nothing to fear from any nemesis – or rather, from that particular one; I make no promises as to others. But this can only occur, I am afraid, if you will secrete yourself in that dressing room with all haste.'

'One moment, Mr Pike,' said Mrs Cheveley, although we heard light, feminine footsteps and her voice began to reach us through the dressing-room door rather than the one opening onto the drawing room. 'Mr Holmes is a friend of yours, I understand. Well, so it may be; I set little store by friendship. But most men do, and I can hardly believe that you are betraying your friend with no reward in mind. What shall I owe you? You must know that I am an extremely wealthy woman, and I pay my debts, but I prefer to know what they are before incurring them.'

Indifferently, Pike said, 'My own income is not negligible, nor are my needs wholly monetary. I hold a great deal of information that never reaches the popular presses, and I have the sources to provide me with a great deal more. I would be a valuable asset in your work, but I do not wish to be an asset. I would like to become a junior partner in your enterprise, and to enjoy a share – a modest share – of what will be very substantial proceeds.' With an impression of venom so convincing that it shocked me, he added, 'I shall also very much appreciate seeing Sherlock Holmes humiliated, but that is by the by. It is always trying, don't you find, when one's friends are better known than oneself, but refuse to acknowledge the assistance that one has given them? Well, perhaps you have not had that experience, in which case I envy you. Are we agreed?'

'We can discuss terms afterwards,' said Mrs Cheveley with an equal affectation of disinterest, 'but I am quite amenable to such an arrangement as you propose.'

We heard the dressing-room door close quietly, and settled back silently to await the arrival of Sherlock Holmes.

My friend had done me an injustice when he suggested that I exercised no discretion in presenting his exploits to the world. I had, for instance, not yet mentioned Langdale Pike in my accounts of his adventures for publication, feeling that my friend's occasional reliance upon a person of Pike's profession was rather sordid and not greatly to his credit. Hearing the hatred, which I sincerely hoped had been feigned, in Pike's voice, I had found myself wondering whether that had been a mistake. Holmes was trusting Pike with his reputation, and they had known each other a long time. How would it be if the sentiments Pike had just avowed were real? How would it be if the doyen of London's gossipmongers was cognisant of some shameful secret of Holmes's to which even I was not privy?

Holmes did not keep us waiting for very long. A minute or so later we heard an impatient rapping at Pike's front door, and a clatter as it was opened.

'Sherlock!' Pike effused, with an unctuousness that was entirely the antithesis of his earlier scorn. 'Always a pleasure to see you, my dear friend.'

'Langdale.' Holmes's voice acknowledged him with a good deal less friendliness. 'I shall not be staying very long. You know what I am here for.'

'But of course, Sherlock, efficient and to the point as always. I have found the perfect fellow for your needs. A young boatman from a thoroughly respectable working family, personable and quite well-spoken, ideal for the purpose.'

My friend asked, 'Will he do all that I have asked?'

'Since he hopes to be paid, it would be idiotic of him not to.'

Holmes had not told us the details of the scenario he had concocted with Pike for Mrs Cheveley to overhear, and I wondered with some curiosity what variety of scandal they had in mind.

Pike continued, 'He will give his oath that as a child on his grandfather's boat he saw Lord Arthur Savile beneath a lamp post on the Embankment, in the very act of pitching Septimus Podgers into the Thames. His grandfather's attention was elsewhere at the time, and the old man beat him for lying. The savage fury on the nobleman's face, he will assure the court, has haunted his dreams for years, so he will have no difficulty in identifying him for the jury.'

'Good,' said Holmes decisively. 'The case against Savile is a little tenuous, and this will shore it up nicely. Now, about the Belgrave Square murder.'

Pike drawled, 'I have spoken to a servant in Lord Illingworth's household. It's only just around the corner, after all. It is a little tricky, as the place has already been searched by the police, but it seems the suit His Lordship wore to the Moncrieffs' ball was being cleaned at the time, and was not inspected. This girl can arrange for the item you mentioned to be found in a pocket. Do you have it with you?'

'I do,' Holmes's voice confirmed smugly. 'A photograph of Timothy Durrington's father in uniform, presumably carried by the victim in order to demonstrate a resemblance to Ernest Moncrieff. Doubtless he passed it to Illingworth on the balcony, and His Lordship absent-mindedly pocketed it before pushing him to his death. It will demonstrate the earl's guilt far more effectively than his half-hearted letter of confession.'

'It will require some wear and tear to suggest that it has been through the laundry,' Pike observed doubtfully. 'But I dare say I can handle that.'

'It must remain recognisable.'

'Of course. When shall you need it discovered?'

'As soon as possible,' said Holmes. 'It will cause Moncrieff some little embarrassment, and considerably more to Illingworth if he is still alive, but it will clear Mabel Goring's name beyond any doubt, and that is all that matters to my client.' Lord Goring was on his feet again, and bore an expression of intense distaste.

'As usual, I shall ensure that the discovery is commented upon in the press,' said Pike. 'I presume that our customary fee applies?'

'Naturally, Langdale,' Holmes said coldly. 'We may be friends, but our business affairs remain always on a professional footing.'

I felt a nudge from Gregson and realised that the inspector was looking at me with silent concern. The distress I felt at hearing my just and honest friend say such base things, no matter that I knew he was dissembling, must have been showing on my face.

I nodded and essayed a smile, but Gregson was already rising to stand by Goring's side. The door between the dressing room and the drawing room had been thrown open, and Mrs Cheveley's voice rang out in triumphant amusement.

'Mr Sherlock Holmes! How very surprising that we should meet here!'

A shocked pause – or rather, the facsimile of one – followed her arrival. Finally, my friend's voice said, a trifle weakly, 'Mrs Cheveley, I presume. I assure you, it is more of a surprise to me than it is to you.'

'Oh yes,' she said, 'I was not speaking of my own surprise.' I wondered afresh whether her voice was truly that of Mrs Nepcote, though I was certain that it was one I knew. 'Although I admit that I had not expected to learn that the great detective, the paragon of probity and the moral and intellectual exemplar of his age, has gained his reputation through grubby lies and purchased perjuries. Of all surprises, I love disappointments the most. The depravity of human nature is so delicious, and so universal.'

Holmes said, 'Most of us love what we see in a mirror.'

Mrs Cheveley gave a delighted laugh. 'Spoken just like a man! Not one woman in a hundred loves what she sees in hers. A man pays no more compliments to his mirror that he does his tobacconist. A woman treats hers like an oracle. We women are accused of self-satisfaction, but in fact it is a masculine virtue. You are very satisfied with your reputation, are you not, Mr Holmes?'

'It has served me well,' Holmes agreed in a pained tone.

'Then I can serve you too, by allowing you to keep it,' Mrs Cheveley laughed. 'Provided, of course, that you render me a little service in return. That's no more than fair, I think.'

'You cannot prove what you have heard,' said Holmes. 'It will be your word against mine, and my reputation will protect me.'

'Ah, there you are mistaken, Sherlock,' said Langdale Pike. 'I will corroborate Mrs Cheveley's account in detail, and may go further. Our past interventions in the course of justice have left their mark on so many of your more famous cases. Colonel Moran's lawyers, for instance, would be most interested to learn where the bullet came from that connected their client to the death of poor Ronnie Adair. On all of them I can cite chapter and verse. I think your friends in the police will listen to what I shall say.'

'And if your reputation is of value to you, how much more is your liberty?' Mrs Cheveley asked sweetly. 'The company in prison is not of the best, so I hear, but you would, I am sure, find a good many who knew you already. What a welcome you should find in your new circle.'

'Very well, you have made your point,' snapped Holmes.

'Langdale, I am disgusted with you, though I suppose I should have expected no better. From you, Mrs Cheveley, I certainly did not.'

I could hear the simper in her voice as she replied, 'For my own part, I try never to disappoint. I feel that those who know me should have no illusions about anything at all. Indeed, I have made stripping away illusions my life's work.'

Holmes growled, 'And what must I do, madam, to preserve intact the illusions others hold about me? I suppose you desire me to cease my investigations, as Lord Goring asked me to do under instructions from you.'

'Oh, there will be no need for that. Your plan to blame Lord Illingworth is perfectly in accordance with my own wishes. It will form a quite satisfactory resolution to the case... for the moment. No, I ask simply for immunity from all your future investigations. You must never make any enquiries about me, and if I warn you that something you are looking into has ramifications that affect my interests, you must desist at once. As far as you are concerned, we shall inhabit separate spheres, never touching. Almost like husband and wife.'

'Under protest, I accept,' said Holmes. 'If that is agreed between us then I take my leave of you, madam.'

'Oh, but that is not all,' said Mrs Cheveley in the sweetest of voices. 'You are a master of information to rival Mr Pike, and information is my stock-in-trade. You have investigated cases for countless clients, from itinerant labourers to members of the noblest families in Europe.'

Holmes said, 'It is true, but I fail to see its relevance.'

'That will not do at all, Mr Holmes. Embellished your reputation may be, but it is well known that you never fail to see the relevance of anything.'

Stiffly, he replied, 'I accept all my cases in the strictest confidence, whoever the client. Were that confidence called into question, I could not operate at all. If private information about my clients were to reach a third party, they would know who to blame.'

'But they would not blame you publicly, not if I warned them not to. Your role in the affair would be as hidden as my own.'

In a voice that sounded almost strangled with pain, Holmes said, 'Watson would know, and it is he who mediates my reputation to the outside world. He has a certain gullibility that has always recommended him to me, but I could not hide such a thing from one so closely involved in my affairs. Your letter made no impression upon him whatsoever, I fear. Watson will never be suborned.'

'Well, that may also be taken care of,' Mrs Cheveley said calmly. 'I, too, have my clients, people who pay me to ensure their own reputations survive. You know already how far they will go, out of gratitude to me, on my behalf. It would be a small matter to remove the good doctor from the picture.'

There was a long pause. Then Holmes said, in a cowed and broken tone, 'Very well. If Watson must be dispensed with, so be it.'

I actually gasped at that, but fortunately Mrs Cheveley was already speaking. 'Really? Then so be it indeed.' She laughed again. 'What a partnership we shall have! The great detective and the Cleopatra of crime!'

'My God, she's turned mad,' whispered Lord Goring, aghast, under the cover of the ensuing peal of laughter.

'May I ask one thing in return?' Holmes asked, still in that small voice. 'It would be to know whether I have accurately discerned the facts of the murder at the Moncrieffs'. Not the story where Illingworth is the sole culprit, but the truth.'

'What is truth?' asked Mrs Cheveley. 'You yourself have amended reality on many occasions.'

'Forgive me, but that is not so,' said Holmes, a little more boldly. 'I have altered others' understanding of reality, no more. The facts in those cases remain the same, even when they are known to me alone. It would give me some small satisfaction to know whether I have correctly understood them in this instance. I believe that I have, now that I understand the calibre of intellect that I have been dealing with.'

'Very well, then,' Mrs Cheveley agreed smugly. 'Why don't you tell me what you believe happened?'

Holmes said, 'The man Durrington was a threat to your operations. He was attempting to blackmail Ernest Moncrieff before you had had a chance to do so, and that made him a random factor. You were determined to remove it, but you thought you might thereby serve another end also.'

Mrs Cheveley's voice was still amused. 'That much would be obvious to anyone who knows what you know. You will have to do better than that to impress me, Mr Holmes.'

'You learned of his existence and intentions, I imagine, because you were monitoring all the correspondence to and from Number 149 Belgrave Square, at least all that was sent through the standard postal channels.'

'Postmen are eminently bribable,' Mrs Cheveley crooned. 'They are paid so wonderfully poorly. Please go on.'

'You wrote to Durrington and asked him to call on Ernest Moncrieff during the evening of the ball. It amused you that he should give the name Bunbury, as a reminder to Algernon that he had not yet secured your silence on the secrets of his past, but that benefit was merely tangential. You hoped, not only to eliminate your unwashed rival, but to make it appear that Mabel Goring was responsible for his murder. You knew of the forthcoming vote on the government bill, and that her brother's voice would be decisive in that debate. And you also, of course, bore a grudge against her brother, her sister-in-law and especially her husband, which goes beyond your business affairs and into the realms of maleficence.'

'I gave you no permission to analyse my character, Mr Holmes,' Mrs Cheveley said lightly.

'I apologise for it. I will confine myself, then, to your business motives, which I believe we have established.' Holmes continued his narrative. 'You had the house under surveillance, of course. You knew that tradesmen were routinely seen in the library. You saw that Ernest Moncrieff, as was his custom, had smoked on the balcony earlier and left it unlocked. I assume that you had a plan of contingency in case he did not, probably to obtain access to the housekeeper's keys by way of Dora Steyne or another servant, but it was not needed. You also observed the Gorings' arrival, and the details of Lady Goring's clothing – the midnight-blue dress, the shawl and the brooch. Although you had your plan sketched out in outline, its finer details depended on the particulars of Mabel Goring's attire.

'Lord Illingworth was not your only agent among the invitees to the ball. There was also Mrs Teville, who is indebted to you for keeping secret her true relationship with her daughter. I do not know the young woman's identity, but I assume she is a figure of some significance in London society.'

'Oh, you would be amused if I told you, Mr Holmes,' said Mrs Cheveley. 'Not that I shall, of course. We all have our codes of professional ethics.'

'Indeed we do, though they may differ in detail,' Holmes noted, with something more akin to his usual dry tones.

Mrs Cheveley said, 'Mrs Teville is most protective of the young lady, however. She has taken drastic action before to defend her reputation, and I expect her to take it again shortly.'

Holmes said, 'Be that as it may, you sent a messenger to Mrs

Teville, describing Mabel Goring's ensemble and telling her to wear as similar a dress as she possessed. She dutifully arrived, dressed in royal purple, a little before Durrington himself. The mink stole which she was wearing when I saw her later that evening would make her outfit superficially dissimilar to Lady Goring's, but could be put aside as easily as the latter's shawl. Indeed, I noted that it was slightly discoloured by a pale dust, suggesting that she had stowed it on some high shelf, or similar out-of-the-way place.

'There was, of course, some risk in this plan, since Mrs Teville is known in the character of a widow, however gay her habitual behaviour, and thus could only have attended the ball in some suitable mourning colour. I may be wrong, but I suspect you mitigated this by conniving with Lady Goring's maid so that her first choice of dress, in eau de Nil, was rendered *hors de combat* and replaced with a gown of a darker colour. I doubt you are a person who willingly trusts to luck in any aspect of her enterprises.

'Acting on instructions he had received from you, Lord Illingworth played on Mabel Goring's concern for her friend Cecily Moncrieff to detain her near the fire in the music room, causing her to shed that shawl, which he purloined. He tore the brooch free and passed it to Mrs Teville, then giving the shawl to the maid Dora to throw from her window.

'The fact that Mabel Goring went directly from the music room up to the library was an unexpected development, but it complicated matters only slightly. Even had she met and spoken to Durrington, it is unlikely that it would have changed anything, except to make her later testimony even more dubious.

'As it happened, though, the room was warm, and the balcony already unlocked. In his nervousness, Durrington had doubtless felt the heat oppressive, and stepped outside. For the few minutes during which Lady Goring was present in the library, each was unaware of the other's existence.

'After Lady Goring left, Mrs Teville entered the library and found Durrington already on the balcony. If any observed her there, as Dora in fact did, she would be easily mistaken for the younger woman thanks to the colour of her dress.

'I imagine she claimed to be acting on behalf of Ernest Moncrieff. Positioning herself carefully above the place where Lady Bloxham's sundial used to stand, she offered Durrington the brooch as a down payment for his silence about Ernest's true identity. It would have represented more wealth than he had held in his entire life; perhaps, since he was an outdoor servant, not present on formal occasions, more wealth than he had even seen. Taking advantage of his understandable distraction, Mrs Teville pushed him over the balcony to his death on the flagstones beneath, then quickly left the library and went downstairs.

'It was all very neat,' Holmes concluded, 'and planned in meticulous detail. I congratulate you particularly for the double layer of obfuscation which enabled the police to construct a perfectly plausible case around Lord Illingworth, after Lady Goring was eliminated as a suspect. Illingworth was involved, of course, and may have been very well aware of what was he was doing, but he was only an accomplice to your true assassin. As a pawn he had reached the end of his usefulness, and could be sacrificed to protect a more valuable piece.'

We heard the sound of Mrs Cheveley's applause. 'Bravo, Mr Holmes. You have described everybody's part in the affair quite accurately. I must say, I wonder that you have had need of Mr Pike's services, if you always hit the mark so well. But I suppose that accuracy is not the same thing as proof, and the courts are so wearyingly insistent on proof, aren't they?'

Holmes said, in an altogether different tone of voice, 'In this instance, I am pleased to say proof will present very few difficulties.'

'That's our cue!' exclaimed Gregson, and at once the three of us burst out into the drawing room.

CHAPTER SEVENTEEN
THE MUSIC OF NAMES

Mrs Cheveley was dressed as if for a ball, in vibrant purple silk with a diamond necklace. She wore also an expression of stunned horror.

I was, as Lord Goring had predicted, impressed at once by her beauty, though her allure was that of a poisonous blossom. I had not seen her grey-green eyes or dark red hair before. They had been obscured by her widow's veil.

'Mrs Winterbourne,' I gasped. Little wonder that she had been able to abstract Ernest Moncrieff's notepaper, or to observe his house so closely during the night of the ball. She had even told us that she had been watching the comings and goings.

Mrs Cheveley herself only had eyes for Lord Goring. 'You have betrayed me, Arthur Goring!' she exclaimed, ignoring Inspector Gregson as he cuffed her. 'You will come to lament this day. I can still bring you down.'

Lord Goring said, 'On the contrary, your only hold on me is broken. The inspector knows who killed Durrington. He knows that Mabel is innocent, as she has always been in all things. You know nothing to my discredit beyond what is public knowledge, and there is nothing to know to Mabel's because she is the best woman in England.'

Mrs Cheveley's eyes narrowed. 'I know all about Robert Chiltern, though.'

Goring sighed elaborately. 'Nothing that can be proven, as we established two years ago. Besides, you are in no position to threaten anybody. You have confessed to conspiracy to murder, in the hearing of a police officer. I doubt you will find many to mourn for you when you hang, Laura. I know that I shall not.'

At the mention of hanging, Mrs Cheveley, whose skin was naturally pale, turned whiter still.

Constable Northbrook had appeared at the door to Pike's rooms. 'She'd left that bloke with the scar and the broken nose hanging around outside,' he reported, 'just like you said, Mr Holmes. We've got the beggar in custody now. Put up a proper fight, mind,' he added, gingerly fingering his own nose, which was beginning to swell.

'Let me take a look at that, Constable,' I said.

'No need, Doctor, I'll get it seen to back at the Yard,' he grinned. 'I don't want to miss bringing this one in.'

'I will ruin you all,' hissed Mrs Cheveley. 'Even from beyond the grave, should it be necessary. I have friends who will still do my bidding. Everybody has a shameful secret, and certainly every man. If you have forgotten yours, Arthur, I will still find them. And yours, Mr Holmes, and yours, Inspector Whatever-your-name-is. Yours I know already, Dr Watson. And as for you, Langdale Pike, I know things about you that I am sure the good inspector would love to hear.'

'All right, all right, that will do,' said Gregson. 'Let's get you down to the Yard. We'll need a formal statement from everybody,' he reminded us.

'One moment, Gregson,' said Holmes. 'I firmly believe you will find that Illingworth is dead—'

'As to that, sir, sorry, sir,' said Northbrook, 'word's come through while you was shut up in here. They've dragged a body out of the river at Greenwich. It's difficult to be sure, of course, but they reckon as it's His Lordship.'

'Thank you, Northbrook,' said Holmes graciously. 'I believe we can assume for the moment that Lord Illingworth is out of the equation. Mrs Teville, however, remains at large.'

'Her real name's Mrs Erlynne,' I interpolated, forgetting in my excitement that it was probably Lady Augustus Lorton.

'Thank you, Watson,' said Holmes, in exactly the same tone he had addressed to the constable. 'Mrs Erlynne is still at large, and Mrs Cheveley made a remark earlier that rather alarmed me. What did you mean, Mrs Cheveley, when you said that you expected her to take further drastic action to defend her daughter's reputation?'

But Mrs Cheveley, the keeper of secrets, smiled like a sphinx and kept her silence, until Gregson and Northbrook bundled her out.

'I must tell Mabel and Robert,' said Lord Goring. 'There is a late sitting in the House tonight. Robert still has time to retract his previous statement.' He bade us goodbye and left, his concern for his wife and brother-in-law palpable in his haste.

'Well, we must set our minds to tracking down Mrs Teville, or Erlynne, at once,' Holmes decided. 'Langdale, I must thank you for your help. You acted the part to perfection, my dear fellow. I could almost have credited that you hated me.'

Langdale Pike laughed loudly. It was the least affected sound I had heard from him. 'And I could well believe your contempt for me, Sherlock. I have often said that you missed your vocation on the boards.'

'I must say, Holmes,' I said, 'I had not expected that Mrs Cheveley would turn out to be Mrs Winterbourne.' I hardly liked now to admit to my suspicions of the ridiculous Mrs Nepcote, who was presumably, given her behaviour, simply another of Mrs Cheveley's victims. Whatever secrets her past held, she must be ashamed of them indeed if she feared Major Roderick Nepcote discovering them.

'I had guessed it, my dear fellow. Did you not hear Gwendolen Moncrieff allude to their shared schooldays when we found them together?'

I remembered now that Gwendolen was also a schoolfellow of Lady Chiltern's, as, I recalled, was Mrs Nepcote. With Mrs Cheveley they must have made an odd quartet.

Holmes added, 'And it would certainly have given her the best vantage to observe and orchestrate the campaign against Durrington.'

I said, 'But is it not a most unlikely coincidence that she was living next door to the Moncrieffs?'

'That is true.' Holmes frowned. 'It was a great help to her in planning the murder, but she cannot have been expecting that when she took the house.'

I said, 'Nor was Ernest of any interest to her, except through his connections. She would have done better to take the house next to the younger brother, since she was blackmailing Algernon, Cecily and Lane. Nobody was blackmailing Ernest but Durrington.'

A look of great alarm came onto Holmes's face. Evidently less used to his friend's moods than I, Pike asked, 'Good God, Sherlock, whatever is the matter?'

'I have been an imbecile, Watson!' Holmes cried in horror. 'We have the architect of this affair in handcuffs, but the murderess is still at large, and there is someone whose safety I have been entirely neglecting. Come, quickly!'

Soon the pair of us had bade a hasty farewell to Langdale Pike, and were once again in a cab to Belgrave Square. During our short journey Holmes enjoined upon our stolid cabbie an urgent haste obviously quite offensive to his sensibilities, which must have been as languid in their way as Pike's own.

Insisting that the man wait for us, Holmes led me at a run up to the front door of Number 149 Belgrave Square, past the scandalised face of Merriman the butler, up the stairs, and into the drawing room. There, we found Gwendolen Moncrieff sitting alone.

'Mr Holmes!' she declared, rising. 'Dr Watson! To what do I owe this precipitate and somewhat intrusive honour?'

'Mrs Moncrieff,' Holmes said without preamble, 'I believe you are aware that your next-door neighbour, Mrs Winterbourne, was once known as Laura Hungerford.'

'Well, of course,' Gwendolen replied with perfect composure. 'She and I were at school together.'

'Were you also aware that she went by the name of Cheveley?'

'When someone has had as many husbands as Mrs Winterbourne,' Gwendolen replied, 'it is not polite to remember all their names. Like childhood pets, each lasts for so short a time, and the mention of them may summon distressing memories. What is the import of these most stimulating inquiries, Mr Holmes? One does prefer to understand the reasons for one's interrogations.'

'One more question, Mrs Moncrieff, if you will indulge me. Has Mrs Winterbourne recently intimated that she might reveal any fact about your past that you would prefer were not widely known?'

Gwendolen opened her mouth to express her disdain for this question with some perfectly crafted retort, then closed it again. She said, 'Oh dear,' in a small voice, sat down and burst into tears.

Baffled, Holmes looked wildly about for a way to circumvent this unexpected obstacle. Sighing, I sat down next to Gwendolen, pulled a clean handkerchief from my waistcoat pocket and passed it to her.

'Come now, Mrs Moncrieff,' I said, patting her hand. 'We only want to help. You can trust us not to let anything you say go any further. But Holmes is worried that somebody may be about to commit violence, and on subjects like that he is, I am afraid, seldom wrong. Won't you please help us prevent it?'

Holmes was gazing at me with impatience, but also some respect. Remarkably, he had the good sense to keep quiet for the moment.

'Come now,' I said again to Gwendolen. 'Why don't you tell us all about it?'

Sniffing occasionally into my handkerchief, Mrs Moncrieff revealed the final piece in our puzzle.

'I have,' she said, 'always had a fascination with the name Ernest. It was one of the first and most profound things that attracted me to my husband. When I was quite young I happened upon some personal effects which I now realise must have belonged to my late uncle, General Moncrieff, and they bore his Christian name prominently. It thrilled me to realise that there were men whose rectitude was written in that way in the very syllables that designated them, but it was more than simply the meaning of the name. The all-but-synonymous name of Frank, for instance, I find clumsy and lumpen. Ernest spoke to me with a music all of its own. I knew then that I was destined to marry a man named Ernest.'

During this her voice had become impassioned and lyrical. Now she paused and swallowed. 'Unfortunately, Ernest

Moncrieff, or Ernest Worthing as he was at the time, is not the first man of that name whom I have known.'

I saw the gleam of understanding in Holmes's eyes, but shook my head as he opened his mouth to speak.

Instead, I hazarded a guess of my own. 'Did this happen at school?' I asked, and I saw Holmes's head dip sharply in approval.

Gwendolen swallowed again. She said, 'He was the groundskeeper's boy, Ernie Preston. The instant I realised what that vulgar abbreviation stood for, I became fascinated by him. I sought his company. We spoke together. I was very young, and my notions were romantic ones. I said things I should not, and so did he. When Matron found out, he was dismissed and I have never seen him since.

'It took many years before I would consider marriage to another man, much to Mama's dismay as she had an alphabetical dossier of suitable candidates compiled in collaboration with her friend, the Duchess of Bolton, but when I found another named Ernest I realised that he, and only he, would be my husband. It was extremely fortunate,' she added practically, 'that Ernest turned out in fact to be his real name.'

Unable to contain himself any longer, Holmes asked, 'How did your matron discover the liaison, Mrs Moncrieff?'

'Another girl told her,' Gwendolen said. 'Laura Hungerford happened to see us together one day. She was as malicious then as she is now, but she had not yet learned the value of keeping secrets. It was only with the most heartfelt pleading, and a substantial cash bribe, that I was able to persuade Matron to keep my name out of the matter when she reported Ernie to the school authorities. I was forced to sell a rather valuable watch that Papa had given me, but I had no choice. If it had reached Mama's attention…' She shuddered.

I asked, 'And was it this secret that Mrs Winterbourne threatened you with?' I may have sounded slightly sceptical. Gwendolen was a grown woman now, and married, and surely could no longer be held responsible for a foolish schoolgirl flirtation.

She looked defiant. 'Dr Watson, you know Mama. If you were her daughter, would you wish her to discover that you had been keeping from her for years a secret that might affect the reputation of the family?'

'No indeed,' I said, but I guessed from the flush on her cheeks that the affair had perhaps extended further than the relatively innocent romance she had described. There had perhaps been unfulfillable promises that could still embarrass the family, were they to become known.

Well, it was no business of mine, and Holmes was interrupting once again, bursting with impatience. 'What has she demanded from you now, in return for keeping your secret? Is it your husband's money?'

'My husband has comparatively little money, Mr Holmes,' she said, with the natural distaste of her class in discussing such things.

'Forgive me, but I had understood that he was somewhat wealthy,' Holmes said with some asperity.

'I said "comparatively", Mr Holmes. Mrs Winterbourne appears indifferent to Ernest's modest fortune. Her interest is in Papa's money. Papa is extremely and exceptionally wealthy,' she added disingenuously, 'regardless of one's basis for comparison.'

'I see,' said Holmes. His look of alarm was returning. 'And how receptive has Lord Bracknell been to this suggestion?'

'Oh, if it was a matter of Papa alone, I believe he would indulge me as he always has,' Gwendolen replied. 'But he naturally defers to Mama in all matters of business and finance, as he does in those of politics, religion, ethics, diet, dress, health, household management and social relations, and she utterly refuses to countenance the idea. I told Mrs Winterbourne regretfully that my mother was an insuperable obstacle, and that has been an end to the matter.'

'Great Scott!' Holmes cried. 'Mrs Moncrieff, this is extremely important. Where is your mother now?'

'She has gone to the theatre,' said Gwendolen, frowning in concern. 'She was to see *The Deplorable Mrs Guildbourne* with Mrs Teville.'

'Mrs Teville, by Jove!' By now I was almost as alarmed as Holmes. 'Which theatre?' I asked her.

But Holmes was looking at his watch. 'The theatre is immaterial, Watson,' he told me. 'Lady Bracknell always leaves at the interval.'

'In that case, I suppose they will be taking tea together at Brown's,' Gwendolen suggested, still absolutely mystified.

CHAPTER EIGHTEEN
TEA AT BROWN'S

We entered Brown's Hotel at a run, Holmes flinging a handful of coins at our sluggish cabman with an exhortation to wait outside on Albemarle Street, in case we needed to follow the trail still further. We hurtled past an angry liveried doorman and an appalled commissionaire, and made for the tearooms where customers sat at linen-draped tables marked out in chess games of china and silver.

Lady Bracknell and Mrs Teville – or, as I now thought of her, Mrs Erlynne – were sitting at a table at the far end. In contrast with her finery at the ball, Mrs Erlynne's mink stole now adorned a simple ivory dress that contrasted starkly with Lady Bracknell's lavish crimson ensemble.

The murderess was pouring tea from a teapot into two cups, to one of which she added milk before handing it to Gwendolen's mother.

'Lady Bracknell!' Holmes bellowed across the crowded tearoom. 'Don't drink the tea, I beg you!'

We hared across the room, scattering waiters and upsetting at least one tea tray. Lady Bracknell sat frozen with her cup halfway to her lips until we had come to a halt in front of her, then she set it down carefully.

'*Mr* Holmes,' she said, in tones that would have withered the whole of Kew Gardens, 'you appear to have developed an inordinate objection to tea. Are you a faddist, sir? I have no truck with teetotalism, but I confess discovering the existence of its opposite alarms me even more.' She once again lifted the cup towards her mouth.

'The tea is unsafe, Lady Bracknell,' Holmes told her urgently. Out of the corner of my eye I saw Mrs Erlynne reach for her own cup, and I dashed it from her hand. She stared at me, paralysed by fury and alarm, as its tarry stain spread across the richly pattered scarlet and gold carpet.

Lady Bracknell paused again, the vessel an inch from her lips. 'Unsafe, sir? At Brown's? I admit that the tea at Claridge's is to be preferred, when that establishment is not, as now, lamentably closed for refurbishment. But there are surely any number of more dubious purveyors of the beverage in the West End alone? If Brown's tea is to be considered unsafe, then taking tea at the Savoy must be perilous in the extreme, and the blend used at the Langham invariably fatal.'

'Lady Bracknell,' Holmes pleaded as she once again made as if to take a sip, 'the tea you are holding *is* fatal. Mrs Teville has poisoned it.'

I had not been altogether sure of this myself, until I had seen the desperate way Mrs Erlynne had clutched at her own cup. But Lady Bracknell was not a person to respond well to statements made with less than absolute certainty.

Her Ladyship went so far as to rise from her seat, though not to put down her teacup. She glared at Holmes and declared, 'Should I find myself in need of a food taster, Mr Holmes, I shall advertise the position in the appropriate trade journals, and you will be most welcome to apply. As matters stand, I have no recollection of inviting you to interest yourself in my affairs in any capacity. You may believe, sir, that your questionable profession entitles you to imagine the most sensational plots on the part of others, but it does not grant you the licence to insinuate that a person of my standing in society has consorted with poisoners.'

Holmes threw up his hands in exasperation. He cried, 'Lady Bracknell, if you drink that tea you will die an agonising death!'

Meanwhile, the headwaiter had arrived. 'Shall I have these persons escorted from the building, Lady Bracknell?' he asked obsequiously.

'I think that would be for the best,' she said with an air of finality. 'I cannot imagine what conspiracies Mr Holmes will uncover when he learns that you serve coffee also.'

Next to me, the supposed Mrs Teville made a sudden attempt to escape from the table, but I was in time to seize her arm. 'Mrs Erlynne,' I said to her hastily, and saw her start at the use of her former name. 'Mrs Cheveley is arrested. We have come directly from the scene, or very nearly. She can do you no more harm now. Your daughter is safe.'

I felt her sag in my arms, and struggled to catch her. I manhandled her back into a chair, while the waiters clutched ineffectually at my own arms.

Mrs Erlynne held up a hand. 'Please wait,' she said to everybody in the vicinity. 'Especially you, Lady Bracknell,' she added, as that lady made to fortify herself with an invigorating sip of tea. 'Mr Holmes is telling the truth. I have attempted to murder you. I placed arsenic in the teapot.'

By now we were at the centre of everyone's attention in the room, and this announcement caused no little sensation among the other customers. Lady Bracknell reacted with nothing more than a blink.

After a longish pause, she proclaimed, 'It is the birthright of all English persons, from the highest to the lowest station, to drink tea if they wish. The same is true in India, I believe, and even in China, although doubtless there are prohibitions against it in the modern republics. Providence has extended to neither Mr Holmes nor any other person the authority to revoke that privilege.' She placed her cup back onto its saucer with extreme care. 'Nevertheless, given the exceptional circumstances, it is one that I shall forgo, for now.'

She sat again. With one deft motion, Holmes whisked away the cup and teapot and placed them on a tray, which he handed to the nearest waiter with the instruction, 'Give these to the police when they arrive.' The man took the tray as gingerly as if it were an angry cat.

'If Brown's is to play host to such revolutionary outrages as this,' Lady Bracknell observed to the head waiter in tones of ringing disappointment, 'then Claridge's cannot reopen soon enough.'

'Yes, Lady Bracknell,' the man said. 'May I bring you some more tea?'

'I think not,' Her Ladyship replied sharply. 'I am not yet so jaded with life that I would hazard it in such a reckless gamble.'

'Dr Watson,' Mrs Erlynne asked me, 'have you tricked me, or is that venomous woman truly in the hands of the police?'

'She is,' I said. 'You may be absolutely sure of that.'

'Then I will confess everything,' the murderess said. 'Everything I have done has been at her behest, and I will tell all if it will help to condemn her. For my own safety I care nothing. But… you spoke of my daughter. Do you know her name?'

I shook my head.

'Do you, Mr Holmes?'

'Madam, I do not,' he told her gravely.

'Then I must implore you on your honour never to find out,' she said passionately. 'I know that you could if you wished, your reputation assures me of it, but I must ask you never to do so. My crime can never touch her as long as her connection to me is unknown.'

Holmes inclined his head. 'She is an innocent in this, and shall be protected. I give you my word.'

'Thank you, Mr Holmes,' said Mrs Erlynne. 'And thank God.' She drew from her pocket her decorated fan, and waved it over her flushed face. For the first time I saw that the curlicues with which it was adorned spelled out the name 'Margaret', and I wondered whether the fan was her own, and if not, whose it was.

One of the quicker-witted waiters had summoned a police constable, who arrived shortly thereafter and took Mrs Erlynne away, with strict instructions that she must be kept apart from the vengeful Mrs Cheveley.

Several of the nearby tables had been hurriedly vacated by the more nervous of Brown's clientele, and Holmes sequestered one, gesturing for me to join him. 'I believe I could feel the benefit of a pot of tea, Watson,' he observed, waving a hand for a waiter, 'while we consider the satisfactory conclusion of our present case and look forward to our next. I imagine that Gregson will be rather busy this evening, and he can surely wait until the morrow for our official statements.'

A babble of voices interrupted us, and we looked up to see the arrival of the four members of the Moncrieff family, who rushed up to Lady Bracknell's table in great concern.

'Aunt Augusta, are you safe?' Ernest Moncrieff asked at once.

'I am not in the habit of being otherwise, Ernest,' Lady Bracknell replied disapprovingly, 'although it seems that doubting the fact has become quite the fashion. I am quite disappointed in your lack of conviction.'

'But Mr Holmes seemed quite sure that your life was threatened,' Gwendolen cried, looking anxiously across at us.

'If Mr Holmes's concern for my preservation were any greater,' Her Ladyship observed, 'I should expect him to petition to have me listed as an Ancient Monument.'

'So there was never any danger at all?' Algernon sounded disappointed. 'Gwendolen promised us danger.'

'On this occasion, Mr Holmes's excessive and overfamiliar vigilance was instrumental in preventing my succumbing to a case of arsenical poisoning,' Lady Bracknell conceded severely, 'but such occurrences are certain to be exceptional. It is the general principle that I object to.'

'We're very glad to see you well in any case, Aunt Augusta,' said Cecily, demurely sitting next to her, 'even if you are disappointed in our lack of conviction. May we join you for tea?'

Nearby, a warm, feminine voice greeted Holmes and me by name, and I looked away from the Moncrieffs' family reunion to see Lady Goring standing next to her husband.

Lord Goring said, 'We were on our way to dinner at the Criterion when we overheard talk of a recent commotion at Brown's. When we gathered that you were here, Lady Goring insisted on our coming to thank you.' After his earlier displays of emotion he had returned to his usual reserve, but his tone was cordial and his handshake firm.

Mabel Goring looked as radiant as always in silvery-grey, with the diamond and sapphire of the spider's-web brooch prominently displayed. She said, 'Arthur has promised to tell me everything, Mr Holmes, of what you have done, and of your contribution also, Dr Watson. From what I understand, though, the true murderer of Mr Bunbury is arrested, and those who tried to blame me are also dealt with. Is it true?'

'It is.' Holmes nodded. 'Except that the man's name was never Bunbury. It was Timothy Durrington.'

Mabel said, 'I shall remember it, although we never met. It

seems strange that our fates became, for a short time, so closely connected. Now, though, I am free to resume my life, and I am very grateful to you both for it.'

Lord Goring said, 'Mr Holmes, I do not claim that I always settle my accounts, for to do so would give other gentlemen of my rank and income a bad name. Nevertheless, I owe you a great debt, and this reckoning I choose to pay. You have my card, sir, and I shall expect to receive your bill. Good night.'

And he bowed cordially and left us, his beautiful young wife at his side.

As they departed, Ernest Moncrieff crossed over to us from the nearby table. He said, 'Holmes, do I really have you to thank for saving Aunt Augusta's life?'

Holmes inclined his head. 'The pleasure was entirely mine.'

'No, I understand my wife's glad of it as well,' said Ernest, smoothing his moustache judiciously. 'I'm also told you have cleared up that business about the man who died. Is there anything that I would be better off not knowing?'

Holmes said, 'Two of your guests conspired to kill the man who was attempting to blackmail you; not from any concern for your well-being, but under the malign influence of your next-door neighbour, who was also responsible for blackmailing both your brother and your sister-in-law.' I noticed that Holmes did not mention Gwendolen, who was observing the conversation a little nervously from Lady Bracknell's table.

'Good heavens,' exclaimed Ernest. 'When you put it that way, I was fortunate not to be involved.' He sighed, and glanced across at Lady Bracknell, who was expatiating now on the lack of backbone shown by modern waiting staff when faced with life-threatening crises. 'It's difficult to imagine a blackmailer causing my mother-in-law any difficulties, isn't it? Or arsenic, if it comes to that.'

'She is as human as anybody else,' I assured him.

'Do you think so? Well, perhaps,' Ernest admitted. 'As a theory it seems fantastical, but I suppose it is the only explanation for her having produced Gwendolen.' He thanked us both and ambled back to their table, passing his brother, who was sidling up to us at that same moment.

'I say,' said Algernon. 'That fellow who died. Darlington, was it? I don't suppose you ever found out why he gave that other name, did you?'

'Mischief merely,' said Holmes opaquely. 'And I can assure you that neither you nor Mrs Moncrieff will be hearing again from those who tried to extort money from you.'

'Well, that's a blessed relief,' Algernon observed. 'On the whole they weren't the sort of people I'd choose to be associated with.'

'That is undeniable,' Holmes said, 'for all that one was a peer of the realm and another went to a respectable girls' boarding school, though one where the conduct of the staff might have been better assured.'

'Really?' Algernon shook his head. 'I must say, the behaviour of the upper classes these days is tremendously disappointing. I blame the servants, personally. They should guide us with a firmer hand.'

Holmes said, 'I would not recommend looking to Lane for moral guidance, Mr Moncrieff.'

'Good heavens, no. Why, only this afternoon I had to reprimand him for his reprehensible laxity in allowing someone to deplete the refreshments he supplied for Lord and Lady Maybridge. Well, good evening to you both.' And Algernon, too, returned to his family.

Quietly, I observed to Holmes, 'We never did discover what he did in his Bunburying days that he is now so keen to see buried forever.'

'No.' My friend shook his head, rather wearily. 'Nor is it

our concern, unless a crime is discovered. If Podgers' murder had never come to light, Lord Arthur Savile would be sleeping soundly in Belgrave Square, undisturbed by the prickings of conscience. In Algernon Moncrieff's case, I can hardly imagine anything so extreme. We can but hope that Cecily's constancy can tame his wild nature.'

The waiter brought our tea, and Holmes busied himself for a few minutes pouring us both cups of the mercifully unadulterated fluid.

As he did so, he mused, 'Speaking of our next case, Watson, following the trail of Savile's crime has given me a taste for revisiting unsolved mysteries. There was a strange account a few years ago that I might turn my attention to, of the baffling disappearance of a portrait painter and the very peculiar death of one of his subjects...' But he could see that he had not my full attention. 'Is something on your mind, Watson?'

'Oh,' I said, 'I am sorry. I was thinking of something Cecily Moncrieff said, though she attributed the thought to Mrs Chasuble. She said that in fiction, good people end happily and bad people end unhappily.'

'Well, Watson, we know from her manuscript that Mrs Chasuble is not qualified to be an arbiter of taste in literary matters.'

'It was a juvenile work, Holmes,' I pointed out. 'I wrote some dreadful tripe myself at that age. But I was thinking that in real life, it's not so easy to tell what people's desserts are. Mrs Cheveley is an out-and-out villain, of course, and if the courts play their part she will suffer for it. But what of Mrs Teville, an assassin who wanted nothing more than to protect her daughter? Or Lord Illingworth, a wicked man whose sentiments approached nobility only where they touched his own child? Or Mrs Chasuble herself, harbouring her guilty secret and suffering its effect on her nerves every day for thirty years?'

Holmes was nodding, a trifle impatiently. 'You are right, Watson, these are imponderables. In this life, at least, there is no poetic justice, only that which we make ourselves. And that is our calling, old friend.'

I was flattered that he included me in this mission, but even so, my train of thought would not be diverted. 'And then there is the matter of Ernest,' I insisted. 'You assured us all that there was no chance that the infants had been exchanged at Victoria Station all those years ago. You said that any such plan would have been nonsensical. Yet Timothy Durrington believed it, and so did his mother – if indeed he was Timothy Durrington, and she was his mother.'

Holmes sat back, sipping his cup of tea, and sighed. 'I admit, my dear fellow, that I may have overstated my certainty upon that point. To be sure, it is not a plan that I would have made, but not everyone is so clear-headed as I. Durrington Senior may have intended that *his* son should be found in the handbag, and brought up as Ernest Moncrieff, while he raised the original as his own child. Perhaps his intention was to reveal the truth at a later date, after each boy had had the time to display the tendencies of his adopted class. It would have been a powerful statement of the irrelevance of birth, albeit one which would have seen the sergeant consigned to prison for making it.

'As we know, that is not how events transpired, but perhaps the scheme failed only through the sergeant's death. Perhaps he intended to report the child's presence to the police once Timothy's mother was on her way with the real baby Ernest, and trust that they would make the connection with the kidnapped Moncrieff child. Absent a serious accident at the station that day, he would almost certainly have been right.'

I said, 'So it is possible, then, that Ernest could be William Durrington's son after all? Might the body we called Bunbury have been none other than the original Ernest Moncrieff?'

Holmes shook his head. 'Such speculation is bootless, Watson. We can never know the truth now. Nor would it do any good if we did. The Nepcotes' gardener was a childless bachelor, whereas Gwendolen Moncrieff may well bear her husband children, if she can overcome her fear of emulating her own mother. Were such a revelation to be made, none could benefit from it and several would suffer.'

We looked across to where the Moncrieffs and Lady Bracknell were conversing, the very picture of a family at peace together. Cecily held Algernon's arm protectively while he tucked into a muffin, as if concerned that he might injure himself with the butter knife. Gwendolen and Ernest exchanged a loving look across their teacups, while Lady Bracknell informed them exactly what their opinion should be of the play to which she had been paying no attention earlier.

I turned back to Holmes, who nodded. 'Whether the man once known as Jack Worthing is actually Ernest Moncrieff, the son of a decorated general, or Timothy Durrington, the son of a disgraced sergeant, is irrelevant. He has a family now, and they have him. He is a good man, or at least no bad one, and we have no business preventing him, at least, from ending happily.'

'In the end, then…' I mused.

'Indeed, Watson,' said Holmes. 'There is no vital importance to his being Ernest.'

AUTHOR'S NOTE

Other than those found in the Sherlock Holmes canon, most of
the characters in this book owe their existence to the remarkable
works, primarily the plays, of Mr Oscar Wilde.

Ernest (or 'Jack'), Gwendolen, Cecily, Algernon, Lady
Bracknell, Miss Prism, Dr Chasuble, Lane and Merriman all
appear, of course, in *The Importance of Being Earnest*, probably
the most perfect comedy ever written in English.

Lord Goring, Mrs Cheveley, Mabel Chiltern, Sir Robert
Chiltern, Lady Chiltern and Phipps are taken from *An Ideal
Husband*; Lord Illingworth and Mr Kelvil MP from *A Woman
of No Importance*; Mrs Erlynne and her daughter from *Lady
Windermere's Fan*; and Lord Arthur Savile and his connections
from the short story 'Lord Arthur Savile's Crime', whose plot is
as deduced by Holmes in Chapter One. Numerous references to
marginal characters are taken from these and other works.

I have striven to be faithful to all of their characters as
Wilde portrayed them, though obviously I have not hesitated to
embellish and interconnect them when it has served my story.
Despite his tendency to reuse names, Wilde was not writing
with any thought of a shared continuity, and in some cases (such

as the two Lady Windermeres) this has required some creative interpretation to reconcile.

Any errors are of course my own, while the brilliance of the characters is all Wilde's. My debt to him is enormous, but that was true long before I began this novel.

PPH

ABOUT THE AUTHOR

Philip Purser-Hallard is the author of a trilogy of urban fantasy thrillers beginning with *The Pendragon Protocol*, and the editor of a series of anthologies about the City of the Saved. As well as writing various other books and short stories, including *Sherlock Holmes: The Vanishing Man* for Titan Books, Phil edits *The Black Archive*, a series of monographs about individual Doctor Who stories published by Obverse Books. He tweets @purserhallard.

For more fantastic fiction, author events,
exclusive excerpts, competitions, limited editions and more

VISIT OUR WEBSITE
titanbooks.com

LIKE US ON FACEBOOK
facebook.com/titanbooks

FOLLOW US ON TWITTER AND INSTAGRAM
@TitanBooks

EMAIL US
readerfeedback@titanemail.com